Visions of Time

By

Peter Brown

Strategic Book Group

Strategic Book Group
P.O. Box 333
Durham CT 06422
www.StrategicBookClub.com

ISBN 978-1-60911-763-4

Printed in the United States of America

Dedicated to my grandson
Charlie Brown for all the happiness he gives.

ACKNOWLEDGEMENTS

TO WIFE SYLVIA, daughter Samantha, and son Michael for their support and encouragement and special thanks to all at AEG Publishing without whose expertise the book may never have been published.

CHAPTER I

THE PANORAMIC VIEW—primitive, even savage—is breathtakingly beautiful. Mighty conifers, reaching for the sky, form a shelter in which the Cycads and Ferns proliferate. Volcanic lava flows shimmer brightly as they undulate, like fiery snakes, down the steaming hillsides, until they throw up giant plumes of steam and reluctantly give themselves up to the stormy sea.

In the foreground, a creature of immense proportions moves lazily through the small coppice, desperately straining its long, muscular neck to reach the succulent, green vegetation in the higher branches of the tree. Once he has consumed the sustenance here, he turns his attention to the next food source, as he must, to sustain life in his enormous body. As he walks, each thunderous step reverberates on the baked earth.

A deep roar resonates through the trees, as another creature, this one a carnivore, announces its ominous presence to warn all who might have designs on its recent kill. This carnivore is the giant Tyrannosaurus Rex, king of the terrible lizards. He looks around defiantly and proclaims his supremacy. The Tyrannosaurus pauses as if waiting for a dissenting voice; but there is none for this savage giant strikes fear in all. The creature roars again before returning to rip another huge piece of flesh from a young male Triceratops unfortunate enough to wander too far away from the protective care of his parents.

High in a clear blue sky, the sun shines brightly, an enormous, fiery, golden orb, its heat causing the forest to steam under the canopy of trees sheltering the small coppice and its light sustaining life on this fertile planet. A dark shadow moves stealthily across the sun's path, temporarily blocking the light and plunging the earth into a murky ether. The creatures that inhabit this planet become restless, momentarily pausing in their eating, drinking, or breeding. The shadow, however, gradually moves away from the sun; the light returns to earth, and the creatures continue with their activities.

Suddenly the figure of a man appears in the scene, shimmering in and out of focus before taking on a solid form. The night sky is gloomy once more; an ominous shadow is again blocking out the sun, turning day into night. The figure gazes in wonder at the dramatic scene laid out before him. He feels hot; his clothes, soaked by his own sweat, cling to his heavy body. He looks skyward, not able to understand or believe what his eyes behold. The gloom of the night sky is illuminated only by continual lightning strikes on rugged terrain. A whooshing sound fills the air drowning the roars and screeches of frightened creatures as they crash through undergrowth, trying desperately to escape the approaching instrument of doom. A hot wind chases the man, its intensity causing him to stumble to his knees. As the pounding gets louder, he rolls behind a protruding rock, clear of the giant, fleeing creatures. As he regains his feet, the earth begins to explode around him. He runs in blind panic, but there is no hiding place for the man or the stampeding creatures.

"Bloody hell," Gene called out as he tried to control his shaking limbs and at the same time unravel himself from the twisted, damp bedclothes, which gave testament to his restless, dream filled night. His flailing arms knocked over the unfinished bottle of Jack Daniels, left from the previous night's binge. The sound of glass shattering, as the bottle met the hard, bare wooden floor, jolted Gene Harman into instant wakefulness.

The trembling man emerged from the sweat soaked sheets and sat on the side of the bed with his head buried in his hands. Gene Harman had had dreams before, nightmares even; but this one was the most vivid and frightening he could remember. Lifting himself wearily to his feet, he stumbled blindly into the kitchen, still shaking. "Bollocks," he yelled as his big toe came into violent contact with a sharp edge on the fridge, another testament to his previous night's excesses. A louder shout of "Bollocks" resulted from the pain pulsating through his toe and halfway up his leg; it made his search for another drink even more frantic.

The bottle of Jack Daniels he'd secreted away for a rainy day proved elusive. He swung cupboard doors wide open and trembled as his search became more frenzied. The comforting feel of a long forgotten, unopened bottle of vintage malt whiskey finally rewarded his frantic search. "Better start the day on a good note," muttered the editor of *World in Focus*, turning the seal off the new bottle. Not bothering with a glass, his trembling hands raised the bottle to his eager lips.

CHAPTER 2

A HAZY, RED light reflects dimly onto the shimmering liquid as it dances provocatively to and fro, like a gentle sunset tide. A ghostly image begins to appear under the glistening, clear liquid. The image takes on a more distinct and solid outline as the seconds slowly tick by—tick, sixty seconds; rock the dish. Grey rapidly turns black, creating dancing images on the expressionless eyes of the onlooker, his face disfigured in the constantly moving liquid—tick, ninety seconds; rock the dish. The black image now takes on a halo of white fluorescence, set in a light grey background. The onlooker's face floats above the emerging image—tick, one hundred seconds; rock the dish. Dark tree shapes, with branches like withered arms, provide a frame in which another object begins to take on a familiar shape. This time the onlooker's face widens in a smile, his teeth taking the form of white tombstones among the constantly undulating scene—tick, one hundred and twenty seconds; now the foreground develops to form the distinctive and recognisable outlines of creatures vanished from earth millions of years ago. The draught from a stifled giggle temporarily ruffles the surface of the liquid, creating a stippled effect on the now recognisable image.

The developed image is moved into a new dish containing a

yellow pungent liquid mixture—tick, thirty seconds; rock the dish—tick, sixty seconds; violently plunge the image into its next resting place, a clear but acid smelling liquid. This is to prevent the image from fading in the light. It will be important that these images are permanent, as they have an important role to play in the coming events—tick, thirty seconds; rock the dish—tick, ninety seconds; rock the dish—tick, one hundred and twenty seconds.

Removed from the evil smelling liquid, the fixed print is dropped unceremoniously into the waiting sink. Clean water cascades from the tap over the clear image, washing away the remaining residue of acid. Twenty minutes later, the printer pegs out the finished print to add it to others on a string line stretched tightly over the sink. A bright, white light floods the room as the printer examines his handiwork more closely. He stands back satisfied, takes a final look around the room, and then switches off all the lights before leaving the prints to dry in the darkness.

Carl Santos enjoyed his work. More specifically, he enjoyed the financial security full employment gave him and his family. Carl worked for a nationwide courier service, which meant, with overtime, he, his wife, and little daughter could live comfortably in their two bedroom ground floor flat, in an old, but respectable part of the lower town district. On this day, March ninth, Carl had a delivery to the multi-storey Goldberg building that dominated the town centre skyline.

This was the home of the Goldberg press group, whose popular publications included the *Western Daily News* and the *World in Focus*. Today Carl had a delivery for Gene Harman, the unpopular editor of *World in Focus*. Since Goldberg was one of their biggest customers, Carl was a frequent visitor to the imposing building with its impressive lobby. Carl whistled as he made his way through to the smiling face housed behind the oak panelled reception desk. The smiling face belonged to Judy Clarke, the receptionist. He always enjoyed chatting with Judy when she wasn't too busy; and even if she was busy, she made time for quick friendly banter with callers. Sometimes, if there wasn't anyone else around demanding her attention, she would offer him a coffee out of the vending machine. Today his luck was in.

"Hello, beautiful," said Carl in his best Humphrey Bogart voice. "Where have you been all my life?" To Carl his impersonation was indistinguishable from the original!

"To Casablanca, Humph," replied Judy, with all the seriousness she could muster. She liked Carl; he always teased her and made her laugh. And she liked that he was a happily married man with no hidden agenda. "We're out of espresso today, Carl. Will ordinary filter do?"

Dramatically Carl clutched his throat and pretended to gag in a way even his hero, Bogart, would have approved. "Yes, that's fine, sweetheart," he joked. "Got any biscuits? I've got a delivery for the miserable sod upstairs," said Carl swallowing the lukewarm coffee.

"You mean Mr. Harman," Judy rebuked jokingly, stressing the "Mr." "Anyway, he's out at the moment; I'll sign and see that he gets it when he comes in."

"Right then, gorgeous," said Carl sliding the slim brown parcel across the counter while Judy signed the receipt. "See you soon, blue eyes," said Bogart waving a hand vigorously as he strode out to his waiting van just in time to prevent the friendly neighbourhood traffic warden serving a ticket on his illegally parked vehicle residing on the pavement outside.

"Not if I see you first," shouted Judy to Carl's retreating figure.

From his office Gene Harman called out rudely to his picture editor, Vincent Craig, "Hey Vince, get in here and bring Archie with you," Archie was Archie Brown, his top graphics technician. Gene, all six-feet-four of him, was forty-two years old, an imposing figure, though too many lunches on expenses and more than a fair share of alcohol had taken their toll on a body now going to seed. As editor of a popular magazine, he was tough, stubborn, and opinionated; when he called, people came. Because he was bigoted and selfish, his marriage to Lois was in trouble after five tumultuous years. They had grown far apart: the spark that had existed between them had long since ended, as had any intimacies, including sex. Gene was also a bully, which was one of the many reasons he was now in the throws of a messy, acrimonious, expensive divorce.

"What do you think of these?" Gene thrust a sheaf of black-and-white, eight-by-ten prints under Vince's nose. He felt like pushing them up the little runt's nose; but he resisted the urge, especially as Craig was old Goldberg's favourite nephew. Vince's first inclination was to say that the prints are just a load of rubbish; experience, however, had taught him that when the editor asked for an opinion, anything less than a positive reply was met with disapproval on a grand scale. "Obviously a manipulated image, but very well done," said Vince hesitatingly, not really expecting to satisfy Gene with his noncommittal.

"Archie, what do you think?" Less than impressed with his picture editor's irrational opinion, Gene tried his luck with Archie.

The graphic technician flinched and sat upright when Gene directed the question at him and demanded an immediate answer. He was always nervous when speaking to his editor, as were many others in the office. Whereas Gene was exceedingly tall, Archie was only five-feet-four and lacked the self-confidence shown by his editor. He also lacked the combative instinct shown by many small men. Archie was extremely good at his job; therefore, his opinion or advice was regularly sought by his colleagues, especially on the subject of image manipulation. "Well, I agree with Vince—it looks like several images superimposed, but whoever did the printing knew how to produce a quality chemical photograph.—Strange though, these days most prints are produced digitally, so this printer must be one of the 'old school'," added Archie warming to his task.

"Do you think it's worth putting in the next issue?" Gene kept probing, aware that, like Ned's parents, Vince had thought of nothing and was all out of ideas.

"Why not? Give it a try," said Vince weakly, trying desperately to regain some of the ground he'd already lost during this discussion.

"I'm looking for a positive reason we should publish it, not a negative one." Gene had already lost interest in the one-sided conversation and was wondering why he had bothered to ask Vince's advice. Better to go with his own judgment anyway. "Haven't you two got work to do?" asked the editor sarcastically, the sharpness of his tone signalling, prematurely, the end of the unsatisfactory meeting. He could only take so much of Vince at the best of times. This was not the best of times.

Gene was aware that with the technology available these days, it was easy to transform an image well enough to fool even the expert. But these were different, as Archie had said: chemical prints were more difficult to fake. He reluctantly had to agree with that little runt, Vince, that the photographs were excellent. He spread them out before him, impressed with the depth of detail exhibited in each print. The first showed a round, black object surrounded by an aurora of what looked like fire. The object, in the centre of the frame, took up about one-third of the picture area—not the best composition, thought Gene, the rule of thirds springing to mind. The clever bit, however, was the framing. While trees provided a frame for the print, something in the foreground, slightly indistinct, looked like a giant lizard. "Yes, well-done," Gene murmured, suddenly realising his voice had carried through his open office door.

"Hmm, looks like a scene from Jurassic Park," he muttered more quietly this time. He'd seen the film recently at the multiplex; he grimaced as he remembered the price of the tickets. It was the last time he had been out with that flighty piece from the main office; he'd spent a fortune on her that night and still got nothing except a headache next morning. He scooped the prints up off the war torn area he called his desk and leaned back into the creaking leather chair, the seat grown hollow over years of being used by an overweight body.

Suddenly the editor felt a cold tingle down the back of his neck. He snatched the prints from his desk and experienced a feeling of déjà vu as he recognized scenes from his dream of the previous night. The two other photographs were similar in content to the first, each showing Jurassic Park like scenes. One of them was a superbly composed photograph of a gigantic dinosaur standing over what looked like an untidy heap of rotting meat. The creature was looking up with his mouth open roaring its defiance to the sky. The blood running down his jaws looked black and shiny on the monochrome print. The final photo depicted a running man with the ground erupting around him. Seeing the photographs of his dream, Gene broke out in a cold sweat. God, I need another drink, thought the editor reaching for his bottle of Jack Daniels. Thinking better of it, he slammed the drawer shut with a loud bang. He needed his wits about him for the meeting with his wife's lawyer this morning. Gene stood in his doorway briefly surveying the rows of bowed heads before yelling to Daniel Weston to bring him a strong coffee and a packet of biscuits.

Daniel, the office "dogsbody," had recently left university with high aspirations of making a career in journalism. Daniel had thought the world was waiting for him, a belief encouraged by his university tutors wishing to raise the profile of their courses. Daniel, however, had learned quickly that it would be a hard grind leading up to his goal. Meanwhile he had to get coffee, whenever and for whoever demanded it. Now it was for that bastard, Gene Harman.

"What do you think of these photographs?" Gene Harman demanded as Daniel walked into the cramped office placing the plastic cup of steaming coffee on his editor's desk.

Daniel hadn't yet learned that to speak your mind to Mr Harman could get you into more trouble than you need at any time let alone when Harman was in a bad mood, like now. "They look real enough to me," he said. "But I've never seen a dinosaur like that one, it's too big for one thing," he added for good measure.

"That's what I thought" said the editor slurping his coffee, mildly impressed with the dogsbody's incisive observation. "Send that pratt Vince in on your way out." His tone left no doubt that the brief dialogue with dogsbody had ended.

Heeding "his master's call," Vince shuffled with trepidation back to his boss's inner sanctum, wondering what he'd done wrong this time and ready to deny vehemently whatever it was. "Put this in the next issue—full-page," the boss ordered Vince, "and get the readers to give comments and to suggest a caption. Get them to e-mail their entries, and offer a couple of rolls of film for the best contribution; perhaps we can get some better ideas than you've come up with.—Shouldn't be difficult," he added as an afterthought, revelling in his subordinate's hangdog look.

Barely glancing at the retreating figure, Gene now concentrated his attention to more important matters. A letter from his soon-to-be, ex-wife's lawyers demanding more money for a settlement, was definitely more important. Gene looked at his watch; his appointment with his lawyers was half past eleven. This gave him half an hour to get across town. He'd better get Danny to drive him there, as it was difficult to park; that way he would save the taxi fare. Old tight arse Goldberg was checking on his expenses recently, so better not give him an excuse to moan on such a small amount. Better wait until it was worthwhile. Then he'd make the old bastard pay.

By the time he had finished with his lawyers, or more precisely, by the time they had finished with him, it was four o'clock; and the only place to seek solace was the nearest pub. And not surprisingly he knew just the place—The Spotted Cow.

The locals called it "Mo's Dump," and it had its fair share of "Homers" and "Barneys" crowded round the bar making it difficult or nearly impossible for anyone outside the circle to get served. Gene's imposing size, however, encouraged the crowd to make way for a man desperate to get his drink. Five hours and enough whiskey to sink a battleship later, Gene staggered to the waiting taxi as he waved goodbye to his new best friends—the Homers and Barneys.

The taxi dropped Gene off at his modest three bedroom house situated in a grubby cul-de-sac off Bletchworth High Street. He'd learnt this afternoon that Lois and the "old bag" of a mother-in-law had plans to get his house sold as soon as possible. Well, they'd have a fight on their hands. But now, the most important job was to take something for his throbbing head.

CHAPTER 3

THE HEAT WAS stifling. An old fan in the centre of the room was wearily spinning just enough to move the hot air around the room, but not to cool the waking man. It was still dark outside, the dim bulb doing little to relieve the gloom of the bare, ten-by-eight room. A grey, ragged sheet slid gracelessly to the floor as the somnolent man stumbled out of the ancient, creaking bed.

Where was he? Who was he? He looked around the room, frantically searching for anything that would suggest an answer to the myriad questions that were whirling around in his head. The only comfort was provided by familiar sounds, such as the ticking of the fan as it laboured on its journey to nowhere, the chirping of insects carried on the still night air, and the sound of a moth self-destructively slamming itself on the small bulb. These connected him with the past.

He walked silently toward the yellow, peeling door and grasped the greasy knob. Oblivious to the slimy feel, he turned the disgusting brass orb first to the left and then to the right. He felt rather than heard the catch disengage as the door opened onto a dimly lit hallway. Instinctively he ducked his head as he moved through the low arch of the doorway. The wooden floor creaked beneath his weight. He turned toward the glimmering light at the end of the narrow passage. He advanced with caution, glancing nervously at a padlocked door that he passed on his right.

As he got closer to the open doorway, the light took on an unearthly quality, softer and tinged with red. He stooped and moved into the room as shimmering faces with furtive eyes followed his progress. His heart pounding, he raised his hands to his face in a defensive reflex action; the eyes continued to stare. Cautiously he lowered his hands and moved closer to them. Eerie, poster sized photographs, supported only by intermittently placed brass pins, depicted faces distorted as if by some unseen terror. The man's head lolled from side to side trying to fathom the horror before him. A tear formed in the corner of his eye as if some memory was awakening within him. He raised his hand to wipe away the tear; but a great jolt coursed its way through his body making him drop to his knees. He screamed, as his limbs became rigid and his back arched almost to snapping point. Another even greater charge brought merciful oblivion to the man.

He was in different, more comfortable, surroundings now; but his body still ached as a reminder of past suffering. Had he been dreaming? Which experience was the reality? Grimy and torn, his expensive clothes looked like rags hanging from his dirt encrusted body. Slowly as his memory began to return, the room took on a familiarity. As his recollections became more vivid, the full horror hit him; and he broke down, his body shaking with the anguish of realization.

CHAPTER 4

"BLOODY AMAZING," COMMENTED Vincent Craig to anyone who cared to listen. Vince looked around expectantly at the chattering masses animatedly discussing last night's TV. The office continued to buzz around him totally indifferent to what he considered was bloody amazing. Although Vince had risen to the dizzying heights of assistant editor of *World in Focus*, no one rated him. His inferior ability, combined with an unpleasant personality, did little to endear him to his work colleagues, superiors and subordinates alike. By common consensus, the only strength Vincent Craig had going for him was his uncle, Jason Goldberg, the owner of Goldberg Publications. "Bloody amazing," Vince said aloud, this time desperate to get some confirmation that he actually existed and had not suddenly become invisible.

"What's that, Boss?" asked Archie trying to show a little interest—after all he did work for Vince, like it or not.

"The entries we got from that competition in the last issue." It pleased Vince to know someone had noticed he was there, even if it was only Archie. "You know, the one the boss said looked like scenes from Jurassic Park.—Some of the comments were good, but we got some flak from some "clever sod" university professor, a bloody woman at that.—She had the nerve to correct one of our captions." Vince paused for breath; now he finally had someone's attention he would make the most of it. "She said we were wrong in identifying the published photograph as a Tyrannosaurus Rex."

"What is it then?" asked Archie, doing his best to sound interested, and failing dismally.

"I don't know; the professor asked for the 'genial Mr. Harman' to ring her at the university—bloody stuck-up cow. She's got more chance of flying to the moon than getting Harman to ring her back," Vince added not waiting for Archie's reply. "Bloody stupid competition anyhow; I don't know why people bother for two rolls of film"; this response was typical of Vince's, attitude—if he hadn't thought about it, it wasn't worth doing. "Look at this." Vince was on a roll now full of his own self-importance as he slid sheaves of paper across his desk towards his nonplussed graphic technician.

Archie scanned some of the other comments, his cheek giving an occasional involuntary twitch as he studied the documents. "Most people see them as manipulated images anyway," Archie concluded looking to his boss for support but not getting any.

Another of Vince's annoying habits was his ability to ignore other people's comments and opinions; too "wrapped up in himself," was the consensus among his colleagues. "Not too much imagination or effort gone into the others—some of them are just plain stupid," was Vince's succinct summing-up of the remaining entries. Vince's speciality was criticising other people's work. Even though he couldn't do as well himself, he felt morally righteous "putting the boot in" to others. Vince impressed some people, until they got to know him.

"What about this one?" asked Archie, looking down at a yellowing sheet of paper. The writing in green ink was a laboured scrawl making it difficult to read by all but the sharpest eyes. "I can't read it," admitted Archie knowing that Vince probably couldn't read it either.

"A fat lot of help you are," Vince retorted scathingly. "Haven't you got any work to do? I'm going to see Harman." Archie scurried back gratefully to the sanctuary of his desk; the less he had to do with that cretin the better.

Although Gene Harman claimed to run an "open-door policy", in reality this applied to all other people's doors, not his. The last person to walk into the editor's office unannounced had felt the full weight of his sarcastic tongue. The next one to walk in was everybody's friend—Vince. "What the fuck do you want?" yelled Gene angrily at the fat little figure mincing into his office unannounced. Luckily for Vince, he was Jason Goldberg's nephew; or he might have received an even less enthusiastic welcome from the irate editor.

"We've got the entries for the competition, boss; but there's nothing too imaginative," he offered smugly. Vince was trying hard to impress his boss by putting forward an opinion. Gene, for his part, was not the slightest bit interested in what Vince thought on any subject, let alone submissions.

"Let's have a look," said Gene holding out a bruised hand. The discolouration of his knuckle was the remaining evidence of the final violent argument he'd had with wife when in a drunken rage he'd put his fist through the kitchen door panel. This had been the last straw for Lois; she'd moved out the next day and was now living with her mother in the witch's cave. As a mother-in law Elsie had sucked; as an old-bag she was perfect. Well, to hell with both of them.

Vince pushed the entries into the big outstretched hand. "So bloody predictable—none of them worth two rolls of film," said

Gene as he glanced down the list.

Vince broke the silence, "There're some on the other page," he ventured, ever helpful. "Oh, and a Trudy Ballinger from the university wants you to ring her; she said it was important."

The speed of the big man's riposte was impressive by any standard. "Bollocks, if she wants to speak to me, she can make an appointment like everyone else," was Gene's succinct retort as he quickly scanned the remaining entries, pausing at the yellowing paper with the green writing. "Hmm, this one's too bloody subtle for me," he said thrusting the old looking parchment under the nose of his startled assistant editor. "Who sent it in anyway?"

"There's no address," said Vince feeling more confident now, "just a quote by Thomas Monson. 'The past is behind, learn from it; the future is ahead, prepare for it'."

Gene felt the hair on the back of his neck bristle; and not for the first time today, with last night's dream still vivid in his mind, he could feel his head beginning to throb. "Well, this one is a waste of time," said the editor stuffing the yellowed paper into his trouser pocket. Quickly looking through the remaining entries, Gene was now anxious to be on his own to consider the latest events. "Publish this one as the winner—it's the only decent contribution," he said referring to a page of text that described in boringly technical detail how to manipulate a black-and-white print.

"Fucking phone," muttered Gene; his head was much worse now, as was his temper. "Fucking phone!" This time he almost shouted as he reached across his desk, knocking over a cup of cold coffee. "Harman," he rasped jamming the phone between his neck and shoulder while trying in vain to salvage some of the paperwork from his now sodden desk. Even worse, a moat of grey coffee surrounded his pork pie, with its pastry crust slowly absorbing the liquid. Well, that takes care of my lunch, he thought miserably, throwing a soaking tissue towards the paper bin—and missing.

"Hello, I would like to speak to the editor," said a refined female voice. "This is Professor Trudy Ballinger from Bletchworth University."

CHAPTER 5

TRUDY BALLINGER WAS professor of Palaeontology at Bletchworth University. Academically she was well thought of with significant contributions to current academic theory. She'd earned her prominent reputation by papers published worldwide and currently was working on her first eagerly awaited book. She was thirty-two years old, but still had a youthful, trim figure. Her colleagues considered her attractive and her students, "a bit of all right." Her blonde hair, worn up in a tight bun at work, framed an oval face complemented by emerald-green eyes and a strong nose turned up at its tip.

Dedicated to her work, Trudy was a slave to her profession. Boyfriends rarely lasted long; intimidated by her considerable intellect, they soon looked for pastures new and less challenging. From Trudy's perspective, once the early physical attraction had faded, few if any, of her lovers could provide her with the mental stimulation she craved. To say she did not tolerate fools gladly was an understatement; Trudy Ballinger did not tolerate fools at all. She was between romances at the moment.

If asked, people who knew her would say her only failing was her tendency to be outspoken. She always strived to have the last word, no matter what the subject; but her spirit fostered many lively discussions with her peers and students alike. Devoted to her career; her dog, Frodo; and photography. It was this latter passion that made her an avid reader of *World in Focus*; and that accounted for her being on the phone now to its editor, Gene Harman.

"What can I do for you, Professor?" Gene's mood had perceptibly lightened. His weakness for the ladies had reached legendary status among the more attractive members of the company's typing pool and had given Lois another reason to file for divorce, besides the influence of her mother.

"It's more of what I can do for you, Mr. Harman," replied Trudy Ballinger icily. "I am a regular subscriber to your excellent magazine and until this week held the photographs and the journalistic information in high regard. This week, however, you have published photographs giving incorrect information, much to my surprise and disappointment."

Gene's lighter mood suddenly took a turn for the worse. "I'm sorry, Miss Bollinger; but we have experts to double check all information published in our magazine," said Gene acidly.

"My name is Trudy Ballinger and its Ms, not Miss," retorted Trudy, taking an instant dislike to this rude man on the end of the phone. "Anyway your so-called experts missed this one," she added, striving desperately to preserve her reputation for having the last word.

"Bloody hell, that's all I need—a bossy woman," muttered Gene under his breath. "So sorry, 'Ms Ballinger,' please enlighten me; where did we go wrong?" As an editor, Gene did not take kindly to criticism; as "macho man," he was even less pleased. The not so subtle blend of hostility and sarcasm in his voice demonstrated his intense displeasure on both counts.

"Well, Mr Harman this "bossy woman" doesn't like your attitude; I'll speak to someone who takes preserving the quality of the magazine seriously," said Trudy Ballinger slamming the phone down so hard it resounded in Gene's already throbbing head.

"Bollocks, Prof," he shouted into the dead phone line.

Just when Gene had thought the day couldn't get much worse, it did. The distinctive chirp issuing forth from the seldom used red phone, his direct line to Jason Goldberg, began to ring. "Harman, I've just had a Professor Ballinger on the phone," the commanding tones of Jason Goldberg coming straight to the point. "I want you to ring her to apologise for your rudeness and arrange a meeting with her at the university. She's unhappy with the treatment she received from you and has threatened to go public. This magazine has had more than its fair share of bad publicity in the past; that's got to stop. If you're not prepared to be polite to our subscribers, then I will have to find someone who will. Think it over." As a parting shot, this was a conversation killer.

Gene had a good job at Goldberg Publications, and it was doubtful whether he would get another job like it at his age. If he was going to come out on his divorce settlement with anything at all, he needed all the money he could get. It was with this sobering thought in mind that he reluctantly reached for the phone. Pausing momentarily to gather his resolve, with trepidation he rang the number of Bletchworth University.

CHAPTER 6

DANIEL WESTON LOOKED furtively around the staff smoking room before sidling in and pulling the door tightly shut behind him. He wanted to be on his own because he was angry. Daniel had always been angry. Born prematurely, he had developed a speech defect that caused him to stutter when he was stressed or under pressure. He thus became the subject of ridicule and bullying by the other children both at school and at play. His teachers considered his reluctance to talk as "having an attitude." Every day he had to run the gauntlet of jeering, bullying, and tormenting from classmates intent on making his life as miserable as possible. If he was lucky, he would get home without any physical damage; but the mental scarring, although unseen, was deep and permanent.

As a child Daniel had lived in an old, gloomy house, its grimy appearance and constantly peeling paintwork testifying to a general lack of motivation combined with low-income. Backing onto the local glassworks, the house absorbed a sickening chemical smell. He lived with his mother but spent most of the time on his own waiting for her to get home from work. She would not get in sometimes until well after dark, leaving Daniel to let his already vivid, imagination run wild. As other children of his age were playing together in the street, laughing and shrieking, Daniel would be in a darkened room talking with imaginary friends.

When Daniel was three years old, his father did not return from work one day choosing instead to run off with another woman he'd met several years before. Left to fend for themselves, Daniel and his mother were not destitute, but his mother had to go to work to earn the extra money needed to keep them in the house. Mean spirited and bitter, her grudge against the world, men in particular, affected Daniel constantly. Although she didn't abuse Daniel physically, she worked out her own frustrations on Daniel mentally. One of the mental tortures she inflicted was to lock him in his cold, gloomy bedroom for hours on end for even the smallest misdemeanour on his part. Consequently, Daniel had little respite from mental anguish and torment; his only relief was to immerse himself in his own fantasy world, blocking out as much of the real world as he could.

He would fantasise how satisfying it would be to kill his tormentors one by one and would imagine different ways to make them suffer. His most degrading and painful deaths, however, he reserved for his father, although his mother came a close second in the painful death scenarios. Daniel had two great redeeming features, his high intelligence, and his photographic memory. These propensities combined to enable him to fly through school subjects with an ease that alienated him even more from struggling classmates. Daniel's entry into higher education was easy; he won a scholarship to a prominent southern university, studying English literature.

A more sophisticated tormenting followed him to university. He found himself menaced by the older male students and ignored by the young women on campus. Even the lecturers made it obvious they resented the time spent with him, preferring instead the company of the more outgoing and communicative students. Girls presented another problem. Daniel's paranoia convinced him that the groups of chattering female students were laughing at him—their faces, like grotesque theatre masks, alternating between laughter and sorrow. Once when he had asked a fellow student named Susan out, she rebuked him saying, "Fuck off, creep." He never again asked any girl out and never would.

While at university, he lived on his own in a dingy little bedsitter on the outskirts of town, leaving his room only to attend classes. After each miserable day at college, when he would return to his lonely room, the bitterness and resentment burned deep inside him. His bitterness would one day erupt with devastating consequences, and someone would pay the price.

The object of Daniel's present anger was the editor of *World in Focus*, Gene Harman. The fat slug—how dare he order me about; he was as bad as the rest of them—the hateful bastards at school, those slobs at university, and, of course, the mother whom he despised fervently. Well, he'd make them pay; one day he would make them all pay. These dark thoughts and many others crowded Daniel's brain. His breathing became laboured, his head pounded, his heart beat a rapid tattoo against his chest, as he slid slowly to the floor, his back leaving a sweaty snakelike trail down the yellow, emulsion covered wall.

CHAPTER 7

HARRY BUTLER WAS about to take a Harry Butler sized bite out of his cheese and pickle sandwich when an old, battered Ford Capri screeched to a halt outside the university security lodge. His security lodge no less. Harry was the Head of Security at Bletchworth University, a title he was proud of. Harry didn't have too much to be proud of, although his colleagues didn't tell him this because Harry had the short man's sometimes pompous nature. Five feet tall and five feet round, Harry was still living at home with his elderly parents. At forty-seven Harry felt short changed in the life stakes, but he was head of security on seven pounds an hour and with an unwarranted degree of authority—that made up for a lot.

The windswept rain was coming down in sheets as the car carrying Gene Harman pulled up outside Harry's lodge. Harry reluctantly placed his half-eaten sandwich down on his plate, borrowed from the university refractory, and searched for the visitor signing-in sheet. "Good morning, sir," Harry addressed his visitor. "Can I help you?"

"I'm here to see Trudy Ballinger," said Gene exuding all his legendary charm.

"Ha, you'll be Mr. Harman then," said Harry already taking a dislike to Gene, a trait he shared with many other of Gene's acquaintances. "The Professor was expecting you an hour ago; I'll ring her office and see if she is still available—she's always very busy," Harry added beginning to enjoy seeing Gene quietly steaming.

"Fuck off, she'll see me," said Gene his charm for the day all used up.

Harry was about to exert his authority and tell Gene he would have to wait when, fortunately for Harry, given the difference in size between him and Gene, Trudy Ballinger's cultured voice echoed down the phone still pressed firmly to the security chief's ear.

"Harry, please send Mr. Harman to my office immediately he arrives," said an authoritative, disembodied voice resounding in the black earpiece still clutched tightly in Harry's sticky, sweating hand.

Professor Ballinger's office was on the top floor of the four-storey university building. Gasping his way up the stairs to the fourth floor Gene was in no mood for pleasantries as he walked into the professor of Palaeontology's small office. "Good morning, Mr. Harman," said an attractive blonde lady, offering her hand; "I'm Trudy Ballinger."

Loss of words was not a state that sat easily with the editor of a national magazine. But speechless he was, albeit only temporarily. Trudy Ballinger was not what he had expected. For a start she was extremely attractive and although short by his standards, had a stunning figure, slim yet full of promise. Maybe the meeting wouldn't be so bad after all. Gene quickly regained his ability to speak and muttered vaguely, "Pleased to meet you." As it turned out, that was the high point of the meeting; it was all downhill from there.

"Mr. Harman," said Trudy, "the reason I phoned you was to ask how you came by that photographic mock-up of dinosaurs you published in the last edition of *World in Focus*."

"May I ask why you want to know?" replied Gene bristling at Trudy's direct approach. Gene was happy when he was the one rasping out the questions; in these situations he expected immediate answers. However, now that the roles had temporarily reversed, his determination to win back the initiative became instinctive.

"Two reasons," answered Trudy already having her preconception of Gene from the previous phone call more than justified. "Firstly, your article wrongly named the large dinosaur in the foreground," the professor was on a roll now and woe betide anyone who dared argue, even the editor of *World in Focus*. "Secondly, I would like to know who created the image. We have only just discovered the remains of this dinosaur; and the discovery is not, so far as we were aware, known outside the fraternity."

Gene paused gathering his thoughts. "I'm afraid the source of our information is confidential," he finally said feeling the balance of power tipping in his direction.

"Mr. Harman," Trudy retorted with an icy tone of voice reserved only for her current and soon to be enemies, "I think there are two factors you should consider here." This was Trudy at her best as many of her students could confirm. "Firstly, if you do not cooperate, I will inform Jason Goldberg; and I know he's not impressed with your handling of the problem so far, especially as he is a patron of the university." This was the second "conversation killer" Gene had received today. *What's next?* he wondered. Goldberg was already gunning for him, and Gene didn't relish the thought of another bollocking off his boss.

"Secondly," Trudy continued, "if you do cooperate, I will help you, by correctly identifying the dinosaurs in the picture and write a short article to accompany your apology for getting it wrong initially." If Gene had to make a choice between the two factors so eloquently outlined by Trudy, the first one, which involved Jason Goldberg, would have been the outright winner. Combined, the two arguments left Gene with no choice if he wished to remain the editor of *World in Focus*. "Listen, Professor, you can't bully me; I'm not one of your students." Gene knew deep down he would have to cooperate with the hard-nosed little bitch, but he was going to go down fighting.

"Mr. Harman," said Trudy ignoring Gene's last desperate effort to gain any initiative from the discussion. "I have students waiting for me now, and as you were late for our meeting, I suggest we schedule another appointment to discuss your problem. Please contact my secretary on your way out to arrange a further meeting this week." It was the second time today Gene had been perfunctorily dismissed. But at least the Professor was more attractive than Goldberg. The thought cheered him up somewhat as he walked slowly to his car.

Sitting in his car, Gene felt like a naughty student told off and dismissed by his professor. Still, she was a spunky little character; he'd give her that. He'd like to give her a lot more, he thought as he drove past Harry's security gate, pausing only to give Harry a well-tried and tested gesture on his way out. Harry who was still busy eating his lunch and was now tucking in to a large slice of chocolate cake missed the proffered gesture entirely.

CHAPTER 8

A TRICKLE OF perspiration ran down Trudy's face and paused on the tip of her nose before finishing its journey as a spreading blob on notes lying untidily on the highly polished lectern. She looked up at the sea of expectant faces before her. God, they look so young, she thought, or is it me getting old? Trudy rather hoped it would be the former although she had to concede that thirty-two was, as they say, "getting on a bit." She could remember when she was one of the fresh faces looking on expectantly, hanging on to the lecturer's every word. Those days are long gone, she thought sadly.

"Next week, boys and girls, we will discuss the second major subdivision of the Middle Jurassic Period." She knew this group of students well and felt comfortable addressing them in a way some people would consider as patronising. "Don't forget to hand in your assignments before next Monday." Trudy had to raise her voice over the sound of fifty pairs of feet moving with indecent haste toward the open door of the lecture theatre. Thank goodness that's over, thought Trudy wearily. This hadn't been one of her more inspired lectures; in fact, she had bored herself, so God knows how her students had felt.

Trudy's meeting with Harman had left her rattled. Revealing

the discovery of this particular dinosaur was to have been Trudy's moment of glory, when she presented it to an astounded world at the Paleontological Society next month. It was obvious that someone from the university, or worse still, her own department, had leaked the information. Trudy's determination to discover the person responsible and make him or her pay, spelled trouble for someone. She'd take no prisoners if they stood in the way of her ambition, as many colleagues could verify from their experiences with her as she rose to a chair at the university. This chair was just a stepping stone for Trudy; so to get the information she needed, her first port of call would have to be that shit, Harman. Although he was the last person Trudy would ever want to speak to, she made a mental note to ring the aforementioned shit in the morning. Meanwhile Trudy decided to confide in the only person she really trusted; Dr. Mike Powell Psychiatrist.

It was after downing his second whiskey and lighting up his third cigarette that Gene began to mull over the events of the past few days. The bloody nightmare had really shaken him. It was strange for him to dream about dinosaurs particularly as he hadn't any interest in the bloody creatures. Maybe it was something to do with that film they'd been talking about in the office. He tried to recall its name, but soon gave up, and instead raised his glass to his lips. Realising it was empty, he did what any right-minded person would do in the circumstances and walked slightly unsteadily to the bar and ordered a third double Jack Daniels. Seated again with a comfortingly full glass of the best Tennessee bourbon, Gene continued his deliberations.

Who was that figure in the dream? Was it supposed to be him; or, if not, who was it? Was the figure significant at all? Who sent those photographs? They looked uncannily like scenes from his dream. Obviously it was a coincidence, but bloody unnerving just the same. That bloody Ballinger women didn't help—Who did she think she was anyway? Now she'd got that bastard Goldberg on his case, he'd have to be civil and keep a rein on his natural chauvinistic prejudice or his job could be on the line. Gene had lost many points with his boss recently and couldn't afford to lose many more, especially now, with his divorce going through. All these thoughts were mulling around in his mind when a grating voice, not unlike Mo from *The Simpsons*, called "last orders." Gene took a second look at his watch, not believing his eyes the first time.

"Bollocks," he said, to no one in particular. He'd only called in for one drink, to calm him down after his meeting with the Ballinger women. Now, several whiskeys and too many cigarettes later, he still couldn't shed any light on recent events. Oh well, "in for a penny," thought Gene walking with exaggerated care to buy his final drink. Funny how the bar got further away after a few whiskeys, he mused and smiled briefly before continuing his unsteady journey to the waiting bartender. "Mo" gave his best customer a disapproving stare as he downed his final drink in one noisy gulp. "Take care," he said, not really caring whether Gene "took care" or not. On a more lucid and less drunk occasion, Gene might have questioned Mo further on his superficial end-of-conversation phraseology; but now he was too drunk to care.

To appease his social conscience, as well as for the simple reason he could hardly stand let alone drive, Gene decided to leave his car at the pub and collect it later. It was a tossup whether to get a taxi back to the office or get that kid Danny to pick him up. Not a difficult decision under the circumstances, thought Gene, looking at his empty wallet. God, my life's falling to pieces, thought Gene, looking at the blank face of his mobile phone, empty of messages and sadly in need of a charge.

"Hey Danny, come and pick me up from The Spotted Cow," said Gene from the pub phone. Mo, the "full of heart" bartender had grudgingly allowed Gene to use the phone; he didn't want an enquiry if Gene had an accident on his way back to work. Other things might come to the attention of the authorities—underage drinking for one.

Danny's face was expressionless as he listened to the disembodied voice of his boss giving him orders and treating him like a servant or worse. They were all the same, but Harman was the worst of them all expecting everybody to jump to his tune. Still, thought Danny, my time will come soon; and then they'll all regret the way they've treated me—those who survive that is.

CHAPTER 9

MIKE POWELL HAD just received a call from Trudy Ballinger. The call had been out of the blue; in fact, they hadn't spoken for at least a month. Mike sighed; he'd planned a quiet night curling up in his armchair and listening to his new Mozart CD and had looked forward all day to playing it. When Trudy contacted him, it usually meant she had a problem to discuss. Often that meant he would become involved and find himself taking on the burden of Trudy's problems. He found it difficult enough to deal with his own problems these days without taking on Trudy's as well.

They had become firm friends during their university years; whereas, Mike was shy and detached, Trudy outgoing and vivacious. They got on well together adding weight to the adage "unlike poles attract." Since then they had gone different ways, pursuing their individual career paths; but they had remained in contact, albeit spasmodically. Occasionally, when Trudy wanted a sounding board, they would arrange to go out for a drink, or sometimes, even a meal. Tonight it was for the meal. Trudy must have a lot on her mind, thought Mike.

It had come at a bad time for him—he was feeling lousy, probably due to this flu virus that was going around. Two of his patients had cancelled meetings with him this week, which in the circumstances suited Mike, although it wouldn't stop him from sending a bill for missed appointments. Trudy was, as always, very persuasive and not deterred by Mike's obvious reluctance to meet. They had arranged, or rather Trudy had decided, to meet at eight o'clock at a local pub they both liked. The pub did excellent food and a good pint of real ale, although Mike mentally decided to give the ale a miss tonight.

The day his mother died Mike Powell's world fell apart. Irene, Mike's mother, had been ill for years; so when she died, it was no great surprise to anyone. He remembered being distraught the day they had committed his mother to Bletchford psychiatric hospital. He knew something was wrong as he turned the corner and saw his aunt's car parked on the drive. "Your mother has gone to hospital," Aunt Maud explained as he walked in through the back door full of trepidation. Only later was it explained to him that they had sectioned his mother under the mental health act and it was his aunt who had signed the forms for committal.

His mother's mental illness was the overriding reason Mike had decided, at an early age, to become a doctor. By the time Irene's mental condition had worsened, Mike had branched into psychiatry. Over the years he developed a greater understanding of his mother's affliction, which stimulated in him an enduring interest in psychotic behaviour. Well-regarded he studied hard and was offered the consultant's position at Bletchworth Hospital, which he readily accepted. He held the post for three years before moving into more lucrative private practice. His mother never did come out of hospital; and many years later, when she died, his close friend Trudy had been the rock that had helped him to keep on an even keel. So when Trudy needed a friend to talk to, he was always there for her. And this was one such occasion.

On the phone Trudy briefly outlined her problem to Mike, trying to stick to facts rather than feelings. They always worked this way and each would be able to make best use of available time when they met. Get the business out of the way first; they could then enjoy the remaining evening socially. If only I can get rid of this wretched headache, thought Mike, reaching in his medicine cabinet for the painkillers he always kept there. He looked in dismay at the empty bottle; perhaps he had better prescribe himself something stronger next time.

CHAPTER 10

"WHERE ARE YOU off to, Danny?" choked Vincent Craig, jamming a last handful of salt and vinegar crisps into the cavernous gap between his greasy lips? Not skiving off again, I hope." Although Vince was a lummox himself, he did command some respect from the lowest in the pecking order at Goldberg Publications.

"I've got to pick his lordship up from the pub" retorted Danny irritably as he snatched his coat from the back of the old office chair. That was something else that annoyed him. Why did Vince and that slob Harman have luxurious, upholstered chairs when he had to make do with a rickety metal object?

"Wait a minute," yelled Vince, as Danny struggled into his coat, still wet from this morning's downpour; "I want a word with you before you go." Although Gene was the big boss, Vince still liked to flex his muscles occasionally with his subordinates, especially when Gene was out and could not undermine his authority by butting in. "I've noticed you have not been performing well in your job the last couple of weeks; your mind is obviously elsewhere." Vince was warming to the task of asserting his authority. "You didn't run that copy through the spell-check last week as I asked you; Harman gave me the bollocking. You've also been getting into work late looking like a tramp, so you'd better buck your ideas up if you are remotely interested in keeping your job," said Vince sarcastically. "Now, fuck off, and remember what I've just said." Vince felt a warm glow of satisfaction. Danny felt a cold rage.

Danny fumed as he walked down the corridor to the underground parking area. He threw a punch at a concrete pillar, and all he got for his effort was a bloody knuckle—the concrete pillar was unscathed. This did nothing to relieve the anger he felt towards the world at large and his boss in particular. He felt a little better running his keys against the side of Vince's parked car, creating a jagged scratch that ranged across the two side doors and finished just short of the wheel arch.

Danny drove the old, red Ford Fiesta recklessly, narrowly missing a pristine, blue Mercedes parked on the roadside. The decrepit Fiesta was a pool car, so why should he worry any damage wouldn't come out of his pocket. By the time he reached the pub a controlled rage had replaced his initial fury. It took all of Danny's self-control, as he turned into the pub car park and saw Gene waiting, to resist aiming the Fiesta at him and splattering him on the bonnet. Instead, he steered the car towards a large pool of water, the spray of which covered Gene's already damp shoes, eliciting his standard response, especially reserved for these occasions.

The ride back to the office was tense, the atmosphere almost unbearable, with Danny still fuming inside and his boss uncomfortable with sodden shoes and the beginnings of a powerful headache. Gene was too wrapped up in his own problems to even notice Danny's sideward, malevolent glances.

CHAPTER II

THE SMOKY, NOISY atmosphere of the pub did nothing to lessen his nagging headache. Mike walked through the saloon bar on his way to the restaurant area where he had arranged to meet Trudy. He cast a quick glance around the cosy restaurant and spotted her sipping a drink at a table in the far corner.

Trudy smiled at his approaching figure. Mike was an intelligent man, but no one could accuse him of being handsome. A rotund figure, standing about five-feet-nine, he wasn't any girl's idea of a dream date. When Mike and Trudy were out together, they looked an oddly matched couple—men would look, wondering how he came to have such an attractive companion. Years ago it embarrassed him; now, many years later, he thrived on their questioning looks.

Trudy got up from the table to give Mike a hug, noticing as she did his haggard look. Mike responded with a dry kiss on Trudy's cheek. With the formalities over they got on to the more important business of ordering their meal. Mike looked up from the gravy stained menu to see Trudy gazing into space, deep in thought. "Come on, let's order first; then we can 'put the world to rights' while we're waiting," said Mike lapsing into his consultation mode.

For once, contrary to her natural inclination, Trudy allowed Mike to have the last word and continued to scan the vegetarian menu. "Vegetarian lasagne with a side salad," said Trudy with a smile to the young, fair-haired waitress poised with pen and notebook at the ready.

"I'll have steak and ale pie with chips," Mike ordered, aware of his spreading figure, but lacking in the will-power necessary to order healthier fare. Trudy ordered a glass of medium white wine, while Mike, head still aching, decided to go for a pint of orange juice topped up with lemonade.

"Well, fire away," said Mike swallowing the last mouthful of his steak and kidney pie. The food had been average at best and the conversation polite but stilted during the meal; now was the time for a serious discussion.

Trudy downed her remaining wine, covering the glass with her hand in reply to Mike's questioning look. "I'll have a refill later, but I need to keep a clear head at the moment," Trudy said cautiously. "I've two main problems as I briefly described over the phone," began Trudy closing her eyes and trying to assemble her thoughts. "You remember I told you confidentially about my discovery of a new subspecies of dinosaur I was going to present to the society next month," she paused, taking a deep breath and continued. "Well, it's now revealed to the readers of *World in Focus*, and before long every internet user will know the intimate details of the discovery. I have spent two years of my life on that dig and at the very least would have expected the pleasure of presenting my discovery to the society," Trudy's raised voice elicited tentative looks from the next table.

"I hope you don't think I've told anyone." Mike cut across Trudy in full flow, a risky thing to do at the best of times and this was far from the best of times. "Anything that's told me in confidence stays that way," Mike continued in a suitably hurt tone.

Well that's answered my next question, thought Trudy, silently relieved she had not yet voiced the question. "Of course not, Mike," Trudy continued. "I have narrowed down to the few in my department who knew about the discovery, but frankly I have no reason to doubt their loyalty. Rival palaeontologist and other people outside the department are more likely suspects."

"So how can I help?" Mike inquired, rather more sharply than he had intended, aware that he had not convinced Trudy that he hadn't let it slip, though unintentionally, to a colleague or friend.

"Well, I was hoping I could bounce a few ideas off you and maybe come up with a way of finding who was responsible for the leak." Trudy realised that this meeting may not provide the help and support she was expecting. Mike had reacted out of character; perhaps this was a side to him she had not seen before. She wasn't sure whether she liked the new forceful Mike or not. She would have to tread carefully or the whole evening could turn out a disaster.

"Well, first you will have to find out who had access to the graphic mock-up of the dinosaur." Mike leaned forward adding emphasis to his next point. "It's obvious that whoever knew about the dinosaur didn't know the name your department had given the newly discovered creature." Trudy looked up abruptly; she hadn't thought of that. She had focused on who knew about the new discovery, not on who had access to the graphic mock-up. This would narrow the field down considerably. Perhaps the meeting would have some benefit after all.

"Another avenue to follow is the identity of the photographer. From what you said over the phone, these photographs look so real it would have taken someone with a good deal of experience to produce them."

"Hmm," murmured Trudy, "there couldn't be many who specialise in this form of photography."

"You could try to get information from *World in Focus*," Mike continued, now full of his own importance and oblivious to what his companion had said.

"Mike," Trudy bristled, "I'm not one of your patients; I came for advice, not a lecture."

"Sorry, let's have another drink," Mike signalled the pretty waitress who took their order. This time Trudy ordered a large glass of wine.

"So, what's the other problem you wanted to 'run up the flagpole'?" Mike's language lapsed into management jargon.

Trudy hated jargon, and it often prejudiced her opinion of the people who used it. Mike, however, was an exception. She had intended to discuss Gene Harman, but the evening hadn't been as relaxed as she had expected. It didn't now seem fitting to discuss her feelings about Gene. "Oh, it's not important; we can talk about it another time," Trudy replied, now keen to draw the evening to a conclusion. Trudy dispelled any other thoughts Mike may have had when she stood up abruptly and leaned over to give her escort a peck on the cheek. "Good night, Mike; thanks for your advice. It's been a delightful evening." As a parting shot, Trudy announced, not with much conviction, "We must do it again soon." With that she hastily made her way out of the restaurant leaving Mike wondering what had gone wrong.

Trudy had always been unpredictable, even when they had been at university together. Perhaps that was one reason he liked her so much—that and her "bloody attractive" figure, he contemplated as a lascivious smile crossing his face. His head was still niggling as he made his way out through the smoky bar;

Trudy was already out of sight. Mike's first inclination was to phone for a taxi; but after consideration he decided to walk home—perhaps it would help him think straight. His memory lapses and those infernal headaches had been a great worry to him lately. Headaches getting worse and memory lapses more frequent all added to his stressed condition, which in turn exacerbated his problems. "Ever decreasing circles," he thought bitterly as he continued a lonely journey through deserted streets, his footsteps beating an irregular tattoo on litter strewn pavements.

CHAPTER 12

GENE ARRIVED FOR work early, at least early for Gene. He had a meeting with Jason Goldberg this morning, and you were late at your peril. He'd received the call about ten-thirty last night, just after the television news had finished. It was lucky he hadn't passed out with Scotland's finest. He usually had by that time. Gene was hoping it was for a bollocking. Goldberg only invited you to an early morning meeting in his office for two reasons, a bollocking, or the sack; and at this moment the bollocking seemed the favourite option. There was a time, thought Gene, when an invitation to a meeting with the boss could have been to congratulate you for a job well-done. Those times had past long ago, as had youth and ambition.

He'd had ambition once; he'd been editor of a local rag before he was twenty. The sky had been the limit when he'd accepted the offer of a journalist position at Goldberg Publications. Unexpectedly, eighteen months later, a vacancy for editor of *World Focus* had presented itself, and to Gene's surprise Goldberg offered him the position. For weeks after, he and Lois had spent many happy evenings planning their future together.

That's when it all started to go wrong. He'd not resisted the temptations on offer with his lofty status and had spent many late nights at the office with Janice, an attractive young woman from the typing pool. If it had just ended there, Lois might have forgiven him; but then there were the late night drinking sessions as well. Sometimes he did not even come home at night; too drunk to drive, he would sleep at Janice's flat and go straight to work next day. The last time had been the final straw. Lois left him. Now he was in the middle of an expensive divorce, and he desperately needed his job. That's why he was hoping for a bollocking.

Amanda, Goldberg's secretary, ushered Gene towards the inner sanctum of Goldberg Publications. "He's expecting you," Amanda said with a look she reserved for many a condemned man. Amanda, over the years, had seen many an employee pass through these portals only to emerge half an hour later shaken and unemployed. It always gave a warm glow, knowing it would never happen to her. She had too much on Jason Goldberg. She was untouchable, or so she thought. She watched the big editor as he walked through the large doorway to the waiting Goldberg, who sat at his desk like a predatory spider awaiting his next victim.

Gene braced himself as he pushed open the large oak door to Goldberg's inner sanctum, acutely aware that many who were summoned to Goldberg's den came out jobless. The spider spoke: "Come in," Goldberg said as he waved Gene towards a leather chair. Aware of Goldberg's reputation for embarrassing visitors, Gene half expected the highly polished leather chair to make a farting sound when he sat down. Relieved when it didn't, the editor of *World in Focus*, concentrated his mind on still being the editor after the meeting.

"I'm interested in those photographs we published in the *Focus* last week," said Goldberg coming straight to the point. "I have spoken to Professor Ballinger at the university, and I want you to find the person who sent them; if there's a story, there I want it."

"They arrived anonymously," ventured Gene, knowing it would not satisfy Goldberg. I've had Archie look over the photographs, and he thinks they are genuine.

"I pay you good money; now earn it for a change," Goldberg retorted. "I've had my eye on you and your creative expenses for a while now." If you had an Achilles heel, Jason Goldberg would find it. "Find who sent them. I want results. If you can't manage it, I'll get young Vince involved." This was a conversation killer to Gene. He'd guessed for a while now that Goldberg wanted his nephew to take over his job. Now it was finally out in the open—he wanted Vincent Craig to be the editor of *World in Focus.*

Gene nearly laughed out loud, but decided against. He knew that Goldberg had to please his sister; she had inherited a large tranche of Goldberg shares in their father's will. She wanted her son to have the editor's job, and it was Goldberg's responsibility to see he got it. "So I'll give you until the end of this week to get me an exclusive with this photographer; otherwise, you might find yourself working for Vince next week." Gene felt like Reggie Perrin after a meeting with CJ as he walked out of Goldberg's office. At least it wasn't a farting chair, thought Gene, searching in vain for anything positive from his meeting.

Amanda was sitting smugly at her desk, drinking coffee from a bone china cup, presented to her for twenty-five years of dedicated service. Gene advanced towards her desk. "Still working for us, Gene?" she asked, barely able to resist breaking out into a broad grin.

"Bollocks, you fat cow," Gene muttered on his way past the self-important secretary, the smile now frozen on her face.

He arrived back at his office feeling slightly better.

CHAPTER 13

VINCENT CRAIG HAD kept a daily diary now for more than six months. Most people keep a diary to record their own daily activities for reference later, but Vince had broken with this tradition—his diary recorded Gene Harman's daily activities. Vince had a good reason to record his boss's movements; he wanted Gene Harman's job. Although the editor of *World in Focus* was good at his job, he was also a "loose cannon," a type not encouraged in Goldberg Publications. Vince knew that if he could build a strong enough case against Gene Harman, his uncle wouldn't hesitate to sack his errant editor and give the job to his nephew. So it gladdened Vince's heart when a shell-shocked Gene Harman walked into the office after his early morning bollocking. "Morning, boss." Vince slipped the diary into his desk drawer as he greeted his editor. "Been here all night," he added glancing around the office with the smug look of someone who thinks he has said something funny and thinks everyone else appreciates the joke as well. No one did.

"Fuck off," Gene was not at his best after a bollocking, but he was still able to ad-lib with the best. "Come into my office and bring me a cup of coffee," Gene ordered. "If you can manage to drag your fat arse out of the chair," he added.

Gene slurped the lukewarm coffee glancing unsmilingly at his hapless assistant. Vince looked on in trepidation, the glory of his brilliant witticism a far distant memory now. "Okay, Crusty, still feeling funny, or can we get on with some work?" The editor was a fan of *The Simpsons*, but less of a fan of Vince? Gene was making his subordinate squirm in the same way that Goldberg had treated him with less success earlier.

Vince felt the blood rush to his face "Sorry, Boss," was all he could think of saying. Unlike Gene, the art of the ad-lib was not his strong suit.

"Right here's the problem—your bloody uncle has a bee in his bonnet, and I need to find the person responsible for sending in those photographs." Vince could guess what was coming next; years of experience as subordinate to the miserable editor taught him well. His boss didn't disappoint. "Now, guess what? My problem becomes your problem," Gene continued, his face twisted in a dark scowl, "so find the bastard, and hurry up about it."

"Any idea where to start looking, Boss," Vince ventured tentatively, aware he was treading on soft ground?

"You could try the top of Everest or deep in the Borneo jungle for all I care," Gene's ability in the art of the ad-lib was even surpassed by his mastery of the sarcastic comment. "Get that Pratt Weston to help; if you can find him, he'll probably have more ideas than you, which shouldn't be too difficult," he added for good measure. Gene was his most gracious, motivational self in these situations and Vince at his most abject.

Vince walked out of his boss's office regretting his pitiable attempt at humour. To say it hadn't gone down well was an understatement. If he had a cat, he'd kick it; still there was always Daniel Weston—not a cat, granted, but any port in a storm. Right now he had to carry on with the job Uncle Jason had given him; then, he'd find out who the mystery person is without Danny's help. Possibly in the future he and Danny would work together; meanwhile, he had another entry to put in his diary. The case against Harman was building up nicely. If he played his cards right, it wouldn't be long now before he'd be sitting in the editor's office; then he'd make the others jump. They'd laugh at his jokes and fawn around him, as they did Harman now. The thought suddenly cheered him up, and a smile briefly lit up his round moon face. He might even promote Danny, as he was the only one who took him seriously. In fact, he liked Danny a lot. Vince wondered if the feeling was mutual as he surreptitiously made another incriminating entry in his diary.

CHAPTER 14

TRUDY RANG THE principal's number for the third time; there had not been any answer to her two previous tries. This time she dialled his home, more in hope than conviction. "Ian Mason." She was in luck, but the tone of the abrupt greeting told Trudy the principal wasn't in a good mood this morning.

"Hello, Ian—how are you?" Trudy responded confidently; then, with the formalities over, she came straight to the point. "I must talk to you. It's urgent. When can we meet?" Trudy had a good working relationship with the principal. They had respect for each other both personally and professionally. Academically they were both well-thought-of in their respective fields, she a palaeontologist and he a geologist with a special interest in vulcanology.

Ian Mason was the person British television news agencies liked to call on whenever there was a need for expert opinion on any natural disaster. "I'm working from home today on a presentation to the local Chamber of Commerce," the principal explained. "I've only got a week to complete it, and you know how important their financial backing is to the university," he added.

"It will only take half an hour," Trudy persisted. I'll come over to your house if it will be more convenient."

"You win—see you in ten minutes." Ian admired Trudy's pushy nature. When the Principal's position had become vacant, he had been selected for the post by virtue of his intelligence and academic abilities, rather than for any management skills he might have. His wife had been the driving force in his early years, but since she had died, two years ago, he had been a ship without a rudder. The virulent cancer reduced what had been a powerful character into a cadaverous shell, totally dependent on the person she had dominated for years. Now Ian would bury himself in academic pursuits he felt comfortable with, rather than with the daily management of the university. Those responsibilities he delegated to trusted senior members of his staff. This was the reason he could often work from home. There was another reason—Ian Mason had a secret life.

The door chimes hadn't finished their resounding introduction to Beethoven's *1812 Overture* when Ian opened the door. Trudy hated these chimes almost as much as she disliked the *William Tell Overture* chimes that several of her friends thought were fashionable. "Hello, Ian—thanks for seeing me at short notice," Trudy said breathlessly even before she had crossed the threshold.

"Come in. I'm working in the conservatory; you go on through while I make the coffee." Ian's reply was almost as hurried as Trudy's greeting had been. As Trudy walked through the lounge to the adjoining conservatory, she was aware for the first time how tasteful and expensively furnished Ian's house was. There must be more perks to a principal's job than she thought. Her apartment, although comfortable, was modest by comparison. God, this glasshouse must be worth more than my apartment, she thought, walking slowly into the conservatory.

"Well, what's the problem?" Ian's distinctive voice jolted Trudy out of her reverie. He placed a mug of steaming coffee on the table in front of Trudy before continuing. "Biscuit?" he asked as he held before her a plate of custard creams and garibaldis.

"No, thanks," Trudy responded as she raised the mug to her lips, taking a sip of the hot liquid before explaining her urgent request for a meeting. It was an abbreviated version of the events she had explained to Mike the previous night. When she had finished, Trudy sat back in the comfortable chair awaiting Ian's comments; her gaze was met by the principal's unblinking stare. His failure to react surprised and unnerved her. "Damn," Trudy exclaimed, breaking the silence and spilling her coffee. Ian shook himself out of his reverie, rushing forward with a serviette to soak up the spill.

The incident marked the end of the meeting for Trudy still smarting from her principal's lack of interest or willingness to help with her problem. After wiping herself down with the proffered serviette and exchanging a few pleasantries, she bid him goodbye. "Look, I'd like to help; perhaps we could arrange a meeting next week when I'm less busy. I'm sorry; but I just haven't got time at the moment for my own problems, let alone anyone else's" Ian apologised as they shook hands-on the doorstep, the sincerity in his voice nonexistent.

"Bollocks," thought Trudy as she walked down the drive, remembering that she must speak to Gene Harman and see what information she could get from him. She felt a tremor of anticipation at the thought.

CHAPTER 15

DANNY SAT CROSS-legged in a lotus position, oblivious to the hardness of the bare wooden floorboards. The room was gloomy, the only light provided by five candles, one in each corner of the small room. The fifth candle was standing on a blackened saucer in front of him, flickering and changing his face alternately from light to dark. He was having an excited conversation with his best friend, David.

The pitch of Daniel's voice rose and the rate of his speech accelerated as he explained to David how he hated his father for leaving his mother and him many years ago. And now he had returned. "Harman is my father," he explained to his attentive audience. "He left me and my mother; now he's come back to kill us," Daniel went on. "So we must kill him first." David sat in silence looking implacably at his friend. Daniel got hastily to his feet and walked rapidly around the small room. David still looked on expressionless, waiting until his friend had calmed down. At last Daniel relaxed, his pace slowed, and the erratic twitch in the corner of his cheek became less frenetic, finally stopping altogether. He sat again in the lotus position, facing his friend, with a new, crazed look in his eyes.

In silence Daniel stared at an object high in the corner of the room. The only sound was the steady tick-tock of the old wooden station clock, one of the few possessions he had inherited from his mother. David said nothing, waiting for Daniel to begin talking again. After a while Daniel lowered his gaze and became aware of his friend sitting silently in front of him. The mask that had been Danny's face relaxed; he looked at his friend and smirked, and his eyes took on a bright luminescence in the fire glow. He now had the composure of a person confident in what he was going to do and how he was going to achieve it. As David's voice gradually penetrated deep into Danny's subconscious, he became aware of the swish on the pendulum of the old station clock.

"What does your mother want us to do?" The voice seemed hollow and faraway. The clock continued ticking; the pendulum persevered in its laboured motion. "What does your mother want us to do?" the voice repeated, more insistent this time.

"Make Harman suffer and then kill him," Daniel shouted. "Kill my father," he shouted again. "Kill him! Kill them all!" Exhausted, he collapsed to the floor, fighting for each ragged breath, his body convulsing in impossible shapes. Meanwhile, the candles continued to create their grotesque patterns, and the clock continued to tick, like someone's admonishing finger registering disapproval. The pendulum struggled, against all odds, to make one last journey there and back. Suddenly Danny's face relaxed; his body ended its convulsions,

David's smile continued to waver in the gloom of dwindling candlelight, as Danny slowly raised himself to his feet and leaned heavily against the wall, his breathing laboured and ragged with the effort. The room suddenly became darker as the light from the saucer candle finally expired, its charred wick sinking into the depths of the grey molten wax.

David still looked on silently waiting.

Danny stretched and looked at his watch; it was three in the morning—time for a walk. He struggled into an old donkey jacket and put on his gloves, revelling in the warmth encompassing his cold hands. Opening the door to the night air, he paused and turned back gazing round the empty room. "Bye, David—see you later," he said, as he walked out into the murky street.

CHAPTER 16

GENE LOOKED HOPEFUL as he opened his battered leather wallet, proudly displaying the initials "G.H." in gold leaf. The wallet had been a present from the early days of his marriage to Lois. These had been the halcyon days when they had plans and dreams and money to buy each other presents. He remembered the day she gave him the wallet: they'd been joking about having too much money when he started his new job at Goldberg Publications. Lois had even thought to have his initials engraved into the leather. Now she wanted the wallet back and all his money to go with it. His reverie ceased abruptly as the unpleasant reality came flooding back. The wallet was, as he had suspected, empty except for a sheaf of good old credit cards. This was a legacy from the later days of his marriage when bitterness and frustration had replaced the dreams.

He recalled that he'd had strange dreams in those days; but there'd always been Lois lying at his side to offer comfort as a young, attractive wife could. Soon he would forget his dream, immersing himself in their close embrace. Now he had to find money to pay for those blissful days.

Gene reached into his wallet and pulled out one of his plastic friends. Armed with a MasterCard, he walked slowly down the street to the cash point, placed conveniently outside his local bank. He didn't go marching into the bank these days; he didn't want to give those patronising tellers the pleasure of reminding him, with a smirk, that he was at the limit of his overdraft. At least the machines didn't smirk when you were short of money; they just gave a cryptic message and kept your card. "Bollocks," Gene uttered the word that made him famous to all who knew him. The machine had kept his card. Gene decided to try his Visa card next; he hadn't used it much lately. Luckily the old Visa came up trumps. He was tempted to draw his maximum for the day but instead settled for one hundred pounds; the receipt told him he was depressingly close to his limit. With his wallet comfortingly bulging, Gene retraced his steps back to the imposing entrance to Goldberg Publications.

"Good morning, Mr. Harman," Judy called across the foyer.

"Might be for you, but not for me," Gene replied oozing with charm. Dealing with difficult members of the public was "all in a day's work" for Judy, so she had no problem handling a belligerent editor who could be charming one day and a bastard the next.

"You've got a visitor waiting upstairs," Judy continued, ignoring Gene's sarcastic reply and austere look.

"Did they give a name by any chance, or do I have to guess?" Gene didn't like playing guessing games especially with a receptionist.

"Sorry, Mr. Harman." Judy realised that the big chief wasn't in the mood for banter. "Her name is Professor Trudy Ballinger."

Gene decided to take the stairs to his fifth floor office to give him time to think before meeting with the indomitable Ms Ballinger. The idea was good, but by the time he reached his office all he could concentrate on was getting his next breath.

Gene's heart was pounding from his recent exertion. He lent against the door frame of the main office, still breathing heavily, and watched Trudy through the window of a three-by two-metre, glass, partitioned box that he laughingly called his private office. As he walked through the main office toward his glass box, he felt like Claris Starling must have felt on the way to her first meeting with Hannibal Lector, as she passed through the cacophony of lewd comments from the "cannibal's' fellow prisoners. The 'prisoners in this instance were employees of Goldberg Publications but their remarks were just as suggestive as those of the fictional inmates. Only Daniel remained silent, but he stared intently at the figure of Trudy silhouetted against the office window.

Gene ignored the comments as he proceeded, with increasing irritability, to his drab office and to the waiting, real-life Ms. Ballinger. Trudy was sitting behind his desk texting a message on her mobile. As Gene entered his office, banging the door against the recently decorated wall, she rose from his plush status chair.

"Good morning, Ms Ballinger—how nice to see you again." said Gene with a hint of sarcasm as he reluctantly shook the extended hand. Trudy's hand was cool, her grip firm, and her green eyes unwavering. He felt his early anger weaken.

"Good morning, Mr. Harman." To get the information she wanted from this meeting, Trudy would be pleasant or, as a last resort, engage in a little flirtation with the man whose hand she was now holding. "I hope you don't mind my dropping in on you like this," Trudy continued with a smile.

It was against Gene's nature to be civil to people who invaded his domain uninvited. Any of his staff would corroborate that. The last meeting had been on Trudy's home ground; this was his territory, a whole different situation. "What do you want, Ms

Ballinger? Make it quick—I'm busy." Gene was giving Trudy a taste of her own medicine. This wasn't going the way Trudy had expected. The fluttering eyes and the intimate handshake would do the trick with most men; obviously Gene Harman didn't fit into that category.

The phone on Gene's desk rang before Trudy could reply. Gene snatched the phone and snapped into the mouthpiece, "I'll be there as soon as I can. Sorry, Ms Ballinger, I've got to go; but we could have a drink tomorrow night and continue our discussion." The sudden turnaround surprised Trudy. She wanted to elicit the editor's help to track down the person responsible for letting the world know about her discovery. Still, after a drink or two he might be more willing to help.

"How about The Spotted Pig? Gene felt he was in control now.

"Sorry I can't make tomorrow night. How about Saturday?" replied Trudy picking up her handbag and phone. She could have made it tomorrow; in fact, it would have been more convenient, but that would make it too easy for him, she thought spitefully.

"I'll meet you in the bar at eight-thirty then," Gene was at his most gallant. Trudy paused in the doorway before slamming the door behind her. She strode angrily out of the main office followed by the lecherous looks of the male staff and the envious glances of the female office workers.

Gene leaned back in his chair with a self-satisfied look on his face–that worked out better than expected. A drink with the professor—who knows what that might lead to; he could but hope. Good job getting Archie to ring him—it made it easier to suggest an evening drink. That she agreed so readily surprised him. Must be his manly charm, he mused reaching for the phone to book a table.

The Spotted Pig was not the best venue to impress a girl on the first date, especially the smoky bar with the locals "f—ing" and "blinding," with the occasional fart thrown in for good measure. At least the restaurant was clean and quiet for most of the time. The problem was that they would have to eat if he booked the table, and most probably he would have to pay. That was the problem. Ah well, good old flexible friend to the rescue. Perhaps he would win the lottery; then all his problems would be over. After all, the odds of fourteen million to one were not that great. Gene's Uncle Roy always bought a lottery ticket when there was a "rollover"; he didn't bother when the prize might be only a couple of million. Right now, with his finances the way they were, ten pounds would be welcome to Gene.

CHAPTER 17

PRINCIPAL IAN MASON was deep in thought as he crossed the busy road that led to the park entrance. He stood on the chevrons in the centre of the road with traffic zooming past him on either side. A large man with a red beard and no sense of humour leaned out of his taxi window shouting something incomprehensible, but the meaning was clear as he raised his finger in salute. Ian waited until the traffic lights turned red to stop the onrushing cars; he then crossed the final hurdle to reach the comparative sanctuary of the park. As he walked slowly deeper into the leafy core of Bletchworth Park, he imagined himself as David Attenborough on one of his many "zoo quests" to remote parts. His reverie was cut short as he spotted the lone figure of Helen in the distance sitting huddled on a park bench.

Why he'd got himself into this predicament he could not imagine. It started three years ago, when he was at his lowest ebb, shortly after his wife died. He had looked for a shoulder to cry on; as it turned out, Helen had offered more than just a shoulder. The result was she had become pregnant. Since each of them had promising careers, they had agreed that starting a family did not fit into their current life plans and that an abortion was the only way forward. Now the situation had turned bitter. Helen's career had fallen short of expectations, and she blamed Ian for not using his influence to help her get the position she had set her heart on. What she didn't realise was that Ian's career was on the wane.

When his wife died, Ian's drive died with her. Now he was fighting for his own career—to hell with Helen, he thought as he approached the bench where she huddled. Ian reached for the packet of cigarettes he'd just bought. When his wife died so horribly from cancer, he'd vowed never to smoke again; but the stress of the past few weeks had weakened and finally broken down his resolve. He could thank Helen for that too, he thought, giving a small wave of greeting as he sat down beside her.

"I haven't received a cheque from you for two months, and the last one was less than we agreed on." Helen did not waste time with pleasantries; such was their relationship that both viewed any pretence at polite conversation with suspicion.

Ian lowered his head and studied his fingernails intensely. When confronted with a question for which he had no satisfactory answer, Ian often reverted to his nails. Some colleagues even measured the success of an interdepartmental meeting by the number of questions they could ask that would bring on the habit. "I can't keep paying for the mistakes we both made in the past," he finally said. "We've got to 'call it a day' and move on," he declared still inspecting his nails.

A dark scowl clouded Helen‘s countenance, and her thin face took on a demonic look. "You bastard," she choked trying desperately to voice the right words. "You ruined my health and career, and now you say let‘s move on; well, if my career is ruined, I shall make bloody sure yours is as well."

As Ian looked at the contorted face before him, he found it hard to believe that he had ever liked this woman; yet, for six months they spent every moment they could in each other's company. How little we know the true nature of people, he thought sadly, shaking his head. "Well, Helen, do your worst; but I'm not paying any more, and I don't think it would be in your interest to take it further." As Ian got slowly to his feet, he looked down on the hunched figure of Helen, anger rising in him as he realised she was attempting to blackmail him. This feeling was suddenly followed by an icy coldness, which came over him as he turned and walked away from the forlorn figure.

CHAPTER 18

DR. MIKE POWELL'S head slumped forward on his chest; the sudden movement jolted him into a semi-wakeful state. The television playing disjointedly in the background gradually penetrated his brain. Figures in multicoloured shirts, with faces distorted by false bonhomie, raced pointlessly about the screen full of their own importance, entertaining millions but educating no one. Mike raised his head and looked towards the blank window overlooking his back garden. God, it was dark outside. How long had he been asleep? What time was it? These questions competed for answers in his befuddled brain. It must be the Prozac; I must remember to reduce the dose, he reasoned, but with all the conviction of a forty-a-day man vowing to give up smoking.

Ironically, remembering or, more accurately, not remembering was his problem. He had not just short term memory loss, but big black holes of memory deficiency. Mike needed help to enable him to cope with the worry he'd had lately; the drugs he'd prescribed himself bridged what he prayed would be a 'temporary bad patch.' The irony of the situation was that patients paid him good money for help solving their problems. Mike, however, was having great difficulty coping with his own problems, and his symptoms were worsening. He'd prescribed himself several different drugs in the last six months to help keep him on an even keel, but nothing had worked consistently. After a brief respite, the dark cloud would return.

He'd spent many hours analysing his symptoms, as he would with his fee-paying patients, but with even greater urgency. When did the memory lapses first start? Could he identify trigger events? Did the lapses start before or after his bouts of depression? His anxiety made these questions difficult to answer. He now knew how his patients must feel under his probing questions.

Mike felt his personality changing from modest and retiring to aggressive and confrontational. The other night with Trudy was nearly a disaster. They had always been comfortable with each other. Last night, however, was different; he could feel his blood rising several times during their conversation, and he was aware that Trudy was upset by his aggressive approach. Perhaps he should ring and apologise for his out of character behaviour. He dismissed that idea and decided on the face-to-face approach. That way there would be no misunderstanding. Hadn't he always given this advice to his patients? So he would go to see Trudy with a bouquet of flowers and pass on his apologies personally. Perhaps she would invite him to stay the night, he mused, suddenly aware that he was thinking about Trudy in a new way. They were good friends and had been since university; now he seemed to want more out of their relationship. The new aggressive Mike was determined there would be more—whether Trudy liked it or not!

CHAPTER 19

AS HE HURRIED through the small copse, he could feel the adrenaline coursing through his trembling body. His mind was in overload; he felt exhilarated and powerful.

The look in her eyes as he had strangled the life out of her writhing body had given him the best feeling ever. A worthless bitch, who wouldn't normally give him the time of day, had begged him for mercy. Pleading for life was a great leveller; it had given him the power of life or death. Sparing her life, however, wouldn't have been much fun, so with adrenaline fuelled strength he had continued squeezing until her eyes bulged nearly from their sockets and the life force drained from her body. He had stood admiring his handiwork for several minutes after all movement in his hapless victim had ceased. It was the sound of happy, yapping dogs that jolted him out of his reverie.

He was reluctant to leave the body that had afforded him such exquisite pleasure; but as the sound of dogs got nearer, he gave one last, lingering look at the pathetic body shrouded in muddy rags before walking swiftly away from the scene of his conquest. As he hurried more deeply into the wood, the yapping now in the far distance, his mind raced feverishly. Why he hadn't done it before he couldn't imagine; God knows the opportunities had been there. He'd thought about it many times, but something always held him back; maybe it was the prospect of being caught or simply a reluctance to take such a leap into the unknown. Now, at last, he had done it. He felt an enormous sense of release, as if he had been granted a new life and the freedom to do what he liked.

Gradually he became aware of the pitter-pattering rain delicately playing a gentle, rhythmic beat on the leaves of the trees. He looked skyward and laughed; the cool rain felt good on his face.

CHAPTER 20

VINCE WAS PANTING heavily, more than just out of breath—his heart was trying to batter its way out of his chest cavity. Not for nothing had he earned the endearing nickname of "little fat git" from colleagues and even from friends. Not that he had many friends. Still gasping, he stood back in the shop entranceway, sheltering himself from the intense rain. The distress Vince was feeling at this moment had less to do with his excess poundage than with his horror at what he had seen after following Daniel Weston into Fircroft Woods.

Vince was driving home late from the office when he spotted Danny crossing the road leading to the forest. It was the opportunity he'd been hoping for—to see Danny outside work and perhaps get to know him better. Vince had decided to drive round to the other side of the wood and wait for Danny to come into view. He would then stroll over, pretending that it was a chance meeting; and if all went well, he might suggest a drink in the new wine bar on the High Street. Vince had waited impatiently for fifteen minutes before deciding to go and see why Danny was taking so long. He cursed out loud as he walked through the wet undergrowth, oozing mud; his fashionable Italian style shoes were more suitable for the dance floor than for country walks. Prickly bushes grabbed at his trouser legs, pulling fibres out of the cheap, synthetic cloth. Miserable and about to walk back to the car, Vince had recognised the familiar gait of Danny as he loomed like a ghostly spectre in the misty rain. Head down against the rain, walking briskly, Danny had barged past the startled Vince, oblivious to his colleague's friendly wave.

The yelp of a little Jack Russell terrier that ran out of the undergrowth had distracted Vince before he was able to run after Danny. Vince, after shouting the obligatory "Fuck you, Danny Weston" to the retreating figure, had decided to carry on walking through the wood. Not wishing to retrace his steps through the quagmire and hoping to have an opportunity to throw a brick at that yappy little dog, Vince plodded on. Five minutes later, however, he had cause to regret his decision, when he stumbled on the body. Vacant, milky white eyes, protruding from a blue, swollen face, stared up at him, eliciting an involuntary regurgitation of a previously enjoyed dinner over the pathetic heap of sodden rags that once was Helen Baxter.

That was the reason for his acute distress as he leaned in the doorway of the television repair shop on the High Street.

CHAPTER 21

DANNY AND HIS friend David were still holding an animated conversation when they passed Vince Craig in the woods. Vince didn't create much of an impact at the best of times; this time he created no impression at all as Danny, wrapped in his thoughts, swept by.

Fircroft Wood's north exit, or entrance, depending on which way you were going, led to the main road that stretched all the way between Hanbury and Bletchworth, some twenty miles or so. Hanbury Road's High Street was always busy housing a cinema, a pub, an Indian restaurant, and car showrooms, all within the space of half a mile. *War of the Worlds* was showing at the Regal Cinema tonight, and a full house was expected. A building less regal than the town's cinema is hard to imagine; but the popularity of Tom Cruise, combined with the reputation of the original fifties' version, helped contribute to the four deep queue now straggling untidily across the pavement. Some of the queuing throng looked on sympathetically as a dishevelled, and decidedly muddy, Danny Weston marched past, still talking excitedly to his invisible companion. Others, less sympathetic, did what all louts worthy of their salt do under the circumstances—they shouted insults after the retreating figure. Danny was oblivious to the taunting, lost in his—and David's—world.

CHAPTER 22

THE TWENTY-FIRST of March was Gene's birthday, and it had been one he would like to forget. In fact, it was a day anyone who had contact with Gene that day would like to forget. For a start, it was Sunday, for most people a chance to lie in and relax, but not for employees at Goldberg Publications; for them, Sunday was just another working day. Gene was, as usual, driving too fast in his eagerness to hand out his regular Sunday morning diatribe to eagerly awaiting Goldberg employees. His route took him down a road that offered plenty of cover for police to hide, hoping to catch motorists doing thirty-one miles an hour. Well, Gene fooled them; he was doing fifty-three miles an hour when he was pulled over by a smiling police officer. Unfortunately for Gene, but luckily for the smiling, uniformed man, Gene didn't have his driving license or insurance details with him. The guardian of the law's ballpoint was a blur as he filled out a document Gene knew only too well.

"Produce your documents to Bletchworth Police Station, was the police officer's parting shot. Gene whispered his reply, not wishing to make matters worse than they were. They would, however, get worse as the day rolled on.

He was in his office when the news came through of another

brutal slaying. This time a body had been found in Fircroft Wood, just six miles outside Bletchworth. The report came through that a woman in her thirties had been found strangled; so far, the body hadn't been identified. The newspaper hacks were already on the story when Vince Craig knocked timorously and walked in to disturb Gene's meditation. "Boss Uncle Jason rang before you arrived," he said. "He wants your progress report on his desk before he goes out at lunchtime.—Oh, and happy birthday, Boss." Vince swayed to avoid the book flying towards him. Looks like another entry in the diary, he mused as the missile struck the door behind him. The rest of the day followed a familiar pattern based on Murphy's law–"Anything that can go wrong will go wrong." On Gene's birthday it often did.

Gene yawned as he drove home, at thirty-one miles an hour; it had been a trying day. All the hacks had been busy pleading with contacts for information that would give them an edge, in a competitive profession, over their colleagues. Gene was mulling over the events of the day when he suddenly became aware of a stationary car suddenly filling his vision. His brakes screeched as he skidded to a vibrating halt, within inches of the vehicle. Gene searched around in his extensive vocabulary to come up with a word befitting the occasion, finally settling for the tried and tested "Bollocks!" He was shaking as he wrenched himself off the steering wheel. "Must remember to get the seat belt fixed," he murmured easing back into the traffic flow.

It was a major effort for Gene to drag his overweight body up the grimy stairs to his small one bedroom flat. I wonder what the professor would think if she knew what a hovel he lived in. Still, it was only temporary; in about ten years he might get a two-bedroom flat. Good old Lois and her mum, he thought. At least he could joke about it; but then it isn't funny, he realised. The red plastic clock on the wall said seven fifteen. His date with Professor Trudy was at eight-thirty. Perhaps she would give him a birthday present, he thought hopefully and smiled lasciviously at the prospect. God, he was tired—best shower, then have a lie down for half an hour, he decided. The lukewarm, slow running shower did little to encourage Gene to luxuriate under the flowing water. Five minutes later, wrapped in his old, red silk dressing gown, with Rocky II emblazoned proudly on the back, he lay down on off-white sheets and pulled his blue duvet up tightly around his neck. He was asleep almost as soon as his head touched the pillow.

CHAPTER 23

DETECTIVE INSPECTOR ANDY Dale was angry; in fact, he was furious. The murder in Fircroft Wood had landed on his desk just as he was about to go home for the weekend. He dreaded phoning his wife to say he was going to be late, especially as her sister and husband were paying a visit for the first time in six months. Secretly he hoped it would be another six months before they visited again, but he daren't tell Joan that. Meanwhile he had to let her know, like it or not.

Being a senior detective in the police force meant the possibility of "call out" even at the most unsociable of times, often interfering with Joan's arrangements. Over the last year this had driven a major wedge between them. He breathed deeply in an effort to steady his nerves, pulled his shoulders back, and reached for the phone. Not surprisingly, Joan didn't understand; in fact, his wife of fifteen years told him in words that would have made a navvy proud that it was the last straw. Decision time—it was either his wife or the job; her parting shot of "fuck you" left no doubt in Andy's mind that she was a trifle miffed; and when Andy's wife was upset, it didn't bode well for the rest of Andy's team.

"What do we know about the murder?" Andy looked directly at his sergeant, D.S. Rob Murray. Rob was due for retirement in six months—not a moment too soon, he thought as he prepared to present his report.

"Well," Rob began, clearing his throat loudly, a habit that always irritated Andy. "The victim is a white female estimated to be in her mid-thirties—strangled, according to Doc Anderson; but the doc said she'd give us more information later when she's finished the examination."

"We are carrying out a thorough search of Fircroft Wood," chimed in D.C. Laura Thomas, trying to impress. She had high expectations of promotion when Rob retired, so upholding a high profile, especially with the boss, could only benefit her long-term prospects. She had other advantages, however, over her male counterparts; and she would use them if necessary, to achieve her objectives.

"Thanks, Laura," Andy butted in just as his office phone began ringing. "Carry on with the briefing, Rob, while I get the phone," he ordered his sergeant, as he walked briskly towards his office. Perhaps his wife was ringing to apologise and beg his forgiveness, he reflected ruefully, as he picked up the black desk phone.

"Hello, Guv; we've found the Fircroft Wood victim's name," the loud voice of D.C. Jon Stone resonated annoyingly against Andy's ear. Unaware of his superior's growing agitation, the young D.C. boomed, "It's Helen Walters, and she worked as a researcher at Bletchworth University." Andy sank back into his black leather swivel chair, head in hands. This was going to be a high-profile case; he could feel it in his bones. That meant working long hours; he didn't dare think how he was going to explain to Joan. Perhaps leaving the country would be the best option. He emitted a deep sigh, braced himself, and then walked slowly back into the briefing room.

CHAPTER 24

A UNIFORMED CONSTABLE greeted D.I. Andy Dale as the detective tentatively made his way through the wet undergrowth to the brightly lit murder site. It was at times like this that dinner with his nagging wife and her boring sister seemed almost preferable. He fought to keep his balance in the slimy mud. Judging by the cursing going on behind him, D.S. Rob Murray was experiencing the same difficulty. Usually his sergeant could fall in a bath of manure and still come up smelling of roses, so Andy was taking a perverse sense of satisfaction from his discomfort.

"Evening, sir," Constable Masters saluted, doing his best "Dixon of Dock Green" impression. "Her name is Helen Baxter, and she works at the university," Simon Masters informed his superior.

Andy's mood lightened to see his favourite police doctor still there. Doctor Grace Anderson, in her early forties, was a striking, intelligent woman. As a single person still living on her own, she was the subject of gossip among many of her police colleagues. Andrew, as she always called him, numbered among Grace's few close friends. "Hello, Andrew," called a statuesque figure dressed in white coveralls. "I thought I'd wait till you got here." Grace smiled warmly, despite the cold wind howling through the gaps in the heavy-duty polythene that covered the area.

Andy pulled out a hand from the comparative warmth of his overcoat pocket. He was from an age group that still wore overcoats; most of the youngsters on the force these days wore anoraks. Sign of the times, he sighed to himself as he briefly shook Grace's hand. "Any information you can give me at this stage?" Andy dispensed with small talk, wanting to get home as soon as possible.

"Well, as far as I can tell, she has been dead for roughly twenty four hours; that would make time of death anywhere between eight-thirty and nine-thirty yesterday evening." Grace could see the impatience growing in Andy's face. "The victim was strangled; and the marks on her neck suggest that the murderer was extremely strong," she concluded. Andy shivered involuntarily; he had seen too many murder scenes, more than are good for anyone; but this one was singularly depressing.

"Not a good place to be murdered," said Rob flippantly, blowing his nose on a grubby handkerchief.

"Where would you prefer? I'm sure it doesn't make much difference to the victim." Grace's sarcastic comment was lost on Rob, whose idea of a good laugh was seeing someone, especially a friend, fall downstairs; if minor injury occurred so much the better. Rob's mobile phone rang just-in time to stop the uneven battle of wits.

Andy looked intently at the outline of where the body had been. Several sets of footprints showed up clearly in the wet mud, including a churned up patch suggesting a scuffle. "Have casts been made of these footprints?" Andy called across to the constable, who, after the success of his "Dixon of Dock Green" impression, was now doing his "constable smoking a cigarette while stamping on the ground for warmth" impression.

"Yes, sir; they found three different sets, including the victim's. Also looks like someone left their dinner behind," he added for good measure.

"Bloody hell! Where do they get them?" Rob muttered to no one in particular. Constable Masters looked on implacably trying to cover up his embarrassment, all his previous toadying now a distant memory.

CHAPTER 25

A MENACING CLOUD hung over the bustling coastal town. Great cargo ships bobbed up and down in the nearby tumultuous sea. Sailors could be seen scurrying about, raising collars and bowing heads to afford a small protection against the cutting wind. A series of deafening booms resounded against delicate eardrums, their owners desperately trying to muffle out the sound with hands tightly pressed against chilled ears.

On a small hill overlooking the harbour, a magnificent building dominates the leaden skyline. Palatial in its proportions, this imposing structure is home to the rulers of this prosperous land. The beautiful and delicate frescoes of bulls and dolphins adorning the walls suggest a highly creative and successful civilisation. People here are hard working but happy, each contributing to the others‘ success. This has been the case now for over three thousand years—an idyll that will end this night.

For several days, a fine grey powder, not unlike polluted grey snow, has rained gently upon the palatial structure, tarnishing its once magnificent decor. Snow is unheard-of in this land of sunshine and warmth; what is now raining from the skies, with increasing intensity, is hot, choking ash.

A tall, distinguished looking man looks out over the harbour.

His worried look invokes concern in the eyes of his dark-haired, attractive wife. The man is wearing the fine silk clothes that befit the governor of a wealthy seaport. He raises his eyes to look out at the smoking mountain in the far distance, across the stormy sea, just as another deafening explosion shakes the palace to its foundations. Panic replaces concern on the face of the governor's wife.

Rumblings from deep in the earth had been frightening the island inhabitants for many weeks. Now, glowing fire belches from the distant mountain, each thunderous explosion throwing tons of hot ash into the air. Much of it is carried away by the prevailing winds; this time, however, the explosions are louder. A beautiful, painted urn falls with a crash from its once imposing position on the richly waxed oak table. The governor's wife turns and moves quickly to the table, but too late to prevent another clay urn from shattering on the floor. Its pieces mingle with those of its erstwhile companion.

Suddenly there is a lull; the only sounds are the creaking protest of tossed about ships and the sea's pounding against the harbour wall. Among the sailors on the dockside a strange figure appears, unnoticed by the milling crowds. The man, if it is a man, looks as if he is from another place or time. His clothes look alien in this land of colourful fabric and fine cloths. His size elicits stares, for he is at least a head taller than most of the thronging masses. The figure turns to look at the distant mountain; a look of terror crosses his face as another explosion throws plumes of burning ash high into the glowing night sky.

The figure instinctively turns and starts to run up the ash covered hill towards the governor's palace, just as a rumble deep in the ground is followed by yet another explosion from the fiery mountain. In his haste to reach the sanctuary of the palace, he misses his footing on the powdery ash and slides backwards grazing his legs on rocky protrusions. As he scrambles to his feet, he hears a roar. He looks behind him and barely has time to scream before a giant wall of water silhouetted against the exploding mountain races dramatically across the open sea and crashes over the harbour wall. Everything now happens in slow motion as the giant wave engulfs him; the silence is overwhelming as he sinks under the weight of the murky water. As he sinks into the blackness of the ocean, an insistent ringing now penetrates the fearful quiet.

Panic stricken, Gene Harman looked wildly from side to side in the darkened room. The ringing suddenly stopped leaving him stunned. That it had all been a nightmare gradually dawned on him as he turned on a lamp. The now familiar shapes of his bedroom furniture showed dimly in the periphery of his vision. He was still shaking when the shrill ring of his phone once again penetrated his subconscious.

CHAPTER 26

A JAGGED BOLT of lightning silhouetted the old church against the scudding clouds. Almost instantaneously a deep throated roar of thunder told him the storm was close, too close for comfort. What was it he remembered from his physics class all those years ago? Every five seconds between the lightning strike and the thunder is equal to a mile. Bloody hell! By that reckoning that last bolt was less than a quarter of a mile away.

He was beginning to regret his decision to come out on a night like this. A glance at his speedometer told him he was travelling at over seventy-five miles an hour—much too fast for the conditions; but this was a quiet road, with hardly any traffic in the day and even less at night. Another bolt of lightning temporarily lit up the sky leaving a blacker, more ominous night in its wake.

Torrential rain bounced off the deserted tarmac road like a mini sprinkler as the Audi A4 slowed gently to a halt opposite an old, but smart looking, detached house. A light glimmered through the bullions in the front door, the only sign of occupancy. The sodium street light gave the normally white stucco front an ethereal, orange tinge.

He reached in the glovebox for the packet of cigarettes he had kept there, as a reminder, since giving up smoking two years ago.

He looked longingly at the scruffy packet of Silk Cut before, with a great effort of will, putting it back unopened. The torrential rain beat a staccato rhythm on the metal roof of the car as he pulled up the fleecy hood of his jacket. A film of water gave a sheen to the surface of the road, as drains, unable to cope with the deluge, gave up trying altogether. As he ran, splashing across the road, a light suddenly appeared in an upstairs bedroom window casting its glow over the small front garden. The words "drowned" and "rat" sprung into his mind while he struggled to open the ornate iron gate leading up the drive. He reached the front door just as an unseen hand drew the bedroom curtains closed. Breathing heavily from his exertions, he paused, just for a minute, before jabbing with a gloved finger at the illuminated bell push. He held his breath as he watched the distorted figure advance, hesitantly, through the misty glass panes.

Drawing her housecoat tightly round her, Trudy Ballinger strained to identify the dark, hooded figure impatiently ringing her doorbell. Trudy hesitated momentarily as a misshapen face pressed hard against the door pane, a circular mist forming around the mouth and nose. Making sure that the recently fitted safety chain was securely in place, she tentatively opened the door.

"Hello, Trudy," said the dripping figure of Dr. Mike Powell.

CHAPTER 27

TRUDY HAD SPENT the last hour trying, without success, to get rid of Mike. Surprisingly she was looking forward to her date with Gene; and when Mike had turned up on her doorstep looking dishevelled and drawn, she could barely suppress her irritation. She felt obliged to be polite because of her long-term friendship with him, but recently he seemed more of a stranger than a friend. The other night had been a disaster—the food awful, the company not much better; and she wasn't about to let Mike spoil the night she'd planned with Gene. Reluctantly she invited him, dripping, into the hall; his trainers formed muddy imprints on her oatmeal carpet. The former Mike would never have been so inconsiderate, thought Trudy. He flicked back the hood of his anorak spraying more rainwater, this time on her hall mirror. It was the leer on his face, however, that grabbed Trudy's attention. She backed away instinctively to put distance between them.

"What do you want?" Trudy stammered, hoping she sounded more confident than she felt?

"You don't sound pleased to see me," said Mike advancing slowly towards Trudy, depositing more muddy footprints onto the oatmeal carpet. "Are you expecting someone else?" he added darkly.

Trudy Ballinger, revered by some and feared by others for her usual, confidently in control, persona displayed none of these qualities now. Her mind was working overtime; for the first time ever with Mike she was beginning to feel afraid—afraid of someone she had known for years, the same person she had befriended all those years ago at university. "I am expecting a visitor any time now," Trudy lied unconvincingly.

"Well, perhaps we can talk while you wait for your visitor," retorted Mike not trying to disguise the contempt in his voice. "If you don't mind that is," he added, as he brushed roughly past Trudy into the living room.

Trudy's confidence, which had temporarily deserted her, now returned, as she stormed into the room after Mike. "I would like you to leave now," Trudy blazed, adding in a more conciliatory tone, "We can arrange to meet another time when it is more convenient."

"I think I'll wait and see your friend when he comes." Was it Trudy's imagination, or had Mike's leer become more demonic? She gave an involuntary shudder as a cold hand grabbed her shoulder. Trudy had never regarded Mike as being particularly strong, so his vicelike grip took her completely off guard as his fingers dug fiercely through the thin material of the housecoat into her flesh beneath. As he was pulling Trudy towards him, he suddenly seemed puzzled. His grip on her shoulder immediately relaxed. "Oh, my God, I'm so sorry, Trudy," was all he could utter as he sat down slowly, like a little boy, lost in the voluminous upholstery of the chair. Anguished, head in hands, he sobbed gently.

CHAPTER 28

BIG, TREMBLING ARMS threatened to give way under the strain put on them by an overweight body, as Gene struggled to reach the Bakelite phone; a relic from before the advent of cordless rubbish. He fell back on grubby sheets as his arms, still quivering with the effort, gave up the lost cause. Relief washed over him as the black monster, seemingly resentful, whose piercing ring was creating such havoc in his befuddled brain, fell silent.

His eye detected a sudden flurry of movement as he lay back staring at a ceiling desperately in need of decoration. A large, hairy spider raced across his line of vision, pausing briefly before finally disappearing behind the cheap, pine picture rail, its mission complete. He was just drifting back into the semi consciousness that exists between sleep and wakefulness when the black monster once again jangled his nerves Gene sat bolt upright; the sudden shock stimulating his adrenal glands and providing the energy necessary to fuel his weary muscles. With a shaking hand he raised the phone to his ear and immediately recognised the strained, disembodied voice of Trudy Ballinger.

"Hi Trudy," croaked Gene, alert now and feeling guilty as he glanced at the luminous bedside clock. "Sorry I'm late, but . . .," Gene trailed off as the dialling tone buzzed loudly in his ear.

CHAPTER 29

SHE THOUGHT MIKE had finally left. After a decidedly tense, one-way conversation, which had lasted for over two hours, Trudy had persuaded him to go home and rest. Roles had been reversed this night—she the psychologist and he the patient. Mike had opened his heart; Trudy for her part had listened making the occasional encouraging comment. Finally, after what seemed like an eternity, Mike lapsed into a meditative silence. After a third cup of coffee, he had reluctantly agreed to go home, much to Trudy's relief. Trudy had been aware that Mike was angling to stay the night with her; but this was a person she didn't know any more, and she felt a deep unease with him now. His personality changes frightened her more than she cared to admit. The former Mike had been charming and considerate; the new Mike was wild-eyed and aggressive.

A shadow rippling across the distorted eye of bullion glass was followed by a frantic pounding on the front door; Trudy's heart skipped a beat. The visitor could only be Mike back on some pretence to persuade her to let him stay. Trudy placed the phone back on its cradle, rather more roughly than intended. Earlier she had tried to ring Gene; but the line had gone dead, and it still was. The banging merged with Westminster door chimes, as frantic fingers jabbed the bell push. She walked angrily towards the front door—more arguments with the neighbours she did not need. It was bad enough that a constant stream of students visited for tutorials late into the night—a fact frequently mentioned, in an admonishing tone, by her next door neighbour. As she impatiently yanked opened the door, to Trudy's relief, the face appearing out of the gloom was that of Gene Harman.

CHAPTER 30

SILVER SPECTACLES REFLECT the eerie glow of the flickering computer screen. Expert mouse clicks open files, images flashing on and off the screen until just three remain: a once beautiful palace now covered in what looked like dirty snow; bustling people from a strange time and place; and the misty outline of a distant volcano, ominously smouldering. As fingers press "Ctrl P" on the dirty keyboard, the sound of an ink-jet printer beginning its labours overwhelms the gentle hum of the computer fan. Gradually the printer regurgitates a likeness of the images onscreen.

Fingers flash once again, and a new image appears on the screen. Fire now engulfs the distant volcano, and a giant plume of ash and steam fills the sky. The drama of the event pleases the technician, whose sinister smile reflects eerily from the screen, as his fingers once again send life to the waiting printer. Puzzled and with sore eyes from the brightness of the screen, he tries to make sense of the glowing image. Understanding dawns as the image strikes a chord in his mind. The final image spews out like a giant tongue; the light from the screen dims; the printer falls silent. Its work is done—for now.

CHAPTER 31

"AREN'T YOU GOING to let me in, then?" asked a bedraggled, dripping Gene Harman. "F—king wet out here," he added for good measure, just in case Trudy had overlooked the obvious. Gene's polite opening remarks tempered Trudy's initial relief that it was not Mike at the door.

Why she liked this man she could not understand. He was just about as far removed from her vision of an ideal man as it was possible to be. Big and loud, his only redeeming feature was his above average intelligence, albeit well disguised by an overbearing and condescending attitude. She was glad to see him but decided that his ego was big enough without adding to it by telling him so. She did request firmly that he take off his wet coat and shoes at the door.

After she apologised for missing his birthday drink and he, in turn, looked suitably hurt, Trudy ushered Gene along the hall and into the kitchen. While she made coffee and related the story of Mike's visit, Gene busied himself trying to hide a hole in his sock offering tantalizing glimpses of a less than clean big toe.

"He seems a bit of a nut case," Gene expounded, not wishing to get too technical." It sounds as though he could be violent," he added, a note of concern creeping into his voice.

Trudy looked thoughtful while she sipped her steaming coffee, "I wouldn't have thought so before tonight, but the way his manner has changed scares me. Perhaps he needs professional help" she said, looking through the steam and waiting for Gene's reaction.

"Possibly does, but the problem would be to get a psychologist to admit he needed help. Besides, if he did, wouldn't his credibility as a consultant be compromised?"

"You could be right," Trudy conceded reaching for the coffee jug and offering it to Gene before topping up her own half-empty mug. "Or maybe he's just been overworking," she added.

After unloading her concerns on a surprisingly supportive Gene, she began to feel more relaxed and suggested that they drink something stronger. Gene readily accepted Trudy's offer of a whiskey. She poured herself a glass of white wine from a chilled bottled in the fridge. Settling comfortably in the lounge, Gene recounted details of his latest dream to a sleepy Trudy. A light snoring interrupted him in full flow; Trudy was curled up in the fetal position, her empty glass resting precariously on the arm of the chair.

"Bollocks, I must be getting boring in my old age," muttered Gene quietly, not wishing to wake her. Placing his glass on the coffee table, he rose stiffly, stretching briefly before padding silently into the hall. Retrieving his coat and shoes from the cloakroom, Gene quietly pulled the door, which closed and latched behind him, and walked out into the murky night.

CHAPTER 32

THE BLUE FORD Focus swept up the long, black tarmac drive leading to Bletchworth University. Screeching brakes, suddenly applied, rent the air as the car skidded grudgingly to a halt outside Harry Butler, the Head of Security's lair, waking the inhabitant. His red face peered through the misty glass panelling of the gatehouse. "What's your business?" he mumbled, with a brief nod of the head, not happy at having his breakfast postponed. Sometimes the job got in the way of Harry's natural tendency to be lazy, a character trait irritating to his employers, who nonetheless opted for a non-confrontational approach.

"We're here to see Ian Mason." Andy Dale flashed his ID card through the car window at a suddenly deflated Harry Butler. Here was someone with even more authority than he had. Harry was a wimp in every way. At that moment, he decided that cooperation was his best option; after all, he didn't want to add the police to his already long list of problems.

"Is the principal expecting you?" asked Harry all politeness and light. "I expect it's about the murder," he added confidentially as one law enforcer to another. Andy, who dealt with people like Harry all the time, had no time for them even on a good day. He ignored Harry's attempt at light conversation.

"Just tell him we're here," Andy's replied sharply. "We'll find our own way to his office," he added winding up the car window and terminating the conversation. He'd spent more than enough time already on the jumped up security man. "Stupid Pratt," he muttered as Rob Murray did a wheel spin sending the protesting Focus speeding towards the main building.

CHAPTER 33

THE BROWN A4 envelope was waiting for him when he arrived at the office. His eyes were drawn to it as soon as he opened the door. Judy, unable to find a suitable space amidst the clutter of the editor's desk, had propped it up against the photograph of a hardly recognizable, slim Gene Harman receiving an award for excellence in journalism. He always kept the photograph prominently displayed to remind himself, and others, of what he had achieved in happier times—days when he had a slim body, lustrous hair, and money to spend, more specifically, pre-Lois days. Significantly, this envelope, which filled him with a great sense of unease, obliterated his past and now somehow threatened to do the same with his future. Last night's dream had obviously shaken him more than he realised.

"Danny, get me a coffee," Gene shouted through the open door, his voice booming in the busy main office. Startled workers looked up briefly before returning to the safety of their computer screens. Gene turned his attention back to the envelope still taunting him, still threatening to obliterate his past, still daring someone to peruse its contents. Strangely he was reluctant to open it immediately; experiencing almost the same reluctance that one would have confronting a letter that you know contains your redundancy notice and the key to your future.

"Morning, Boss," Vince called from the doorway, holding a plastic cup of steaming coffee and waiting for the invitation to step over the threshold of Gene's inner sanctum.

"Where's Danny?" snarled Gene impatiently, holding out his big, grimy hand for the still steaming cup. This was the nearest to an invitation to step inside that Vince was going to get today.

"He's not at work today, and he hasn't rung in." Vince was still fuming from the snub he'd received from Danny in the woods; so, under the circumstances, "putting the boot in" felt good.

"He'd better have a good excuse; otherwise, he'll be another statistic on the dole queue," said Gene, tentatively sipping the hot, muddy looking coffee. Gene's sympathetic nature was feted within the walls of Goldberg Publications. He watched Vince saunter through the main office pausing at Archie's desk for a brief chat before moving on to his own little cubicle. *To think that jumped up little bastard wants my job.* The thought of it made Gene's blood boil.

With Vince gone and coffee in hand Gene's attention turned back to the brown envelope. Decisively he reached across the cluttered desk and tore open the tucked in flap. As three large photographs spilled out, Gene instinctively knew they would be images of last night's dream. He wasn't disappointed.

CHAPTER 34

IMAGES FLOATED IN and out of focus; the room fell silent as though frozen in time. The only sound was the heavy, dull beating of Gene's heart as the photographs tumbled out on to the untidy desk. Breathing became an achievement rather than the norm, as the horror of his previous night's dream was with him once more. Scenes of devastation crowded his mind—of crying children being scooped up by panic stricken parents, of stifling heat, of giant waves, and then of merciful oblivion. He sat back in his chair stunned, the significance slowly dawning on him. Gradually the spell broke and reality returned as sounds from the busy office filtered through to Gene's subconscious. Déjà vu flooded over him as one by one scenes from his dream spread out in vivid images before him. He felt the room closing around him again; he had to get out; he desperately needed someone to talk to.

Gene's list of friends was hardly extensive. Most of his so-called friends had been Lois's friends, and they had deserted him soon after the separation. With hindsight he realised they'd never really liked him, just tolerated him for Lois's sake. So, bollocks to them. Gene's powers of deduction narrowed down the field of people he could confide in considerably. Still shaking, he picked up the phone and dialled Bletchworth University.

CHAPTER 35

METAL BANGED AGAINST metal as Ian Mason hastily put the document he was reading into the filing cabinet locking the flimsy chrome lock. Not much of a deterrent if anyone wanted to open it, thought the principal slipping the key into his desk drawer. Harry had warned him of the impending police visit, and Helen's final letter was the last thing he wanted them to see. He'd watched enough police programmes on the television to know how badly this murder could reflect on him. When details of his relationship with Helen got out, the local press would have a field day; and his career would surely be over.

DI Andy Dale knocked briefly and, without waiting for an invitation, entered the principal's comfortable office followed by his sergeant, Rob Murray. Ian rose to greet the two detectives. Brief introductions over, the police detective came straight to the point. "How well did you know Helen Baxter?" In Andy's experience blunt open-ended questions often threw the interviewee off guard requiring them to think more deeply about their answers and, hopefully, provide more information for use later.

"I knew Helen as a valuable member of staff and a first class researcher." Ian's throat went dry anticipating the next question.

"Did you know Helen personally?" The question was a crossroads for the principal. If he admitted their affair, then it could mean the end of his career; if he did not, it could lead to serious problems later.

"No, I only knew Helen on a professional level." Ian instantly realised he had made the wrong decision; Andy's next question left him floundering.

"How do you account for twenty-three phone calls made to you from her mobile in the last two weeks, five of them during the early hours of the morning?"

Rob who had been quiet up to now added pointedly, "Do you always talk to members of staff at three-o-clock in the morning?"

Ian's mind was in panic mode; he was getting in deeper all the time and, under Andy's unsmiling gaze, was beginning to crack. At staff meetings he found it difficult to handle conflict situations; and this time he didn't have his wife or Trudy Ballinger to support him. Now he was on his own, and he wasn't handling it very well. Ian had been a good chess player in his youth, but the way he had managed the opening of this situation didn't bode well for the middle and endgame. He felt like resigning now. "Helen had this obsession with me that was difficult to handle; and, yes, she would ring me at all hours, but I tried to keep her at arm's length. I told her I would report it to the police if she continued."

Thirty years of experience had honed Andy's skills in spotting lies and people who had something to hide. This man may be intelligent, thought Andy, but he wasn't good at lying. "Can you account for your movements between eight and twelve on the night of Helen's murder?"

If only he had an alibi, further questioning would be unnecessary. His private life would remain private instead of public, which it now threatened to become. Principal Ian Mason did not have an alibi, and he knew the detective didn't believe his explanation for the late phone calls. For the first time during this ordeal, he felt panic stricken.

CHAPTER 36

DANIEL WESTON HAD an excellent excuse for not being at work today. He was completing his plans to kill Gene Harman, his father incarnate. In fact, Daniel's plans also included that fat little "gay boy," Vincent Craig. He could feel the gay boy's eyes boring into him all the time at the office. David wanted him to kill Craig the other night when they saw him in Fircroft Woods, but that would be too quick. What he had in mind would entail suffering before they died—much more satisfying. He'd take almost as much pleasure killing Craig as he would Harman—almost, but not quite. He giggled excitedly at the irony—killing the two people he hated most, now that his mother was dead, both at the same time. If she was here now, perhaps, at last, she would be proud, give him a hug and say she loved him. Maybe even his father wouldn't have left them if he'd known what a clever person his son would turn out to be. Daniel sang in a quavering voice, and David joined in as they sat at the table, light glaring from an old spring angled reading lamp, admiring the appliance they'd just finished making. It had taken weeks to prepare; getting the materials had been difficult, but now he'd finally completed it. The Internet was a wonderful place to get information; there you could find out how to make anything

Daniel had looked at sites where, if his mother had known, she would have locked him in his room and never let him out. Luckily she was dead—another irony, Daniel thought, using the office Internet to find out how to make the bomb that was going to blow up Gene Harman. Vincent Craig's death would be a bonus. Daniel's giggle got louder, finally metamorphosing into an insane laugh. David laughed too.

CHAPTER 37

TRUDY HAD FORGOTTEN her mobile phone. This was not unusual. She detested the instruments; she disliked hearing people using them with no consideration for those around them. In pubs, restaurants, supermarkets—it seemed that nowhere was mobile free. Even her students walked around speaking animatedly into a mobile glued to their ears. Good news for the telecommunication industry, but a damn nuisance for those who had to put up with the intrusion.

Events of the past few days had overtaken Trudy's desire to track down who was responsible for leaking details of her recent discovery. She had decided to hunt through recent research submissions for clues. Trudy breathed a sigh of relief as she drove into the only space available in the university library car park. The joke among the students was: "If you see a parking space, run off and buy a car." Not so stupid as it seems, thought Trudy, as she walked up to the library reception desk.

Deborah Moon at forty-four had been the chief librarian at the university for fifteen years. Unmarried, she still lived with her elderly mother; her father had died of a heart attack two years ago, just a year after his long anticipated retirement. Trudy and Deborah got on well professionally. Trudy was good at her job; as was Deborah hers. They respected each other. Deborah was the person you asked if you needed any information on current research or thesis submissions. What she didn't know she'd soon find out using her database, the Internet, or as a last resort the dusty old files she kept deep in the bowels of the library building

Blue ink flowed smoothly from the Waterman fountain pen onto the white velum paper as Deborah listed the information Trudy needed. Deborah flatly refused to write with anything else but a fountain pen or to use any but the best quality paper. Deborah's fingers were a blur over the keys as she, with Trudy looking over her shoulder, searched databases and the Internet for clues that would help identify the source of the information leakage. Finally, after a thirty minute, exhaustive search, Deborah had to admit it was proving more difficult than expected; and she would have to make further enquiries later when she had more time.

"Dreadful news about poor Helen," said Deborah as she and Trudy walked out onto the concrete forecourt in front of the research block. "She was researching in the library on the day she was murdered. She looked distraught, as though she had been crying," Deborah added as Trudy walked out the door to her waiting car.

CHAPTER 38

THIS TIME HE woke up in surroundings more familiar to him. A dazzling light flooded the small room creating grotesque shadows on white walls. The memory of his night's work still lingered in the back of his mind. Vague images flashed through his brain but grew less distinct each time. Silver, mirrored spectacles lay on the floor at his side. He gazed at his distorted image reflected in the cracked lens, the convex design giving his nose undue prominence. As he reached to rescue the spectacles from the hard, stone floor, his hand grew to giant proportions. His light sensitive eyes, watering from exposure, gained immediate relief as the spectacles were once again in place.

Vague recollections of pain and anguish from a previous time convinced the man not to explore his surroundings. Sleep gradually began to overtake him; but suddenly he became alert to the sound of scurrying in the far corner of the room. Malevolent orbs glowed red as bright light reflected off the retinas of small eyes. The man sat there momentarily transfixed as they moved closer, but suddenly the spell broke and the man kicked out at the glow that threatened to absorb his very essence. Frantically searching for a weapon, his fumbling hands clamped around a hard solid object. Then he lost consciousness.

CHAPTER 39

Recent events had given him plenty to think about, both at the pub at lunchtime and back in the office two hours later. Work had run a poor second in the contest to gain his attention, a factor that hadn't gone unnoticed by Vince, who added another entry into his log. Now, Vince had gone home, and the office was deserted except for a few skeleton staff. The place looked desolate, which was how he felt at the moment. Even the drink at lunchtime hadn't done anything to help. That was worrying—he could usually rely on Jack Daniel's to help him get through troublesome periods; now even Jack had deserted him.

It was well past six-thirty on a dusky, miserable March evening. He gazed out of the window watching workers hurrying across to the tarmac trying in vain to protect themselves from the incessant rain. Cars pulled out of allotted spaces taking their occupants home to their families and friends. "Bollocks!" Why should they be so happy when he had nothing to go home to? Even Trudy was avoiding him.

His eyes smarting, his head throbbing, and his heart aching, Gene sighed as he looked at the photographs for the hundredth time. Reaching into his desk drawer, he pulled out his Bausch & Lomb magnifying glass—a concession to his worsening eyesight.

Previously he had been looking at the erupting volcano image so intently that he hadn't noticed the unusual object in the foreground. The stone, or piece of rock, was about the size of a man's hand; it was painted red with a strange image etched into the surface. He moved closer to the light, but even with his magnifying glass he couldn't distinguish any more detail. Perhaps Archie could help by digitizing the image and enhancing the stone. He'd get him on it in the morning; it'll give the lazy bastard something to do.

It was nearly half past seven when his phone rang. He considered not answering, as it could be old Goldberg taking the opportunity to call him up for an early evening bollocking. To his relief, it was Trudy's voice he heard on the other end of the phone.

CHAPTER 40

"WHERE THE FUCK have you been?" Gene asked, turning on the charm. "I've been ringing you all day."

Trudy struggled against her natural inclination, which was to slam the phone down, deciding instead on a less antagonistic approach. "I've been trying to find out who leaked information about my discovery," she said in a voice that was neither aggressive nor submissive, but pitched at a rational adult level as defined by Canadian-born US *psychiatrist Eric Berne* in his theory of systematic *psychotherapy* for personal growth. She had attended courses in his Transactional Analysis as part of her training, but it didn't stop her from lapsing into the Critical Parent mode when the need arose.

After his opening gambit had fallen on stony ground, Gene himself decided on a more tempered approach. "Okay, I accept your apology," said Gene with more than a hint of sarcasm. "It's important we have a talk."

Trudy's disappointment at her wasted time in the library showed, with her less than enthusiastic reply to Gene's suggestion. "I'm busy tonight; perhaps we can make it later in the week." Trudy determined she wasn't going to jump when this man called; as the saying goes, "Treat them mean and keep them keen."

"It might help explain your so-called leaked information," Gene added knowing this was the hook that would grab Trudy's interest. He had some experience with playing games with varying degrees of success. This was one of his more successful efforts.

Trudy's attention immediately focused—perhaps he was going to divulge his sources; whatever else she was going to do tonight could wait. "Come to my house about eight-thirty; bring a bottle of wine, and I'll do some supper," she said, trying not to sound too enthusiastic.

"All right, but the earliest I can make it is nine-thirty," said Gene secretly gloating for having had the last word. "'Bye," he added, putting down the phone and not waiting for Trudy's reply.

CHAPTER 41

THE LOCAL TV news correspondent who had been at the scene of yesterday's "ghastly murder in Fircroft Wood" had just finished delivering his report, ending with a police phone number to call with any useful information. The presenter looked suitably sombre and proceeded to the next item.

The television sat mutely in the corner like a blind Cyclops awaiting the arrival of Apollo. Dr. Mike Powell, apparently having turned it off, sat staring at the blank screen. How long he'd sat there he had no idea. Sitting in his dressing gown, he suddenly felt very cold. The central heating, timed to shut down at half past eleven, must have gone off early, he thought, as he looked on the mantelpiece at his Ormolu eight-day clock. Half past three—he couldn't believe his eyes, yet his clock was ticking unswervingly, daring him to doubt the accuracy of its message. Had he been asleep all this time? Mike tried to focus his thoughts and remember details of the evening. The harder he tried, the bigger the barrier became. He couldn't remember coming home or getting undressed; in fact, the previous twelve hours were a complete blank. As he became aware of the pounding in his head and the dull ache behind his eyes, he felt very afraid.

CHAPTER 42

A BOTTLE OF cheap red wine vibrated against an equally cheap bottle of white, as they lay side by side on the seat of the red Fiesta. The old car rattled and protested its way to a halt outside the big white house. The big man grabbed the bottles from their resting-place and eased himself laboriously out of the driver's seat. It was nearly a quarter to nine when Gene arrived at Trudy's. He stretched his cramped muscles and looked up and down the deserted street before proceeding to walk up the driveway to the house.

"You're late," complained Trudy standing aside to let Gene, smelling of cigarette smoke, into the hallway.

"Sorry," said Gene flashing his best winning smile. "I had a 'happy families' phone call from my soon to be ex-wife," Gene said bitterly. "We were debating whether I should be allowed to have a shirt on my back after the settlement," he added feeling a rush of anger well up within him. Trudy suddenly felt sorry for the man—he might think he's big and tough, but at the moment he appeared small and vulnerable. Easily resisting the temptation to give him a hug Trudy ushered the big man into the kitchen.

Trudy had set two places at the kitchen table; she'd thought about lighting a candle but had decided that it would be too corny for the occasion. This is purely business, she tried to convince herself. Stilted conversation accompanied the supper, with Trudy talking about her work as a palaeontologist and Gene about the problems with his estranged wife and that "bastard," Goldberg. For their supper Trudy had cooked a vegetarian quiche with a tossed green salad and baked potato. To Gene, whose culinary horizons didn't extend past microwaving instant dinners and preparing toast and marmite for breakfast, this was a feast worth savouring. And savour it he did, consuming most of the quiche and finishing off the remaining salad.

The big hall clock had just chimed eleven when they finally finished their meal. The sound of chimes dispelled the cosy haze that had threatened to overcome them during supper. Spell broken, they picked up their glasses holding the remainder of the wine and retired to the lounge. The time for serious discussion had arrived.

CHAPTER 43

HE WAS FRANTIC. Despair crowded his mind, blocking out all rational thought. The sinking feeling he had in the pit of his stomach threatened to overwhelm. He desperately needed a drink, anything to take away his anguish, albeit only temporarily. He knew his dead wife wouldn't approve; but then, if his wife had still been alive, he wouldn't be in this situation. His hands shook as he poured a large measure of brandy into an old glass tumbler.

Usually Ian Mason drank his Old Hennessy V.S. Cognac from a crystal brandy snifter, but refinement was not on his mind as he drained half the measure with a single swallow. Feeling more relaxed, as he sank into his armchair clutching his glass, He tried to apply logic to his predicament. He desperately needed an alibi for the night of the murder, but whom could he trust?

He mentally sieved through lists of his colleagues; most of them wouldn't give him the time of day, so an alibi was out of the question. A brother who lived in Australia was his only surviving close family, but the two hadn't spoken for over ten years. A feeling of hopelessness overcame him again as he realised how alone he was. "Billy No Mates" was a term often used by students around the university; for the first time, he became aware of a sadness that lurked behind the jibe. Ian staggered as he refilled his glass, sloshing brandy down the front of his new cavalry twill trousers. Sitting down again with exaggerated care, Ian came to the obvious conclusion that of all his acquaintances the only one he could really trust was Trudy Ballinger.

CHAPTER 44

"YOU'LL PROBABLY THINK this is a load of bollocks," he began cautiously, trying to sound more confident than he felt. They had seated themselves comfortably in the lounge still hanging on to their drinks, talking nervously. The soft glow of a single table lamp cast indistinct shadows, as Gene began to tell his tale. He started with his first dream providing as much detail as he could remember: the prehistoric setting; the dinosaurs; the mystery person: and, above all, the shadow that blocked out the sun.

Trudy listened intently as the story unfolded, intermittently asking questions to clarify points. She was astonished, however, when Gene reached into the pocket of his jacket pulling out an ineptly folded envelope containing photographs he had received following the first dream. "What do you think of these, Prof?" he asked, thrusting them under her nose with a flourish? With exaggerated care Trudy unfolded the envelope and removed the photographs; she had seen one of them in the magazine, but the others were new to her.

The realization finally dawned on Trudy that the man had been sincere all the time and that the dreams worried him more than his macho image would allow him to admit. Silence pervaded the room as Trudy studied each photograph closely and, then, without a word, got up to refill their glasses. She broke the silence by proceeding to bombard Gene with a myriad of questions. Gene felt he'd undergone a third-degree by the time she'd finished. He'd not even started to tell her about his second dream yet. Not for the first time, he spared a thought for her students; they wouldn't get away with anything. Relief showed in Trudy's face as she realised that the news of her discovery had not been leaked intentionally. This relief, however, was short lived, since now there was an even greater mystery to solve.

Volcanic eruptions, tidal waves, and earthquakes—details of Gene's second dream—unfolded before an astounded Trudy. The drama of the story heightened as Gene described the giant wall of water that finally engulfed him. His voice sounded faraway as he relived the horrors of his dream and the shock upon receiving a second batch of photographs. Reaching into his pocket, he pulled out a second envelope, which contained more photographs, this time of the second dream.

"Well, it seems likely that your first dream related somehow to the extinction of the dinosaurs," Trudy began after much deliberation. "Dreams like this are not that unusual as these theories are much in the media recently and could easily have influenced you."

"What is more difficult to explain are the photographs," Gene interrupted, "I've had them checked out by specialists, who unanimously agree they are not manipulated images; they are actual photographs."

"Well, we both know they couldn't be," said Trudy with a touch of annoyance. "They were obviously done by someone even more clever than your so-called experts," she added sarcastically. "Someone could have composed the images with little or no knowledge of prehistoric dinosaurs and by chance picked up an artist's impression similar to the recently discovered creature." Trudy had now satisfied herself that the leak, if any, was not intentional and, more to the point would not affect her forthcoming paper.

Gene interrupted her speculation: "So how did the sender know about my dream?"

"You must have told someone," came the sharp reply, "and they decided to play a joke."

"Okay, so you've got an explanation for the first one; let's see if you're as clever with the second dream." Gene had listened impatiently while Trudy sounded forth her theory. His irritation at Trudy's attempt to make light of his concerns began to show.

"Well, one explanation is that the dream is the memory of some film or TV programme you've seen lately."

"Great, I presume the same person decided to try for another side-splitting joke. I suppose you bloody well think I'm making it up," he snarled.

"Sorry, but I'm trained to work logically," said Trudy trying to defuse the situation, not wishing to hurt Gene's feelings. "I do agree the odds of it happening twice are great, but what other explanation could there be?

Appeased by Trudy's, as he saw it, "climb down," he responded more calmly, "I don't know, but there must be something we're missing."

Knees touching, aware of their closeness, they sat together studying the photographs, bouncing ideas around, but nothing fit the facts. After an hour, they decided to give it more thought tomorrow when they were both fresher. Gene staggered as he stood up, the effect of sharing two bottles of wine and devouring several whiskeys on his own.

"You can sleep in the spare bedroom if you like," Trudy offered, wondering if she'd made the right decision offering this man a place to sleep for the night. She tried to convince herself that she didn't want him to get the wrong idea. Gene, on the other hand, would have been happy to latch on to the "wrong idea," but didn't want to spoil any future relationship they might have.

"Thanks, but I'll get a taxi and pick up the car tomorrow night; then perhaps we can continue our discussion."

Trudy sighed wistfully as she waved him goodbye at the door. It hadn't been such a bad night after all.

CHAPTER 45

TO THE EDITOR of *World in Focus* it felt like a "kick in the bollocks." After considering all available evidence; sickness in the pit of his stomach; throbbing pain in the groin; lack of interest in anything except clutching his stomach and screaming, Gene was lead to believe it was as he first suspected. And who should be the deliverer of the aforementioned kick but bollocks kicker extraordinaire, Daniel Weston.

Gene had been dozing in his overstuffed armchair after a pleasurable evening with Trudy. Their meeting had not resolved much but left plenty to think about. He was beginning to regret not taking up Trudy's offer of a bed for the night, especially when the taxi-driver who dropped him off demanded a "king's ransom" for the privilege. Gene, too drunk to argue, paid up with as much grace as he could muster muttering the immortal words "f—kin' robber" as a parting shot in lieu of a tip. After too much booze and too many late nights, Gene had drifted off into a fitful, uneasy sleep.

In his dream, night had fallen. Gene was sitting in an empty derelict building, vaguely reminiscent of his office at Goldberg Publications. He became painfully aware of his charred and smouldering chair. Wisps of smoke breathed from trousers scorched by an intense heat. Tear ducts worked overtime in a vain effort to clear the dust and smoke from his gritty, sore eyes. He coughed and sputtered trying to clear the way for much needed oxygen to a befuddled brain. The air around him suddenly went cold. A chilling cackle stopped him in his tracks. Through tear filled eyes a wizened man-boy with a hideously distorted face loomed out of the gloom. The face moved slowly closer filling his vision. Gene imagined he could feel the rancid breath hot on his face, burning into his very soul, filling him with dread that tested the limit of human understanding. As he looked on helplessly, resigned to whatever fate had in-store, the face of the man-boy began to fade, to be replaced by the face of Daniel Weston—first one, then the other challenging for permanence.

The face, smiling on one side and a bloody pulp on the other, advanced insanely, with arms reaching out beseechingly, to a terrified Gene Harman. A parcel tied with a big, blood-red bow appeared in the outstretched hands of the phantom, who so beguilingly pushed it ever closer into the face of the petrified man. Gene crossed his arms over his face as if this action would form a protective barrier against all things evil. The man-boy slowly faded, finally becoming an indistinguishable entity, as Daniel fought to regain supremacy.

Gradually the dark malevolent face of Daniel regained control. Growing ever bigger filling Gene's vision, the bloated face emitted an inhuman scream that awoke the slumbering Gene.

CHAPTER 46

THE TABLETS HE'D prescribed himself didn't give any relief from his, now continual, headaches. He rang his secretary, Jean, to postpone his appointments for the day.

"Are you sure?" she said reproachfully. "Mr. Harrison was annoyed last time we cancelled his appointment; I'm afraid this time he may cancel altogether." Jean disapproved of the doctor's cancelling his appointments; she didn't consider it professional. This was the second time she'd had to rearrange his schedule in the last two weeks. If he carries on like this, he'll soon lose all his patients and I'll be out of a job, Jean thought to herself reaching for the phone.

Mike had more important problems on his mind than unhappy patients. "Yes, cancel them until further notice," he said harshly slamming the phone down.

Mike decided to take a taxi to Fircroft Wood. When the taxi pulled up outside the small shopping mall squeezed between the cinema and the car showrooms, he fumbled in his pocket for change and tipped the driver twenty pence, all he had. The cabby drove off thinking it was his lucky day.

Mike didn't really know why he'd come here or what he was going to do; he just felt compelled. He'd just written out a prescription for himself; he'd get that filled at the chemist in the mall. Good idea to spread them out when they were prescriptions for his own use. After what seemed an endless wait, his prescription was filled, and Mike walked slowly towards Fircroft Woods.

CHAPTER 47

ANDY HAD JUST come out of a meeting with his governor, Chief Superintendent Ryan. As usual the meeting was a one-way affair, with CS Ryan doing all the talking and Andy doing all the listening. Ryan was a bastard at the best of times; his ambition got in the way of common sense. As an Oxbridge graduate, fast tracked for higher things, he had little time for those who couldn't influence his betterment within the force, or for that matter influence his social standing outside the force. His current position was just a stepping stone, and Andy just one of the minions to tread on if necessary. Head buzzing from his governor at work and his governor at home, Andy was considering the Foreign Legion as a favourable alternative to his current situation.

The assistant chief constable was a governor of the university, as was Jason Goldberg, the media tycoon. Goldberg wouldn't hesitate to condemn the police in his newspapers if results were not forthcoming, and the unfortunate officer in charge bore the responsibility. In this case the officer was DI Andy Dale.

The team were busy working, heads down, when Andy got back, still fuming from his non-productive meeting with his boss. "Rob, come into my office," he said beckoning to his sergeant.

"We need a result on this one fast." Andy had already made up his mind that Principal Ian Mason was guilty of Helen Baxter's murder. "Take Laura with you and bring him in for questioning. He's as guilty as sin—all we have to do is prove it and get a confession."

Rob shifted uneasily; he knew his boss was quick to make judgements even if there was little evidence to back it up. Rob wasn't convinced that the principal was guilty, and with only six months to retirement Rob didn't want any complications that could affect his plans. "There isn't any evidence against him; he just hasn't got an alibi for the night of the murder," Rob insisted.

"He lied about knowing the victim personally, so he probably lied about everything else as well." Andy wouldn't let go; his mind was made up. "I'm going to speak to staff who knew Helen and see if I can dig anything up, so 'fuck off' and do your job—bring Principal Ian Mason in for questioning. Ask him to come voluntarily if it will make you feel better," he added sarcastically. "On your way out send that lazy bastard Stone to fetch the car 'round. We're going to see the librarian in charge of the research centre; that's where the victim spent a lot of her time.

CHAPTER 48

"HELLO, TRUDY—THIS is Ian. Please come to my office as soon as you pick up this message." Trudy was about to ring Gene when she picked up the principal's cryptic message on her answer phone.

Trudy had arrived at her office later than she had anticipated still nursing a hangover from last night. She'd lain awake after Gene had left mulling over their discussion. Finally giving in to insomnia, she had dragged herself out of bed, padded downstairs, and made a strong, black coffee. The next hour Trudy, now wide awake, had made notes detailing the contents of Gene's dreams. As a university lecturer Trudy always stressed to her students the importance of a sound methodology when analysing a problem. Thus, not surprisingly, by the time Trudy had finished, discarded sheets of paper containing all manner of diagrams and scribble littered the surrounding floor. The results of her labours, although not conclusive, had thrown up several interesting theories, one of which was extremely compelling. She needed to talk to Gene at the first opportunity.

She hadn't any lectures scheduled for today; she would use the time to finish her academic paper in time for next month's presentation. Trudy looked at her watch, a Rolex Oyster, at least forty years old. It had belonged to her dad; so when he died, she had asked her mother for it and had worn it every day since. Ten-thirty-five, later than she thought—well, she wasn't going to give an excuse for arriving late; goodness knows how often she had worked overtime for Ian's benefit in the past. She dialled the principal's number. "Hello, Ian; is it all right to come up now?" she asked expecting at least a "Good morning."

"Yes." Ian's impatience showed through in his monosyllabic reply.

Declining to take the lift, although her hangover begged otherwise, Trudy walked slowly up the stairs to the principal's office. What could be so urgent to demand a meeting immediately? Ian's message didn't give any clues, and neither did his curt reply to her call. His ability to cope with stress had always been questionable. Not surprisingly, coping with the murder of a staff member must be affecting him badly. All these thoughts were going through Trudy's mind as she wearily dragged herself up to the third floor.

Framed in the doorway, Principal Ian Mason was waiting impatiently for Trudy as she walked into the outer office. "About time," he snapped shutting the door as Trudy, without being invited, sat demurely in the visitor's chair. Suddenly Ian's demeanour changed; sitting down opposite Trudy, he visibly wilted as the anger drained out of him to be replaced with a look akin to panic. "Trudy, I'm in serious trouble and need your help," he began. "I desperately need an alibi for the night of Helen's murder."

Stunned, Trudy felt cold and numb as the principal, in a faltering voice, explained: "I was out on the night of the murder, but I panicked and lied to the police. You've got to believe me, Trudy; I didn't have anything to do with Helen's murder, but I feel as if I'm the number one suspect. The only way I can avoid suspicion is to say we were out together discussing university business.— Perhaps I should tell you the whole story about Helen and me."

Ian went on to tell the story of his relationship with Helen, giving details of their affair and subsequent acrimonious breakup. He did not, however, tell her about the abortion; he'd heard Trudy's opinion on that particular subject in the past, and he needed her support. Trudy listened in silence as Ian rambled on getting more and more animated as he revealed intimate details of his and Helen's liaisons. After several minutes of what was blether to Helen, Ian sank back in his chair eyes glazed as if the effort of baring his soul was too much for his fragile mental state.

It was a bombshell to Trudy who was beginning to feel let down by all those around her—first Mike, now Ian. Who would be next, she wondered—Gene perhaps?

"Well, are you going to help me or not?" snapped Ian, rousing from his momentary trance. His question went unanswered as DS Rob Murray followed by DC Laura Thomas walked unannounced into the principal's office flashing their ID's.

CHAPTER 49

THE POLICE WERE still working at the murder site as Mike made his way slowly towards Fircroft Wood. A diversion marked a path through the woods for members of the public and casual strollers. A police constable guarded the site and encouraged people to go about their business attempting to discourage those of a morbidly curious nature. Constable Masters took his duty seriously. He didn't intend to be a uniformed police constable all his life. His father had been a constable for twenty years and retired without having achieved promotion. Simon Masters intended to do better than his dad. Impressing the DI in charge of this case wouldn't do him any harm at all. As these thoughts ran through his mind, he caught sight of a loan figure ambling towards the murder site, ignoring, or oblivious to, the diversion signs.

Mike suddenly became aware of a uniformed figure striding quickly towards him; instinctively, he turned and ran in the opposite direction to the now sprinting policeman. A stinging blow to the face from a low hanging branch sharply focused his mind. He could hear cursing as the chasing constable slipped in the muddy undergrowth. Mike ventured a quick look back, in time to see the uniformed figure haul himself up out of the mud shouting at the running Mike to stop. Mike ran more deeply into the wood weaving to avoid straggling branches, and the voice of the constable trailed off.

Mike's one thought was to get out of the wood and to the safety of his own home. He would have to go through the woods and across the fields to a little known path, which came out at the back of the car showrooms. Breathing heavily, he ran unerringly along deserted pathways; his face and hands were cut and grazed from the constant attention of branches, which showed little regard for the frailties of the human body. Open fields, dotted with scrub, loomed up ahead; he made for a small gap hidden in the tangled mass of poorly managed hedgerow. As Mike struggled through the narrow opening, he felt his anorak grabbed by thorns seemingly determined he wasn't going to get past them unscathed. The sound of material tearing rent the air, but sheer panic and distant voices, carried on the wind, drove him on.

He kept low, as if this would make him less visible to a good pair of eyes. Gasping with the effort, he made his way painstakingly across the open field. He instinctively headed towards the yellow arrow that marked the continuation of a little known public footpath. Stillness pervaded the night air, relieved only by his heavy breathing and the thumping of his heart as it fought desperately to keep blood and oxygen circulating through his body. His legs weary from unaccustomed exercise, he reached the relative cover of the tree lined footpath. He slumped against an overhanging oak still dripping from an earlier rain shower. Sliding down the wet trunk, he waited agitatedly while the oxygen did its healing work. His mind was racing with questions. Why had he come to Fircroft Woods in the first place? How did he know about the shortcut through the woods? He'd never been here before. What was his fascination with the murder? He didn't even know the victim.

Distant sounds jerked him out of his reverie. Forcing his protesting body upright, he continued, as if in slow motion, along the overgrown path. Chain link fencing appeared on the periphery of his vision. Cars parked haphazardly in the chain link compound reinforced in him the certainty he was near the main road. He edged furtively along the fence expecting to see a uniform patrolling his escape route; except for a few stragglers, however, it was deserted; so Mike stepped cautiously into the road. No one took any notice of the bedraggled man as he walked head down away from the flashing blue light, now a surreal image in the distance.

CHAPTER 50

WISH I'D HAD a bloody education; I wouldn't be pratting around digging up other people's dirt; I'd have a life of my own, he thought wistfully. Andy was not a happy man—what with trouble at home, trouble with his governor, and now the need to spend the day with that 'university toff,' Stephen Green. At least they'd not had any trouble from that jumped up security man; just as well he'd been ready for him. In fact, truth to tell, he'd been disappointed; he needed to work out his frustration on somebody, and Harry "bloody" Butler would have done nicely. A full car park did not deter Andy—he double-parked, blocking several people in. So what? The university "bods" were a waste of space anyway, he thought, as he marched up to reception.

Detective Constable Stephen Green had studied at Durham University and had come away with a first-class honours degree in business studies. His family considered a career in the police force a waste of a good education. His friends considered it fraternizing with the enemy. Although he'd had a good upbringing, in his early youth he had mixed with some dubious characters. Stephen's strong mind and good family values helped keep him away from any serious trouble. Concerned for their son's future, the family moved across town away from bad influences, which threatened to disrupt his early life.

The move was a good one. The young Stephen started to excel at school, and his four top grades at "A" level ensured him a place at the university of his choice. He still kept some of his early acquaintances; but now friendships were guarded, with suspicion endemic, on both sides. Entering the research centre brought back many happy memories of a time when his only responsibilities were to learn and to enjoy himself. Now, responsibilities abounded; his life had changed, but not for the better. Andy Dale didn't like him and harboured resentment for what he called the "silver spooned university kids."

Jenny Smith's disinclination to provide any service showed through as she finally condescended to look up from her book. Customers spoilt the job, be they students or lecturers, always wanting help or advice or, sometimes, even a basic service. Now a scruffy old man in a raincoat was trying to attract her attention; well, he'd have to try harder than that.

At forty-five Andy Dale was not an old man, although he felt like one sometimes; and he wasn't about to be messed with by a "kid." "Police," he bellowed, continually banging the desk bell. Jenny jumped; a can of coke deposited its sticky, brown liquid over her desk and jeans on its way to the floor. "I'm DI Dale and this is DC Green," he said, waving a dismissive hand in the general direction of Stephen. "Who's in charge here?" he asked gruffly, flashing his warrant card.

"I am," Jenny responded. "Miss Moon isn't at work today—I'm standing in for her," she added, her earlier bravado dissolving by the second.

"What's your name, Miss?" Stephen asked more gently than his superior. "We're investigating the murder of Helen Baxter." People make decisions in life—some good, some bad. Jenny's decision to cooperate fully with an already exasperated Andy Dale ranked as one of her better ones.

"My name is Jenny Smith," she choked. "I am Miss Moon's assistant."

"Right, then, Miss Smith," Andy cut in. "I want some straight answers and no time wasting. Where can we talk in private?"

Ensconced in Miss Moon's private office, Jenny provided answers to questions fired at her from the two detectives. "Yes," she knew Helen Baxter, and "Yes," Helen did use the research centre often. "Yes," it was common knowledge that Helen and the principal had a thing going. "Yes," she'd seen them late at night whispering in the study section. "No," Helen didn't have many friends at the university; in fact, most of the staff thought she was a little odd, but "No," she didn't have any real enemies. "No," Miss Moon hadn't phoned the office, and "Yes," this was unusual.

After twenty minutes of intensive questioning, Jenny felt exhausted and frightened. The detective called Stephen had been nice; but the other one, Andy, had given her a hard time. Well, she hadn't told them everything; let the "pigs" find out for themselves.

CHAPTER 51

SUNDAY WAS A write off for Vincent Craig, as were most other days of the week. This was the norm for Vince, as he didn't have many friends queuing up just for his company. Thus, he spent more time on his own than his peers would have considered healthy. Truth was, Vince's only social life came from work; his status as the boss's nephew provided the key to his success, or lack of it. If people invited him out, they did so wrongly supposing Vince could influence his uncle in their favour; he couldn't, but strangely he never let on to the pandering few. They soon realised, however, the extent of Vince's power to influence, which varied between nil and nil—hence, his lonely weekends.

This Sunday, however, was written off for a different reason. In fact, he still could hardly believe that he'd seen a dead body and not an ordinary dead body but a murdered one. Of course, most television dramas these days produce dead bodies in abundance, and they all end up on a pathologist's slab. The more gruesome the bodies, the greater the audience appeal. Real life, however, was different, as Vince had found out. Try as he might, he could not get the ghastly picture of bulging eyes and protruding tongue out of his mind. Even copious amounts of alcohol, greedily consumed, could not dim the vivid image bounding around his befuddled brain in glorious Technicolor.

Vince's first inclination when he stumbled on the body was to call the police, but on second thought he decided not to. Daniel had been in such a hurry to leave the woods on Saturday that he'd barged past Vince without any apparent recognition. In Vince's mind there was no doubt that Danny was the murderer. Vince had seen all the Sherlock Holmes films, including the old black and white B-movies: thus, he felt qualified to judge the merits of the case. He imagined himself as Holmes and Danny as archenemy Moriarty. In the end, Sherlock was always right.

When he had recovered from the initial shock, Vince's thoughts focused on the best way to exploit the situation to his best advantage. Given that he fancied Danny, many ideas flitted lasciviously through his mind. First he would let Danny know that he knew his secret and, then, his continued silence would come at a price.

CHAPTER 52

ANOTHER FUCKING DREAM! At least this one, thought Gene, wasn't an epic like the others. Strange, bloody, frightening, but it hadn't affected him in the same way as the previous dreams had. That lazy bastard Danny Weston had figured prominently in this latest production. Bad enough he should have these bloody dreams at all, but of Danny Weston! What would a shrink have to say about that? Well, he himself would have something to say to the last "toe rag when he came back to work—things like, "Fuck off" or even, "You're fired, you lazy bastard." After a moment's consideration, Gene decided on the latter of the two options; at least, it made him feel better to think about it. In fact, the more he thought about it the more excited he got. Contemplating the sheer unadulterated pleasure he would get from sacking Daniel gave Gene the motivation he needed to get to work early. As it turned out, it was a decision that may have saved his life.

He had been tempted to ring Trudy as soon as he woke from his slumber; but they had arranged to talk tonight, and that would be soon enough. Anyway, how could she help? While true that she didn't talk only about fluffy kittens, like many women of his acquaintance did, she hadn't come up with any earth-shatteringly useful theories either. It was this chauvinistic attitude that endeared him to Lois and her "bag lady" mother.

While savouring the thought of his mother-in-law as a "bag lady," Gene rang for the taxi to take him to work.

CHAPTER 53

GENE WAS MESMERISED by the rapidly ticking taxi meter, the numbers on it a blur like a demented slot machine at an amusement arcade. Why was it that taxi-drivers always manage to find the longest way around? Was this part of the training: find the longest way and then go as slow as you can. Gene's mind wandered as the whirling numbers clicked up remorselessly. Goldberg will love this one he thought watching yet another pound ping up. Oh well, the mean old bastard—I'll book it as client expense. He smiled faintly at the thought, but he turned his mind to more important matters. The most pressing was Daniel Weston.

The Goldberg building, which houses Goldberg Publications, stands at the end of a long road littered with assorted banks, building societies, and charity shops. Six stories high, it is just one of many company buildings scattered around the country. Today the taxi carrying a worried editor cruised down Bank Street towards the ostentatious building. The taxi-driver, determined to squeeze every last penny out of Gene, slowed to let a familiar person, at least ten metres away, cross the street. The figure, whom Gene recognised as Danny Weston, walked furtively up the steps that led into the Goldberg building.

Angrily Gene muttered to himself, "I wanted to get in first and be waiting for him." Half the pleasure, he mused, would have been seeing the shock on Danny's face upon seeing him.

"That'll be twenty-five pounds, Squire," said the taxi-driver hardly able to contain his glee at the look of horror that crossed Gene's face. Counting out two ten pound notes and searching through his pockets for enough change to cover the rest felt like déjà-vu. Was it only last night that he was struggling to rake together the fare from Trudy's? A tipless taxi driver waved happily to Gene as he screeched down the road, suddenly finding his accelerator. Gene marched purposefully on up the steps of the Goldberg building.

Danny was about to tape the small brown package under his editor's desk when Gene stepped out of the lift into the main office. Fortunately for Danny, the lift gates were noisy. Unhurriedly he placed the package back into his open rucksack; a roll of silver-grey fire tape vanished quickly into his anorak pocket and walked out into the main office in time to see Gene striding towards him. "I've put the post on your desk," called Danny brusquely to the six-feet-four "avenging angel" bearing down on him.

CHAPTER 54

TEN MINUTES AFTER the police left Trudy still hadn't stopped shaking. She had been about to reply to Ian's question when they had barged unceremoniously into the principal's office. DS Rob Murray had asked the startled principal to come to the police station to answer questions regarding the murder of Helen Walters. It had only been a request to help with their enquiries, but there was no doubt that refusing wouldn't be an option. Ian had looked imploringly at Trudy as if begging her to come to his rescue and provide the alibi he desperately needed. As the two police officers were escorting Ian down the stairs towards the waiting car, Trudy had stood, face impassive, ignoring Ian's unvoiced pleas. The whole scene had seemed surreal, with everything happening in slow motion. Voices slurred and low as if playing a forty-five record at thirty-three. It was the sound of the police car screeching away through Ian's open office window that had jerked Trudy back to reality.

Was he guilty? she wondered. *He hadn't said where he was on the night of the murder. Why had he lied to the police?* A few weeks ago Trudy would have been in no doubt that Ian was innocent, but recently she realised that people weren't as predictable as she had previously thought. She had been living in a fairy-tale world believing everybody was as honest as she was herself. Welcome to the real world. It had taken her thirty-two years, but she was there now.

Strange how things had changed; a few days ago she would have rung Mike Powell for a shoulder to lean on, but recent events had changed even that. I'll give Gene a ring; he'd bloody well better not let me down, she thought, as she walked down the stairs to her office.

CHAPTER 55

"BLOODY HELL!" EXCLAIMED Daniel, seeing the angry face of his loathsome enemy bearing down on him. It had been a close thing; he'd nearly been caught placing the bomb under Harman's desk. Luckily he'd had the forethought to pick up Harman's post in case he'd needed an excuse for being in his office. Whether the excuse had worked he'd soon know. He was tempted to detonate the bomb now and take everyone with it. If Harman didn't accept his excuse, maybe he would. Self-preservation wasn't high on his agenda; but there was, after all, his friend David to think about. "Kill him! Kill him! He's your father, and he ran out on you." David, who had been quiet up to now, started shouting frantically in his friend's ear, his voice getting ever more shrill. Daniel started humming to block out the sound of David's voice. The louder David shouted the louder Daniel's humming got, finally reaching a wailing climax.

Gene pulled up in amazement seeing Danny Weston's hands pressed against his ears as if trying, unsuccessfully, to keep out the sound of his own frantic humming. This wasn't going as planned. Gene had expected to invite Danny into his office for what is commonly known as a "bollocking," and if all went well, a termination of his contract. The spectacle of Danny cavorting about and humming was unnerving and warranted a change of plans. "What's the matter with you?" Gene asked, managing to keep any semblance of sympathy out of his voice. Gene's bellow penetrated the rapidly closing curtain that shielded Danny from reality. David's pleading voice gradually submerged deep into the shadowy depths of Danny's brain.

"Good morning, Mr. Harman," the sarcasm was clear. Now temporarily free of David's goading influence, Danny jolted back, just in time to deal with the urgent demands of reality.

Gene's office was not the tidiest, cleanest, or most well organized office in the universe; but it was, for the time being anyway, his territory to defend. "Unless I invite you in for a bollocking, keep out of my office," he told Danny. Gene had always favoured direct language no matter how much it hurt a person's feelings. Many considered it rude; surprisingly, however, few complained about it to Gene's face.

The disturbing scene he'd witnessed had, as they say, "taken the wind out of Gene's sails" and had altered his original plan to sack Danny. He was not a tender and caring man, so it was an act totally out of character when a look of mild concern replaced his previously thunderous expression. "You look bloody rough," Gene said, trying to summon the sincerity of a recently notable, if failed, American president. "You'd better go home and call a doctor."

Danny couldn't believe his luck. The fool was sending him home; the irony was too delicious. It won't be me who will need the doctor; in fact, come to think about it, neither would Harman—an undertaker yes, a doctor definitely not. All he had to do was prime the detonator and leave Harman to it. David's excited voice once again forced its way to the forefront of Danny's mind; this time it was welcome as they marched away to the small stationery store where he and David could work together undisturbed.

CHAPTER 56

VINCENT CRAIG HAD decided to take the lift to the third floor this morning. It wasn't much of a decision really. For a fat, lazy person like Vince it was the only decision, the alternative being to use the stairs; and that required physical effort, which he detested. Vince was looking forward to getting to the office today, an unusual instance in itself. He had spent a long time—three days, in fact, deliberating on the best way to approach Danny to let him know that he, his saviour, would stand by him, despite Danny's being a murderer. Anyway, it was only a woman he had done away with. The temptation to ring Danny at home had almost overwhelmed him, but Vince reasoned that at least here at work they could find a quiet place and discuss their future and the cost of his continuing silence.

The collision occurred as Danny, on his way to the stationery room, and Vince, on his way to the staff room, met on the corner by the lift. Danny and David, engrossed in earnest conversation, and Vince, contemplating the pleasures the day held in store, collided forcefully under a disapproving portrait, in oils, of Jason Goldberg. Danny was barely able to suppress his rage. "Look where you're going, you fat git," he hissed, grabbing frantically at the rucksack sliding off his slim shoulder. Just in time, he prevented it and its deadly contents from dropping to the floor. All of a sudden, the need for him and David to survive became paramount. This instinct hit him with a blinding flash. This would be his destiny.

"What did you say?" Vince called indignantly to Danny's rapidly departing back. With more important matters than "fat Vince" on his mind, Danny walked swiftly to the comparative seclusion of the stationery store.

CHAPTER 57

A DEXION CABINET, filled with outdated stationery, obscured the view from the only window in the stationery store. Old copies of *World in Focus* leaned against grubby walls in untidy piles gathering dust. A flickering fluorescent bulb provided the only light in the space.

Safely ensconced out of the sight of prying eyes, Danny gingerly opened the rucksack. Inside, neatly wrapped in brown, greaseproof paper, was the instrument that would solve all his problems and put him on the path to fulfil his destiny—the culmination of his and David's labours. From his jacket pocket he produced a small digital timer, so much better than a cumbersome alarm clock, sometimes used by so-called bombers in films. It took less than five minutes for Danny to connect the timer, which would detonate the device. Many practice runs at home, first in the light and then, when proficient, carrying out the exercise blindfolded, now accounted for his speed and dexterity in the final preparation. He'd got in early hoping to time the bomb to go off at ten o clock, just when the editor would be drinking, or in Harman's case slurping, his first coffee of the morning. Harman's getting in early called for a change of plans.

"Danny, you bastard! Where are you?" called the whining

voice of Vince, still smarting from his encounter with the elusive Danny, but now even more determined to make him pay.

Danny's heart thudded in his chest. Reaching into the rucksack pocket, his hand felt the comforting contours of the hypodermic syringe filled with a fast acting poison. The toxin derivative used by the Indians of South America to subdue their prey was just as effective on "fat gits."

The heavy door protested as Vince, with all the stealth of a herd of elephants, barged his way into the deserted staff room. Indication of the night staff's hurried exodus lined tabletops, as well as any other convenient surface. The partially eaten sandwiches and half-empty mugs of cold, muddy coffee bore witness to the evening shift's revelry. "Dirty bastards," muttered Vince glancing around the empty room, his gaze coming to rest on the yellowed door leading to the stationery store.

"Vince, you lazy git, come here." The abrasive tones of Gene Harman echoed down the corridor. Disappointed that he couldn't sack Danny, he decided to "have a go" at his number two as consolation for an otherwise frustrating morning.

Danny breathed a silent sigh of relief as the door, protesting indignantly when being so rudely opened, now protested equally indignantly as it slammed shut behind Vince. Circumstances had changed; he could set the bomb to go off in thirty minutes and be well away before the blast. "That wouldn't be so much fun though, would it?" David's voice echoed from deep in Danny's subconscious. Perhaps they should hang around and watch the fun—have a ringside seat from the cafe over the road. Nero fiddled while Rome burned, so why shouldn't they play rock and roll on the jukebox while Harman burned?

CHAPTER 58

GENE SAT BACK contentedly sipping his second cup of coffee. Crushing Vince's confidence so early in the morning was greatly satisfying to Gene, but the episode with Danny was worrying. It looked as though he was having a fit—a bit scary, if truth be told; that's why he'd sent him home, not out of consideration for Danny. If word got around that he was being thoughtful, then his street credibility would take a bigger dip than Tony Blair's did after the invasion of Iraq.

What was it that niggled at him? All thoughts of work had long since faded, if they were ever there in the first place. Goldberg Publications would not be getting value out of the *World in Focus* editor today. Recently Gene's lack of enthusiasm for work was becoming a problem, as Goldberg had taken great pains to point out at their last EMB (early morning bollocking). Suddenly it hit him like a bolt of lightning. All other thoughts emptied, without explanation, from his mind. Some long forgotten image, which had burned deep into his subconscious, surfaced, wiping out all other thoughts.

The empty, derelict building; Danny Weston; the intense heat and smoke; and the grotesque face—this dreadful scene was straight out of his dream. As Gene's gaze wandered down the main office, his eyes focused on Danny's now empty desk and he had a sudden realization: his dream was a premonition. The derelict building was this office. Panic induced in him the choking sensation he had felt in his dream. His breathing became laboured and erratic as his throat constricted. He tried to shout out a warning to everyone around, but his words took on a language and a will of their own. Something told him to get out of the building as fast as he could. On legs behaving as though they belonged to some drunkard after a night's binge, Gene ran frantically towards the stairs. Instinctively he bypassed the lift, remembering advice given by some self-important trainer in an otherwise forgotten fire safety lecture.

Archie had also started earlier than usual for the office this morning, due to a row with his son over a phone bill, which looked more like a lottery win. Arguments with James were a regular feature of the Brown household. James had left school and taken a fashionable year off before going to university. Unfortunately, the year had now turned into two years and promised to exceed all expectations by running very predictably into three or four. Why was it that Archie's wife, Jane, always came out on the side of her darling offspring, when it was Archie who had to foot the bill for a lazy son still living at home? Sometimes Archie felt like an outsider in his own home.

Archie had almost made it to the top of the stairs. Trying to convince himself that the exercise was doing him good, he was shocked when Gene burst through the door shouting, "Fucking get out!" as he roughly brushed past his colleague in his frantic haste to act on his own advice. Archie turned and followed in the wake of the fleeing Gene.

Vince didn't hear Gene's garbled shout. Vince was too busy licking his wounds and plotting revenge after his early morning visit to Gene's office—not his best decision ever in the light of future events.

CHAPTER 59

IN A CAFE across the road from Goldberg Publications, Danny sipped his coffee as he waited expectantly. He had chosen a table that afforded him the best view of the action about to begin. Far enough away to be safe, but close enough to witness the result of his, and David's, handiwork in all its splendour. Surprisingly, David wasn't with him to witness the event, encouraging, egging him on; he felt strangely alone, bereft even.

Barely able to contain his excitement, his hands shaking and his face twitching, he caught the attention of a middle-aged waitress busying herself leaning against the serving counter. Danny's state of exhilaration was broken as a hand came to rest suddenly, but with gentle pressure, on his shoulder. His gaze fixed on cracked, but clean, nails attached to red, sore fingers. Turning his head further, he looked into the rheumy eyes of the concerned waitress.

"Are you feeling all right, luv?" she croaked in a voice distorted by years of heavy smoking. "You looked as though you were having a turn."

"Tell her to get lost!" yelled David, his voice booming from the depths of Danny's ear. Confidence returned to Danny now that his friend was back. Repulsed by the physical contact of the waitress, Danny flung her hand fiercely from its resting-place. She was at first surprised, then outraged, and finally made afraid by Danny's violent reaction. She feared the manic look in his eyes, as well as the uncontrollable torrent of abuse directed at her.

The proprietor attempted to come to her rescue. He had been running his cafe for over ten years, during which time he had been called on to handle many difficult situations. A big man, well over six feet tall, he had been a good amateur boxer in his day and still worked out at the local gym with the steroid monsters. Never into steroids himself, when provoked he was aggressive enough without any chemical help. This was one of those times. As he heaved himself out of his chair, a massive explosion took away all thoughts of Danny and concentrated his energy on getting himself to safety.

CHAPTER SIXTY

THE MAN WENT flying through the air as the blast lifted the figure off his feet before finally depositing him in an untidy, quivering heap among the smoking rubble. The world was deafeningly silent around him. Ghostlike images moved in and out of focus. Bricks and rubble rained down, but he didn't feel any pain, as a deep numbness crept over his mangled body. He tried to call for help but could only emit a choking croak, as his mouth worryingly filled with blood from who knows where. A multitude of different coloured lights pulsated on the periphery of his vision, reminding him of Christmas and happy times; but this relief was a temporary illusion as reality crowded in on him once again. God, the heat, getting hotter with each passing second! He was burning up! "Help!" he screamed; he didn't hear himself scream, but he just knew he had. In the distance, through the shimmering haze, he could see movement—backwards and forwards, backwards and forwards. It was an arm pushing through the debris, frantically trying to attract attention, anyone's attention. Shadowy figures in the gloom moved in slow motion towards the frantically waving arm.

Falling masonry created an even denser blanket of dust particles that obscured the man's view even more. Through the haze he watched as the figures worked frantically to remove debris, finally exposing the body attached to the waving arm. They worked for what seemed like a lifetime but could only have been a few minutes, before revealing the face and body of a big man he recognised only too well.

Gene Harman was being eased gently from the wreckage that once was Goldberg Publications. More shadowy figures, struggling to lift the big man onto what must be a stretcher, faded in and out like images in the fog. Why could no one see or hear him? He was sure he was screaming, but people walked straight through as if he didn't exist. He knew it must be his imagination brought on by the shock. Like a whirlpool, his head spinning, he was being dragged down, ever deeper into unconsciousness, as the pressure of the rubble became unbearable, and mercifully, he blacked out.

CHAPTER 61

DANIEL WESTON WAS overcome with excitement. It took a major effort of will to resist running into the burning building and crying out, "Look what I've done!" to the distressed victims. A warm glow of pride shrouded his whole being as he mingled with the small, gathering crowd. Flashing lights from first police cars, then fire engines, and finally ambulances gave a carnival effect to the whole proceedings. Daniel and David wanted to join in the festivities. So did the throng drawn together outside like vultures trying to get a better view of the gruesome scene. A cordon hastily drawn around the incident did little to keep morbid onlookers away, and Daniel on tiptoe could look on with pride of accomplishment.

"Roll up, roll up, all the fun of the fair," David's voice tinkled in Daniel's ear. Onlookers, so engrossed in their own morbid curiosity, failed to notice and condemn Daniel's sudden burst of laughter. Daniel, for his part, couldn't care less; he was having far too much fun.

DS Rob Murray was first on the scene; he'd been on his way home when the call came out. Having worked half the night on a caseload that got heavier every day, Rob was going home for his breakfast and to make peace with his wife. He hoped she was still talking to him, but doubted it. Roll on, retirement, he thought. Less than a mile away, as the crow flies, when the call came out over the radio, he felt obligated to at least show willing until another senior officer arrived. Braking sharply, he did a left turn and roared up Chapel Road towards the Goldberg building, oblivious to the gesticulations of the driver he'd just cut up.

Upon arriving, Rob saw uniforms earnestly scurrying about their endeavours in a scene of chaotic confusion. He screeched to a halt, as cops do in films; opened the window; and beckoned to a familiar police uniform. Constable Jim (Smelly) Smith showed his relief upon seeing a senior officer; it meant he could hand over responsibility. They are paid more than me; let them have the problems, he thought—an attitude that explained why he still remained a constable after twenty-five years of service.

"Hello, Jim. What's happening?" Rob hadn't much time for "Smelly Smith" at the best of times, but he still made an effort to be civil.

"There's been an explosion," said Jim, who seemed to have a degree in stating the bloody obvious. Being sarcastic wasn't in Rob's nature, but he was about to make an exception for Smelly when a familiar blue Ford Focus drew up alongside him.

CHAPTER 62

WHY ARE PEOPLE so morbid? Andy asked himself as he looked around at the gathering crowd. It had been the same when he was in traffic division all those years ago; there had been nothing like a gory accident to bring out the oddballs. He didn't like it then, and he didn't like it now. They must have a screw loose, he thought uncharitably, as he walked briskly up the drive to get a closer look at the scene. He'd sent Rob off home, poor old bloke, in trouble with his missus like most of them. It's not the best job in the world for domestic relationships. Talking of oddballs, look at that one in the crowd, laughing his head off. I'd like to knock it off-the disrespectful moron, thought Andy, turning away in disgust.

"Sorry," a nudge from behind eased Andy out of the way. Two ambulance drivers, one of them a paramedic, with a bright yellow sash proclaiming his status, shouldered their way past carrying a stretcher. As Andy glanced down at the blackened face looking up pathetically from the contrasting white stretcher, he felt a fleeting pang of recognition. Bloody hell, that looks like Gene Harman, he said to himself. Although far from being a celebrity, Gene had his photograph attached to a glossy editorial column in the popular weekly publication, *World in Focus*. Andy thought his pompous pronouncements were crap, but then everyone has his own opinion. Well, he didn't look so clever now. The vindictive side of Andy was always close to the surface as anyone who crossed him could testify.

Daniel felt guilty—not for the devastation he had caused; no, that was great. His mother would be proud. The guilt he felt was from the look that that "pig," the detective in the grey suit, had given him. It was a knowing look, a look that said, "I know it's you; you're the guilty one." Eyes boring into the back of his neck, a more sensitive person would have felt the intense energy generated by his fury. Not surprisingly, as a police officer Andy Dale had no such sensitivity; so he was not aware of the new and deadly enemy he'd just acquired.

CHAPTER 63

THE LIGHT BLINDED him as he opened his eyes, momentarily, before squeezing them tightly shut. The second time his watering eyes remained open long enough to see, swimming in and out of his vision, a hard face, partially covered by a veil, leaning over him.

"How are we feeling today, Mr. Harman?" asked the nurse behind a surgical mask. The face leaning over him wasn't as bad as he had initially thought. In fact, it was nice looking, as faces go. He felt a cool, soothing hand on his forehead, as he registered the full appeal of the face peering down at him. Now that she had removed the mask, he could see a corona of blonde hair framing a pair of the deepest blue eyes he had ever seen. He heard her voice call, this time more urgently. "Doctor, Mr. Harman's awake."

Another figure walked into the room, that of a man in a long, white coat with what looked like a stethoscope hanging around his neck. "Hello, my name is Dr. Watson, and this is nurse Richards," said the white clad figure leaning over, peering into Gene's watering eyes. Seemingly satisfied with his deliberations, the doctor stepped back, much to Gene's relief; gazing into an attractive nurse's eyes was one thing, into a fat-faced, male doctor's was another. "You had us all worried for a while, Mr. Harman. Can you remember what happened?"

Gene squinted hard against the bright light bouncing off the ceiling and all the other white things surrounding him. The room began spinning moments before he spewed forth the remains of last night's supper and, more recognizably, this morning's breakfast over everything within a metre's radius, including Doc Watson's immaculate white hospital coat. The oath muttered by the good doctor on his way out wasn't the Hippocratic one usually associated with the medical profession.

An intense weariness overtook Gene; having had enough excitement for one day, his body lapsed back into a drugged sleep, oblivious to the frantic activity going on around him.

CHAPTER 64

"TERRORISTS STRIKE IN Bletchworth"—The headline dominated the front page of the Bletchworth *Evening News*. "One killed; many more injured."

This was only the second scoop the *News* had run in years, the previous one being the murder of Helen Baxter in Fircroft Woods last week. This story was even bigger, so they made the most of it by not letting the facts get in the way of a good story.

The *News* was wrong on several counts that day. It was not a terrorist that caused the explosion neither were there many injured. Reporting one death was, in fact, the only accurate statement in the whole article. A more accurate headline would have read: "Daniel Weston Strikes in Bletchworth.

One person killed and several people injured." It could have gone on to read: "Gene Harman, editor of *World in Focus* was among the injured as was the proprietor of the local cafe'. Vincent Craig, nephew of Jason Goldberg, was killed in the blast."

This was the news that took the recent murder of Helen Baxter off the front pages.

CHAPTER 65

IT WAS DARK next time he woke up, head throbbing and everywhere else aching abominably. As his eyes gradually adjusted to the dim light, he could make out the indistinct outline of a figure sitting in the visitor's chair at the side of his bed. As he struggled to raise his head, the shadowy figure moved cautiously towards him. He automatically recoiled until a voice, gentle with compassion, enunciated, "Hello, Gene; I'm so glad you're back with us." It was the voice of Trudy Ballinger.

The smile on Gene's face at hearing Trudy's voice changed rapidly to a grimace as the pain from his charred skin vent its condemnation at being stretched. "Hello, Prof; excuse me if I don't shake hands," his voice trailed off as Trudy kissed him lightly on an exposed area of his forehead.

"They tell me you'll be as good as new in a few weeks although," Trudy continued, "you may never play the piano again."

"The old ones are always the best," riposted Gene sitting up, much to the disgust of his wounded body, as a jolt of pain reminded him to be more considerate in the future. They chatted idly for the next half-hour, Gene feeling more relaxed as his pain-racked body temporarily eased its grip. Dim lights created a feeling of tranquillity in which they both languished.

The mood, however, changed dramatically, without warning, when Trudy ventured, "Gene, did you know that one of your colleagues died in the explosion?"

CHAPTER 66

THE NEWS DEVASTATED Gene. A coldness crept over him as Trudy went on to explain how Vincent Craig had died in the explosion. It's not as if Gene had any great feeling for Vince; it was more realizing how close he had come to death that shocked him. "Bloody hell! And to think I only gave him a bollocking this morning," was all Gene could say.

"The police think it is a terrorist bombing," Trudy went on, trying to distract Gene from his propensity for self-pity.

"Well, they're wrong," said Gene breaking out of his melancholic mood; "it was that bastard Danny Weston."

Trudy sat stunned and silent as she listened to Gene's account of his strange vision. Her expression of concern for Gene changed to one of horror as more lurid details emerged. Although Trudy had been sympathetic and had feigned rather more interest than she felt in Gene's previous accounts of his dreams, this time she took them with a deadly seriousness. Premonition as a concept was alien to Trudy's scientific upbringing, but Gene presented enough compelling evidence to shake the foundations of her beliefs. As details emerged of Daniel Weston's strange behaviour just before the explosion, Trudy became more and more convinced that this could be, and probably was, something beyond her understanding.

"I think he's had enough for today," Nurse Richards, now fully recovered from her drenching by the contents of Gene's stomach, said. "Doctor will be 'round in ten minutes to check on our patient's progress."

Trudy squeezed the outstretched hand bringing tears to Gene's eyes. "See you tomorrow," she whispered seductively on her way out.

CHAPTER 67

IAN HAD SPENT an uncomfortable night in the police station, answering the same questions again and again—slightly different slants each time, but the same questions nonetheless, each designed to trap him into another false statement. How he regretted lying about his whereabouts when first questioned; it was rebounding on him now with interest. It was obvious they had convinced themselves of his guilt, and nothing he could say would convince them otherwise.

Trudy hadn't come forward to provide him with an alibi; so he'd admitted to the lie and given a lurid, but false, statement of his whereabouts, embarrassing though it was. He knew enough about the workings of the police mind-set to realise they were more likely to believe his salacious exposition than an explanation less lurid but nearer the truth. The contempt in their faces was palpable; if they could have flung him in a cell and thrown away the key, they would have. Lack of evidence dictated they couldn't hold him any longer. Reluctantly, with the solemn warning not to leave town, they'd let him go, for now.

At home and on his third large brandy, Ian pondered his predicament. He'd lied and was now paying the price for the lie. The police suspected him of murder; and on top of that Trudy had let him down. When word got out, his career prospects would be zero, even if, indeed, they weren't much greater than that before the incident. Trudy would be next in line for his job at the university; maybe that's why she hadn't come forward with an alibi. When this mess was over, he'd find a way of paying her back; but right now his mind was in turmoil, every road a cul-de-sac. The more he thought, the blacker seemed his future.

He'd started off with such high hopes. Where had it all gone wrong? He squinted across the room—the brandy bottle seemed far away, too far away. He made his way unsteadily in pursuit of the distant bottle to pour another large drink. If his wife was still here, she would reprimand him sharply, telling him he'd had enough; and that would have been an end to it.

But she wasn't here, was she? If she had been, he wouldn't be in this mess now anyhow. So when you thought about it, she was to blame, not him. Bossy bitch, he thought; he was better off without her. His face contorted briefly as memories, long forgotten, flashed briefly through his befuddled mind. A sudden spark of anger surged within him; clutching the bottle protectively to his chest, he retraced his steps back to the sanctity of his chair. This time the bottle was reassuringly within reach of his shaking hand.

CHAPTER 68

"FED-UP" WASN'T the word for it. They didn't pay her enough to take all this responsibility and flack from "full of themselves," tutors parading about with their adoring entourage in tow. The students were as bad; just because they were at university doing their easy option courses, they thought they were better than she, a girl from a council house, who never got further than Bletchworth Comprehensive. Well, at least she was earning her living, not relying on someone else to fund their so-called degrees—soft option media studies, most of them, not worth the paper they were written on. Her brother was a carpenter working on building sites in all sorts of bad conditions, while these softies almost swooned if the temperature in the classroom dropped by a couple of degrees.

When Miss Moon came back, they'd all be telling her tales, exaggerating of course, describing in great detail how the service had deteriorated while she was away. On top of that, the police were sniffing around investigating Helen Baxter's murder, trying to make everyone feel guilty. Mind you, Miss Moon would be in trouble when she came back. Everyone had to ring in if they were sick, even the principal—for all his importance

She'd put off this chore for days now, but finally the time had come. "We'll sort out those files in the vault," Miss Moon had said, and then promptly gone off sick leaving the responsibility with her assistant. Dr. Ramsay had requested the files in question two days ago; he was getting impatient and would stir up even more trouble if she didn't get them soon. Reluctantly Jenny put on the official blue overall, the cheapest money could buy, as the dust would soon ruin her own clothes. Muttering to herself, she grudgingly made her way down to the dusty vault.

CHAPTER 69

SHE FUMBLED BLINDLY in the dark trying to locate the switch that would bring light to the black eerie place they called the underground filing room. More like an underground junk store; everything not needed above in the centre found its way below into the vault. Like heaven and hell, except the research centre above was about as far from heaven as you could get. Cursing loudly as a sharp object caught her sleeve, her probing fingers finally located the dusty switch.

Darkness suddenly became light; she blinked, temporarily blinded by the white glowing orbs. Gradually, with eyes adjusted to a glow of half a dozen one hundred watt bulbs lining the centre of the long underground catacomb, Jenny stumbled down the steep, concrete steps. No handrail, she noticed—so much for health and safety. Maybe if she slipped, compensation in the form of a big cheque and a long holiday could be coming her way. All the adverts now for litigation lawyers—"no-win no-pay"— developed a whole new way of thinking, even for a girl from Bletchworth Comprehensive.

The light from two one-hundred-watt, shimmering light bulbs tried in vain to reach the far dim recesses of the long musty vault. Falling short, leaving mysterious black shadow worlds providing grist for the mill of vivid imaginations. The sight of dusty files piled up in stacks against the far wall soon jolted Jenny out of her reverie. "Damn," one of the bulbs was out at the far end, just where she was going to do the sorting. Oh well, she thought, she'd have to drag the files up to the lighted area to work. Bloody hell—this is going to take the rest of the day. As Jenny walked tentatively down the underground vault, rats sprang into her mind. One of the lads who helped out occasionally said he'd seen them scurrying about. She hoped he was joking and only saying that to scare her. He was a bit snidey and rat-like himself, always hovering around her. She smiled at the thought of little "rat boy" nibbling on a chunk of cheese at lunchtime.

However, as she got nearer the far end of the vault, all thoughts of rats, "rat boy," and cheese vanished from her mind. A tentative glance down revealed a twisted and broken pair of spectacles, belonging to Miss Moon, lying on the floor. A bare foot with red painted toenails, now ripped and torn, extended from a naked leg partially covered in dust and torn skin Jenny screamed, as she ran in a blind panic, falling up the stairs, oblivious to any pain in her effort to get away from the dreadful scene.

CHAPTER 70

WHY DID MIKE Powell feel this compulsion? Going to Fircroft Wood— what a no brainer; if the police had caught him, he'd have some explaining to do. They'd be asking questions even he didn't have answers to. What was happening to him? His life had turned upside-down. The determination and logic that had made him successful in the past had now forsaken him, leaving him feeling helpless and afraid. Some force, over which he had little control, had taken away his resolve—indeed, his very essence.

As a trained clinical psychologist, who had completed his medical school training and psychiatric residency, Mike should have been in control of his life; but he wasn't—far from it. At university, he was described as an introvert; and certainly, at times, he relied heavily on his friend Trudy to help him, especially socially. Latterly, however, as he progressed through medical school, his confidence and self-assuredness had grown exponentially.

The decline had been gradual, during the first months hardly noticeable, even to the trained observer, which Mike was. The speed of deterioration had accelerated in the last few weeks. The periods of blackness, with no recollection, now exceeded his lucid periods. Drugs had little or no effect relieving the psychoses affecting his judgment and emotion.

What to do? That's the problem. He could confide in fellow professionals and seek their advice; however, if word got 'round, it would ruin him. Potential and existing patients would not have confidence in a consultant with a history of mental disorder himself. Worse still, he could find himself sectioned under the bloody mental health act.

Maybe there was some power controlling him, and he was not responsible for his actions. Mike suddenly realised that he was displaying classic symptoms of schizophrenia—disordered thinking and withdrawal from reality. Now waves of drowsiness washed over him; he could barely keep his eyes open. He'd experienced similar feelings after having preoperative sedation before undergoing surgery last year. Was he about to have another blackout? What did he do during the periods of which he had no recollection? Did he go out? Did he roam the streets? He could be a Mr. Hyde, the antithesis of his Dr Jekyll self.

He'd been reading too many books—maybe it was all in his imagination. God, it was getting more difficult to keep his eyes open; perhaps a strong coffee would help. He didn't think so, but anything was worth a try. His legs felt like lead; perhaps he would rest for a few minutes before making the coffee. That was Mike's last thought, before he fell into a deep sleep.

CHAPTER 71

ANDY RECEIVED THE call shortly after four o'clock. "There's been another murder at Bletchworth University," Superintendent Ryan had said.

That was all he needed. He'd spent the morning making inquiries concerning the fire at Goldberg Publications. Another bloody murder—what was happening to this town? It used to be so quiet. Now it seemed there was a murder or a major incident every day; he might as well be back in the Met. He'd come here for the quiet life, but it hadn't worked out that way. Bloody hell, he thought; that meant he might not get home till late again tonight. Oh, well, so much for domestic bliss; he might as well get a divorce now and save trouble later. He'd spent so much time at the university recently he might as well take up residency and get a bed. He wouldn't be welcome at home—his wife would see to that.

Pandemonium had broken out at the research centre by the time Andy arrived. Dishevelled and bad tempered, the senior detective snarled sharply at the harassed young police constable, who would have been more at home on traffic duty than at a murder scene, demanding a detailed account of what had happened.

"Seemingly," the constable referred to his notebook, "the facility assistant, Jenny Smith, went down to the stores beneath the centre to do some filing." The constable glanced down at his notes again. "There she stumbled on a body whom she presumed to be Miss Moon. She's in no fit state to identify the body, so we've sent for one of the senior lecturers to come over and do the honours." The constable realised by the look on Andy's face that it was a mistake being too flippant. "Sorry, sir," he said sheepishly, averting his eyes from Andy's stentorian glare.

Frightened, Jenny Smith was sobbing fretfully in a small office that doubled as a syndicate room when bookings were scarce. A concerned looking Laura Thomas placed a comforting arm around Jenny's shoulder. The room was full of smoke when Andy walked in. Although this was a no smoking building, even he, a non-smoker, felt it churlish to call it to the attention of a distressed looking Jenny Smith. Laura looked up and smiled when her boss walked in. "Hello, Boss; this is Jenny Smith, the one who discovered the body," said Laura by way of introduction.

"Hello, Jenny; we've met before," said Andy solemnly. "I hope you're going to be more cooperative than last time we spoke." Andy's stern reprimand invoked another burst of sobbing from Jenny and a look of reproach from Laura.

Leaving Laura to try to repair the damage caused by his unsympathetic interrogation, Andy made his way wearily down into the now brightly lit vaults beneath the research centre. Grace Anderson had already arrived, looking resplendent, wearing plastic coveralls over a smartly tailored blue suit. Seeing Grace looking so attractive even in such unflattering attire sent erotic thoughts flitting briefly through Andy's mind as he approached the scene of death.

"Looks like the same M.O. as before, Andy," she said, getting straight down to business apparently unaware of the senior detective's lascivious smile. "She was strangled the same as the last victim; but this time it looks as though she was hit with a blunt instrument as well just to make sure. It does appear this was a more frenzied attack than the previous one. I'll know more though when I've carried out the post-mortem."

"How long has she been dead?" demanded Andy, all erotic thoughts a distant memory.

"As near as I can judge, about twenty-four hours," replied Grace wearily to Andy's probing question.

"Thanks, Grace; when forensics have finished, I'll get the body over to you as soon as possible. Maybe we can get together soon over a drink and discuss your findings."

"Are you trying to date me?" responded Grace with mock coyness.

"Of course not—just need to talk to someone with more than half a brain cell," Andy replied with more bluster than intended. If the situation doesn't improve at home, I probably will be dating you, thought Andy, walking briskly away.

CHAPTER 72

DEVASTATION WAS ALL around—buildings crumbling, fire, water, bodies everywhere, people screaming, panic. The onlooker cried upon seeing faces he recognised, but was powerless to help. Family, friends, loved ones, even enemies—all appealed to him with suffering revealed in their eyes. Intense sorrow tore at his very soul as he gazed at the incredible carnage around him. Buildings that were once a familiar part of the landscape now lay in smoking ruins as far as the eye could see.

What nightmare was this? Could it be he was in hell, the final resting-place of the damned? A small figure with a face barely more than shrivelled skin stumbled blindly, wailing pitifully through a cavernous lipless hole where a mouth should have been. The pitiful figure turned slowly as if sensing the man's presence and reached out with a burnt stump for an arm. Dead, blackened eye sockets, which pitted the grotesque visage, fixed on him accusingly, before melting like hot molten wax running down a candle, into a smoking heap of burned rags fluttering animatedly in the ever-increasing wind. Ugly, leaden clouds scudded desperately in a frenzied quest to block out the sun's warmth. Scenes of destruction burnt their grim images on the man's brain like light on a sensitive film emulsion as taken by

Yoshito Matsushige at the scene of the Hiroshima bombings.

Despite the devastation there was a vague familiarity about the scene. A figure carrying a child—where had he seen that face before? A big man, now stooped under the burden of survival, stumbled forward aimlessly. Another familiar figure, this time a woman, caught up with the stumbling man, her clothes hanging like rags on a scarecrow. Even in her wretched plight, she held herself upright and aloof, appearing to encourage the man with incomprehensible mumblings. As the forlorn souls moved towards him, he reached out to put a consoling hand on the woman's shoulder; but he could feel nothing. The image just shimmered, without substance, before him. Despair overcame him as he stared at the wandering figures before him. His gaze fell on the strange looking stone around the woman's neck. Memories came flooding back overwhelming him with their intensity.

Recollections in a vivid panorama of colour, from a bygone age—happy memories, sad memories, memories of lives torn apart by anger and greed. He fell to his knees, with his arms open wide, looking up in terror at the apocalyptical sky. "Trudy," he cried; but no one could hear him.

CHAPTER 73

HE SENSED HYSTERIA—high-pitched alarms wreaking havoc with delicate senses; the sound of running feet on polished floors; starched, white and blue uniforms scampering in all directions, each with its own job to do; the sound of placatory voices, not expecting to calm the terror of impending death, but going through the motions just the same.

"You'll be all right, Mr. Harman; hold on; doctor is here," the voice gets slower and deeper before finally stopping altogether.

A cool hand gently stroked his fevered, distorted brow. Torn between two worlds, he felt he must hold on to reality, but which is reality—the frantic activity he could sense nearby or the distraught figures fading, shimmering, transparent, briefly snapping back into sharp focus, fading again—the big man and child, the imploring woman reaching out, the unearthly cry from deep within the bundle cradled protectively in the big man's arms? His body racked with jolting pain, this time the agony more intense, he felt he must get back to reassure them that everything is going to be all right. Jolting pain again—will it never stop?

White faces lined with worry hovered above him anxiously; his pain is their pain. "Clear,“ "bang"; "clear," "bang"—"We're losing him again, Doctor".—Trudy, the child, must hang on—figures fading; everything spinning rapidly; a whirling down into a vortex; a pinpoint of light approaching rapidly, getting ever more intense until too dazzling for the eyes to endure—then, relief, blessed darkness, silence, oblivion.

CHAPTER 74

THE OLD BUILDING looked strangely uninviting as Andy walked up the long drive to Bletchworth Hospital. He leaned heavily on a cold handrail as he dragged himself wearily up the black tarmac.

Pushing hard against the big swing-door, he mused that one could come to hospital relatively healthy and go home with a hernia, an idea that struck him as funny and brought a smile to his usually solemn face. Still, these days a hernia was the least of the patient's worry with MRSA rampant. The door gave way reluctantly to Andy's forceful push. A blanket of warm air, emanating from old, struggling, cast iron radiators, enveloped Andy, triggering a spontaneous bout of coughing. People milling about, voices raised—not the place you came to by choice, thought Andy, making his way to reception.

A harassed-looking receptionist grudgingly gave Andy, after he produced his identification, the directions to Gene Harman's room. Rob was supposed to be meeting him here—lazy git—wait till I see him, thought Andy, making his way up the corridor to Gene's room.

"You can have five minutes with Mr. Harman," said a frazzled Nurse Richards, finally nearing the end of a long, stressful shift, "but please don't tire him out too much. He is still seriously ill and not out of the woods yet," she added for good measure, suddenly realizing she was talking to herself. Andy had already barged his way unceremoniously into Gene's room.

Gene's gaunt, grey face peered up out of voluminous snow-white pillows. Tubes snaking out of every orifice in his body were linked to alien looking machines, beeping softly and blinking greenly. Bloody hell, he looks like an alien, thought Andy, grabbing a chair and scraping it up close to Gene's bed. Andy introduced himself, flashing his ID for effect. The patient, more interested in his own suffering, gave a curt nod, mumbling through his pain, "What the 'fuck' do you want?" Although Gene's body had broken, he was still convivial to a fault.

"Do you feel up to giving us a description of anything that happened before or after the explosion that may help us in our investigations?"

Gene's face contorted with fury, "It was that bastard Danny Weston." The nearly unintelligible, croaking voice emanating from a face filled with medical tubes had become stronger, fuelled by the broken editor's passion. Andy nonetheless edged closer, not wanting to miss any detail of Gene's whispered account.

"I think Mr. Harman has had enough for today." A large, fresh-faced doctor, with a stethoscope as a symbol of authority hanging around his neck, bundled his way into Gene's room.

Although they'd only been talking for ten minutes, and that had been haltingly, Andy felt he'd got enough to pull in Daniel Weston for questioning.

Bloody hell, two murders and an explosion with fatalities to investigate—that's too much for one person; he'd have to start delegating he felt sure. He was a good detective, but a poor manager; and he didn't trust anyone else to do the job as well as himself. His governor had threatened many times to send him on a management skills programme, but Andy had always resisted, using his high case load as an excuse—a chicken or egg scenario, if ever there was one. Superintendent Ryan had pointed out this circumstance on several occasions. At the moment, he was juggling too many balls in the air and hadn't got a grip on any single one. Rob Murray was coming up for retirement; perhaps he should hand one of his many cases over to him. Give the lazy git something to do before he retired—if he hadn't already retired, a premise held by many at the station.

Strangely, his mood had lifted by the time he walked down the drive towards his car. He didn't even have to hang on to the rail.

CHAPTER 75

THE LUSH FOLIAGE of a large, pink azalea bush concealed the crouching figure of Daniel Weston, watching as Andy Dale walked thoughtfully across the car park to the waiting Ford Focus. Daniel Weston had a new target. Mind you, he still had to complete the job he'd started, the one on Gene Harman, but that would be easy now. Harman was helpless, no longer the big, tough, bully boy that everyone was once afraid of, now just a weak invalid. "How are the mighty fallen . . .!"

A detective inspector—now he would provide a much more formidable opponent! If he could kill a police officer, he'd show his true mettle; the thought lingered deliciously in his mind. His mother would be even more proud; she might even start speaking to him again. Gene Harman had been easy, too easy; in fact, Gene Harman had been a big disappointment. He had expected to feel relieved, a sense of achievement after blowing up old Goldberg's offices and, as he thought, killing his pseudo father. But the reverse had happened; he felt more dissatisfied than ever, and so did David—especially David; and David wouldn't be denied. Not that Daniel had any intention of denying David; in fact, he couldn't if he wanted to. David was now in control or, more to the point, out of control.

CHAPTER 76

THEY MET IN the small lift on their way up to the third-floor. "Hello, Miss Ballinger," he said as the lift groaned and squealed its way slowly, inexorably up to the third-floor. Trudy emerged from her reverie with a start. She had been thinking about the events of the past few days—Gene's injury's, the explosion at Goldberg's, that unnerving phone call, and the uncomfortable feeling of being watched. All this, to say nothing of the murders and Ian's problems, hung like a lead weight round her heart.

It was all a million miles from palaeontology and the petty politics of the university. Perhaps this was real-life, not the artificial, cloistered environment of university life where everyone felt self-important but, in reality, contributed very little. Ian was a typical example; now she could see him for what he really was—a pompous, little man, lucky to be a university principal. Why had he lied to the police? What secret life did he have? Had he killed Helen? Now that doubt had crept in, she could not be sure of anything or anyone, even Gene. Then, of course, there was Mike; with the events of the last few days, she'd forgotten about him. He, too, had changed; everything had changed and not all for the better unfortunately.

All of these thoughts vanished abruptly from her mind as she looked up at the grim unsmiling face shaded beneath a black trilby hat. "Hello, Miss Ballinger," said the man again impatiently, this time removing his hat.

"Hello, Inspector Dale," replied Trudy.

CHAPTER 77

THE WARM SMILE Gene afforded Trudy faded as Inspector Dale followed her into the room. "Are you two an item then?" queried Gene sarcastically, giving Andy the look reserved only for turning an unfortunate recipient to stone.

If Andy had had a pound for every time someone gave him the stare, he'd be a rich man, having retired years ago and living by the sea. However, that was not the case; no one ever gave him anything, he thought sadly. Forcing a smile, he approached Gene's bedside and sat down heavily opposite a peeved Trudy, who busied herself arranging grapes in a large glass bowl. "Do you feel like answering a few questions today, Mr. Harman?" began Andy. "I won't keep you long, but I need you to answer a few questions while the incident is still fresh in your mind."

A look of anger crossed Trudy's face, noticed by Andy, who said quickly with impeccable timing, "Please stay, Miss Ballinger. I'm sure your opinion will be helpful."

Gene had felt almost the least important player in the scene, as though he were invisible; but as he started answering the detective's questions, he gained more confidence. As the story unfolded, Gene became more animated. Prompts from Trudy helped him describe his previous dreams and the photographs received afterwards. He then went on to tell of his latest dream, the one that sent him into cardiac arrest. Listening intently, Andy began to warm to Gene and despite himself found his story both interesting and believable. Fifteen minutes later, Gene finished his tale, exhausted by his efforts; sank back; and closed his eyes. The high pitched hum of air-conditioning cutting in broke the silence as Andy and Trudy assimilated the importance of Gene's narrative.

The acting postman for the day, Joey Jones, whose job description identified him as the hospital porter, breezed in and threw a large envelope on Gene's bed. After uttering the immortal words, "post gaffer," he continued his way out.

At Gene's request Trudy carefully slit open the manila envelope and spilled its contents out onto the bed. She picked them up and could feel two pairs of eyes boring into her, as the colour drained from her face. "What the fuck is it?" asked Gene raising himself up with an ease that belied his delicate state. Andy took the photographs out of Trudy's shaking hands and flicked through them, before finally handing them to an impatiently waiting Gene. He placed them face up on the bed,

Almost breathtaking in their brilliance, the photographs depicted vivid scenes of devastation, which gave Gene a weird feeling of déjà-vu. Details that would perhaps go unnoticed to the naked eye were revealed dramatically in the images laid out before them. Three pairs of eyes were transfixed by the chilling scenes. The most chilling of all was the scene depicting the man carrying a child with a woman hanging on his arm. Three pairs of eyes simultaneously recognised the pathetic, care-worn figures.

Andy was the first to speak, "You two haven't matured too well," he said looking intently at the aged versions of Gene and Trudy.

CHAPTER 78

JOEY JONES DIDN'T have time to scream as the knife ripped through his ribcage severing the left pulmonary vein before shattering his beating heart. It's doubtful if he felt any pain at all; at least that's what the doctor would say to his distraught mother after he'd carried out the post-mortem.

As temporary postman on the wards, Joey had an easy working day. Actually every day was easy; Joey saw to that. He was an expert at looking busy, but doing little. Now he was going home for a quick shower and a leisurely tea in front of the television then down to the pub to meet his friends. When the pub closed they would go on to a local nightclub for more drinks, and with any luck they would pick up a few girls. "Well, you're only young once," he kept telling his worried parents. As a concession to them, he would take a taxi tonight; then he wouldn't have to worry about driving later. Joey just completed one drink driving ban and didn't want another. He wouldn't be able to get insurance, or if he did it would cost a fortune; and it was too inconvenient using buses. Therefore, he'd better be safe than sorry. As it turned out, it didn't matter anyway; but as he went to the locker room to change, whistling happily, he had no idea how short the rest of his life would be.

The locker room situated beneath the small annexe that housed the orthopaedic clinic was a damp place. Staff were forever complaining to management, who for their part had intended putting in heating; but there was always a better way to spend the pitifully small budget—not the least being new computers for the I.T. department. It was in this sad place that Joey met his death.

CHAPTER 79

IT SURPRISED GRACE; it shouldn't have, but it did. She'd been a pathologist now for as long as she could remember, and it took a lot to surprise her. Now, however, after checking her notes for the third time, she realised that the murder of Helen Baxter had a different modus operandi than that of Deborah Moon. The Helen Baxter murder was straightforward, as far as murders go—killed by strangulation with a silk stocking. Deborah Moon's death was different. She'd been tortured so severely over many hours that she'd died of a heart attack. A silk stocking had apparently added some malicious pleasure for the torturer. Obviously the thrill for the murderer was in the strangling, whether the victim was alive or dead. The murderer, if it was the same person in both cases, was graduating to a more vicious approach to the job—a worrying development.

Severe rope burns gave testimony to the frantic, agonising struggle Deborah had put up while the murderer had smashed fingers on both her hands with a heavy blunt instrument, probably a hammer. Five fingers having been smashed in total—three on the right hand and two on the left, Grace could only imagine the pain the poor woman went through before her heart finally gave out. Strangely though, there was no sign of the rope used to restrain her. Her first thought was to phone Andy, to let him know of her discovery.

Doesn't anyone answer the phone in Andy's office? thought Grace after letting the phone ring out irritatingly for over a minute. Infuriated, she was about to slam the phone down when an angry voice rasped, "DI Dale's phone."

"Hello, Rob; is Andy in?" Grace was fond of Rob; she knew he'd a lot to put up with working with Andy. Poor man—I bet retirement can't come soon enough for him, she thought. Rob's manner softened on hearing his favourite doctor on the end of the line.

"Hello, Grace, luv; Andy is out at the moment. He's gone to see that bloke Harman who got injured in the explosion at Goldberg's; I've only just picked up his message. Try him on his mobile if you like, but I tried half an hour ago and only got his answering service."

"Thanks, Rob; it can wait," said Grace affably. "How are your retirement plans coming along?" she added on a more personal note.

"Can't come bloody soon enough, luv," was Rob's parting comment as he gently placed the phone back in its cradle.

CHAPTER 80

IT FELT WARM and pleasurable as it moved slowly, seductively up his leg. He lay back, gratified by the ecstasy of the moment. As the feeling gradually worked its way upward, a pungent smell allayed his nostrils causing him to heave momentarily, warm bile rising in his throat and temporarily blocking vital airways. He shivered fitfully, suddenly becoming aware of the intense cold. The warm feeling moved slowly up his body and became even more pleasurable in contrast to the rest of his body. Like a blanket, the pitch-black night bound his eyes, providing an effective shield between him and a reality it was better not to know.

A sudden, agonising pain shot through his body, emanating from an assault on his lip. A scream of horror ripped from his throat as a large, brown rat, frightened by the violent reaction, hung on for a moment to the man's hideously torn lip. Finally releasing its hold, it bound off into the night with a shriek, leaving the man panic stricken and alone. As he hyperventilated and gasped for breath, hysteria swept over him in waves before subsiding into an abject whimper. He rocked back and forth, embraced in his own arms. Gradually his rapidly beating heart returned to normal, as he gained control, uttering only an occasional cry. With eyes slowly adjusting to the gloomy darkness, he tentatively looked around and disgusted by what he saw, squeezed them shut again. Garbage was strewn all around, including empty cans and dog turds; red and blue lights glared—could this be hell? It would be some people's meaning of hell; in fact, it could be most people's definition of a nether world in which the dead continue to exist miserably and in torment.

Were there neon lights in hell, and did they flicker erratically, their multicolour making the head spin? He didn't think so. No, he was in a dark alleyway, lying on top of a pile of rotting food and other foul trash, surrounded by hostile rats. Slowly, muscles protesting, he eased himself upright against the greasy wall. As he staggered forward, a glow from the end of the dark alleyway beckoned him; it became more insistent the closer he got. A sign reading "The House of Beijing," beamed down on him courtesy of huge red and blue lights, which flooded a tatty looking Chinese restaurant with a purple hue.

For twenty minutes he walked on autopilot, not knowing where he was going, but somehow an inner compulsion drove him on and on into the dark night like a zombie reanimating a dead body. Finally reaching his destination, he slid slowly to the floor and lost consciousness.

CHAPTER 81

AT THE GRAND old age of twenty-four, Joanna Richards had felt life was passing her by. Devoted to her job, Joanna was an ideal nurse; this dedication was good for her patients, but not so good for her private life. Yesterday however, everything had changed; she was in love again. She'd met the man of her dreams, or specifically the man of her recent dreams, in the shape of young Dr. Mackenzie. He was taking her out tonight, although she would probably have to pay. Young hospital doctors were notoriously poorly paid for the hours they worked. Nurses also worked long hours for low pay; but when you had wealthy parents, a quick phone call to Daddy would swell the bank account as if by magic.

She had been nursing Gene Harman for the past few days; once you got past the bluff and bluster, he was appealing in a rough kind of way. The woman who visited him was different. While attractive, she spoke clearly and precisely and gave the impression she was lecturing you rather than holding a conversation. But she was obviously fond of Mr. Harman.

She didn't like the man who visited him, the one who was a policeman. She hadn't been told he was a policeman, but she knew straight away. He had a way of looking at you that made you feel guilty of some unspoken crime—bad enough if you were guilty of something, but very disconcerting when you were innocent. Another of her patients, an old gentleman, had just vomited over the floor; and she couldn't find that lazy Joey Jones anywhere. As usual he had switched off his mobile. If anybody could get out of doing work, it was he, she thought angrily; so she'd rather clean up herself than await his convenience. Flat healed, sensible shoes beat a rapid tattoo on the hollow sounding pavement as she half ran and half walked to get her coverall from the staff locker room. Joanna was always conscientious about her uniform, unlike some of her friends, who would even go shopping at lunchtime wearing the same uniform they wore when tending ill patients.

Nurse Richards had seen dead people before, in many different death poses. Although she never became blasé about death, at least she could accept it with the dignity and decorum of a true professional. That was before she found Joey Jones with a large knife sticking in his stomach and his entrails spilt over the highly polished floor.

CHAPTER 82

THREE ASHEN FACES stared in disbelief at the photographs spread out before them—six images, each depicting a scene of devastation and tragedy. Trudy was the first to break the silence. "It can't be," she said, almost inaudibly. Trudy's control was hanging on by a thread and bringing looks of concern from both Gene and Andy. "Somebody tell me it isn't!" Her voice rose to a hysterical shout as she looked first at Gene then at Andy, without expecting an answer from either. Gene, his face pallid before, was now devoid of any colour.

Andy looked stunned; a life devoted to logical and sometimes not so logical deduction found it difficult to comprehend the evidence in front of him. Cynicism was the watchword in his job. Feted by his colleagues as a grand master in the art of being cynical, his fame had spread to the higher echelons of the force, notably the chief constable, who regarded cynicism as a flaw in Andy's character—not the best news for an ambitious DCI. The current situation, however, was for real he had no doubt; the looks on both Trudy's and Gene's faces evidenced that.

"Can somebody tell me what is happening here?" Trudy's was the only voice breaking the gloomy silence that had descended on the room like a damp fog.

Gene who had been uncharacteristically quiet, now levered himself up looking at Trudy with a mixture of unease and concern. "I tried to explain about the dreams before, but I don't think you took me too seriously," he began.

"Is there anything else you haven't told me?" Andy cut in, more abruptly than he intended. Gene bristled at the interruption. Although still ailing from his injuries, the old fire was still there; and the adrenaline was starting to course through his veins. He was about to let Andy have a piece of his mind when a loud scream erupted from the corridor outside. As if on cue, the scream from the bloodstained nurse had broken the charged atmosphere that had built up in Gene Harman's room. Being privy to something beyond their understanding bound their thoughts together and threatened to reveal all when the scream so rudely interrupted their deliberations.

As the senior officer on the scene, Andy quickly took charge upon the discovery of the hospital porter's murder. Trudy and Gene were too shocked to protest. The murder of Joey Jones was the latest incident in what was beginning every day to sound like an Agatha Christie thriller, sadly without Hercule Poirot, or even Miss Marple, to help with the investigation.

CHAPTER 83

BLETCHWORTH POLICE STATION was under siege. At least it felt like that. It was a long time since the station had been so busy or received so much attention. The activity inside the building equalled that of the activity outside, as media, press, and the odd inquisitive passer-by thronged outside the main door hoping for statements they could relay to anxious news editors.

A crisis meeting was in progress, and Andy Dale was feeling the heat. With three murders in town, as well as a bombing, which also included a death, the eyes of the national press were on them. What were they doing about it?—That's what Superintendent Ryan wanted to know, and it was Andy and his team he was directing his questions at. Unfortunately for all concerned, Andy didn't have answers to give, at least none that would impress the chief constable. Gene Harman's description of events before the explosion was the only positive lead they had.

Steve Green was already on his way to pick up Daniel Weston for questioning. As for the murders at the university, Ian Mason was the only suspect they had; and he fit the bill perfectly. "Bring him in and lean on him a bit, and he'll break," said Andy out loud, more in hope than any strong belief. The chief constable had threatened to get one of the elite Met units in to take charge of the investigation if results weren't soon forthcoming. That would have been embarrassing for Andy; having transferred from the Met, he could imagine old colleagues with scores to settle really capitalizing on the situation and revelling in his humiliation. A discussion with Grace earlier had shown up one or two anomalies, which his team would need to follow up; but apart from that they were no further forward.

Getting back to his office he sank into his chair with a sigh. He had forty-eight hours to come up with results; otherwise, the chief constable would carry out his threat to bring in the Met. What a life! Not for the first time, he envied Rob, with his few weeks to go before retirement—even the prospect of mowing the lawn and cleaning the car had appeal.

For the next hour he concentrated on delegating the less important cases to junior members of his team. It would be good development for Laura Thomas and Steve Green to take more responsibility themselves, he thought, only half convinced of the validity of his logic. But it was the best he could do for now, he thought, pulling the last case-file from his untidy filing cabinet. Now the decks were clear, he could concentrate on the murders and the explosion. Was there a link, or was it the silly season for committing crimes in Bletchworth?

Recent events dominated his thoughts. Gene Harman and his strange dreams—what did they mean? That last one was especially weird; and those photographs—well, all three of them were shaken by those. He had read somewhere that directly before the passenger ship Titanic had sunk on its maiden voyage, many people had reported premonitions of its sinking long before the big ship hit the iceberg and sank to its watery grave. Could Gene's dream be a premonition of some catastrophe? In the past he would have ridiculed such an idea, but recent happenings had given him cause to doubt even what was black-and-white and to consider the shades of grey. He would talk with Gene and Trudy again soon; a common bond was forging between the three of them, and they had a lot to discuss.

His office door burst open as he was mulling over recent events when Laura Thomas strode into his office with the news: "Daniel Weston is nowhere to be found, Guv; it looks as though he has gone on the run." What Laura Thomas didn't know was that far from going on the run, Daniel Weston was at that moment looking at her and Andy through high-powered binoculars from the shelter of wooded wasteland behind the police station.

Daniel Weston was now David; more precisely the personality that was David had now taken over Daniel's mind. Occasionally, David would relinquish his domination, fading into the background; then without warning take control again. Such was the situation now, as they were watching Andy and Laura holding an animated conversation and looking like shadowgraphs framed by the dimly lit office window. The drizzling rain adding to the grim atmosphere, only lightning and the occasional clap of thunder missing from what could be a scene out of a horror movie.

"Right, get an arrest warrant; I want that bastard locked up before he strikes again." Andy sensed that this could be the breakthrough they had been waiting for. Not a moment too soon, thought Andy little realizing that "that bastard" was less than one hundred yards away looking at them through eyes rapidly losing touch with reality. As an avid reader of Sherlock Holmes stories, the breakthrough excited Andy. "The game is afoot," Holmes would say to Watson as they chased the criminal down, usually in Sussex. Andy felt like Sherlock; all he needed was a Deerstalker and pipe, as he picked up his phone to call Rob

Murray, his trusted Watson.

Trudy shook her head in disbelief. In stark relief to the duck egg blue, chosen after much deliberation, the red spatter formed abstract patterns that would have done justice to Pablo Picasso. Among the many swirls snaking their path around the hitherto plain bedroom walls and over the recently re-silvered mirror, an observant eye could detect shaky lettering. Trudy's disbelief turned to horror as individual letters combined to reveal a message so chilling Trudy sank to the floor sobbing uncontrollably.

CHAPTER 84

HE DIDN'T WANT to be here. He'd gone out of his way to make that clear to Sergeant Stone, but his appeal to the sergeant's legendry better nature fell on "stony ground"—he was still here and hating it. Joining the police force and then after much sucking up to the people with influence, finally graduating to the firearms unit, his aspirations were higher than looking after some fool editor who got himself blown up.

After serving with the British Army in Northern Ireland, he needed action, not bloody babysitting duties. The murder of the porter had prompted the gods on high to post a twenty-four hour armed guard outside Harman's room. A vindictive Sergeant Stone had assigned him the graveyard shift. Well, to hell with old "Stone heart"; he'd had worse shifts in the army. It didn't bother him then, and it wouldn't bother him now. Still, it was surprising how eerie a hospital was at night, especially up here in the isolation area.

As an avid reader of Robin Cooke's medical novels, he realised that the mind could run amuck with weird imaginings. Rampant deadly viruses, corpses everywhere, megalomaniacal doctors striding about like colossuses—thank God it wasn't like that in real life. Or was it? The programme he'd watched on TV the other night about the Ebola virus didn't fill him with confidence. He half expected to feel the warm trickle of blood as it leaked from eyes and nose and all other available orifices. They say that fact is stranger than fiction, but even a practical, down-to-earth ex-soldier was entitled to have doubts, especially in the small hours of the morning.

Three o'clock in the morning is regarded, by some, as the time when people are at their most vulnerable. Well, it was about three now, and they were right. Strange how flickering shadows exude an aura of menace, even to the most logical mind. His peers thought him well reasoned and rational—someone to depend on. Even so, he gripped his gun more tightly, taking comfort from its cool authoritative feel and daring the shadows to do their worst. He was ready for anything, or so he tried to convince himself. The people who knew him best weren't as convinced of his bravery, one of several reasons being that the army had decided they could do without him.

They weren't taking any chances moving Harman up here in the isolation area away from the main wards. At least with fewer visitors it was easier to check people coming and going—not that Harman had many visitors. He wasn't that popular apparently, just an important material witness, according to Andy Dale. If Dale thought Harman was so important, he should be up here "babysitting," not wasting his time and talent.

He hoped that Trudy "what's her name" would be visiting again soon—nice legs to go with her trim figure. God knows he needed something to brighten up his day. What she saw in that Harman bloke was beyond him—couldn't be his personality or looks, and he certainly didn't seem over endowed, financially, or any other way for that matter. Still, there's no accounting for taste as his dad often said, referring to Sophia Loren, the world's most beautiful woman according to his dad, and Carlo Ponti, her husband, "not exactly an oil painting."

At the far end of the gloomy corridor, the door leading to the now-deserted reception office complained noisily as it opened, breaking the silence and causing a nervous intake of breath by the big police officer. The butterflies in his stomach flitted away on seeing a white-coated figure, with a stethoscope as a symbol of authority, emerge from the darkened doorway smiling. With a wave, a smile, and a twitch of the stethoscope, the apparition in white continued his way through the double doors at the end of the corridor.

"F—kin' Pig!" The jerky, uncoordinated walk gave evidence to the turmoil deep inside him as he fought desperately to keep control of his emotions. He'd not expected to see that fat pig of a policeman wallowing outside Harman's room. It took all his control to prevent running at the pig and tearing the eyes from his fat head. Instead, he'd raised a hand and waved inanely before hurrying to the safety of the reassuring darkness beyond the big double doors.

CHAPTER 85

"GOOD EVENING, LADIES and gentlemen. Here is the ten o'clock news." The news presenter smiled sincerely into the autocue. The autocue, unfazed by the gleaming teeth and a cocked eyebrow, blinked back a cryptic message in return. The presenter's smirk metamorphosed into something more akin to a genuine smile before taking on a more solemn look as a breaking newsflash danced across the screen.

"Remember, folks," the presenter continued, "when in 1998 NASA announced the discovery of two new near Earth asteroids to pass in 2026 but assured us that neither of the objects posed an immediate threat to Earth? Well, it seems they have revised their calculations, and lo and behold the new prediction coincides with the Mayan calendar."

The front man paused for effect before finally continuing. "They are now saying there is a significant probability of a collision with Earth, but the good news is it won't be soon. The Mayan calendar predicts 2012 as Armageddon, so we'll have to wait a while to find out if the new calculations are any more accurate than the old ones." The presenter postulated wisely, cocking an eyebrow to his audience. "Perhaps they'll come up with even newer and better calculations to amaze us in the future, if there is a future," he added on a dramatic note, shuffling his papers, signifying the end of the programme.

The cameras panned out leaving the familiar news service logo for enraptured viewers to ponder on. Numbered among the captivated audience were Gene Harman, Andy Dale, and Dr. Mike Powell, each reflecting on the news item with a singular degree of interest.

CHAPTER 86

"SHUT THE FUCK up; I'm trying to listen," bellowed Gene irritably, frantically prodding the TV remote in the vain hope of hitting the volume button. Nurse Rita Patel, acting as a replacement for Joanna Richards, gave him the scolding look as practiced by nurses everywhere, particularly on patients who had the temerity to step out of line.

The news item, frivolously included to provide the presenter with a vehicle to display his devastating turn of wit and superior knowledge, resounded in Gene's brain, triggering a dormant train of thought.

Gene's mind had been in a whirl over the last few weeks. The murder of Joey Jones hadn't helped his state of mind. That bloody, fat policeman posted outside his room didn't help either; thank God he'd be out of here soon. Trying to make sense out of recent happenings kept him constantly awake during the long, lonely nights, punctuated by the agonised moaning of other patients, which added to the chilling atmosphere. His developing friendship with Trudy was an added complication. He wasn't vain enough to think his manly good looks had bowled her over, and it couldn't be his financial circumstances either. Whatever his attraction, he'd like to know what it was, so he could give her more of the same to keep her interested.

Andy Dale worried him, moreover, sniffing around on the pretence of work when it was plain to everyone that he fancied Trudy. These concerns were minor, however, compared to the explosion at Goldberg's and the death of that little fat git, Vince.

While Vince was alive, he was a useless sod; but after his death, he gained saint like qualities that even Mother Teresa would have been proud of. Goldberg had already offered a large reward for information leading to the capture of those responsible for his nephew's death. Goldberg's compassion for his editor, however, hadn't even extended to a box of chocolates; he should be lying in bed with a bloody catheter stuck up his dick and see how he liked it. The half smile drifting across Gene's face at the thought of ramming a catheter up Goldberg suddenly turned to horror as another thought hit him like a bombshell.

Disaster, annihilation, destruction—the words barely distinguishable, at first, became progressively dominating until they crowded out all other thoughts. Words chased around in his head, each fighting for dominance. Harrowing images previously confined to his nightmares melded to the words giving a frightening significance to their meaning. With the sudden realization that his recent vivid dreams could be related to great disasters of the past came the more horrifying realization that the latest of his dreams could be a premonition of the future. He needed to share this revelation with Trudy; if it was possible to separate her from Andy, so much the better—if not, bollocks, he thought. It wasn't just Goldberg he'd like to stuff the catheter up. Andy Dale would do nicely as well. A grimace creased his face as he reached across to the phone.

"Bloody catheter," he shouted to no one in particular as he dialled Trudy's number.

CHAPTER 87

HER COMFORTABLE MIDDLE-class world was in tatters. This only happened to people in films or on television. Storytellers and producers stretching the bounds of credibility to come up with new slants on tired old plots would not have come up with such a bizarre plot as this. It couldn't happen in real life, but it was; and it was happening to her right now. An overwhelming sense of despair threatened her very sanity—Doctor Trudy Ballinger, a pillar of society.

"FUCK YOU, BITCH." The letters, daubed in crimson paint, or perhaps blood, pulsated as if they had a life of their own, threatening to detach themselves from the wall and swamp their victim. They filled all available space on the wall, forming ominous rivulets of blood, which trailed down the blue painted surface to the white painted skirting board. The crimson streams completed their journey forming a ghastly oasis of blood in the sand coloured carpet. Crimson footprints, gradually fading, made their way down the stairs, vanishing completely before reaching the lower treads. With eyes desensitized by the scene around, Trudy's gaze shifted towards the disappearing footprints, seeking further denial, refusing to accept the chilling message filling the back wall—"You're next."

Her senses, dulled in trying to deny the reality of the chaotic scene, jolted back to reality as the harsh cry of an outdated phone rent the air. Her hand shaking, Trudy reached to silence the nerve jangling sound being emitted from the archaic black monster. Holding the phone away from her ear, as if that would lessen the full force of the voice she expected would spit vitriol from the phone, Trudy listened with increasing horror.

It was like a bolt out of the blue—the phone call from hell. She had never experienced such a malicious call as this before. It would leave her completely unnerved. The strange, robotic voice spewing forth obscenities sent shivers down her spine. Sounding more like a 'Dalek' than human, the cold voice made Trudy's flesh creep. She wanted to slam the phone down, but some inner compulsion made her listen transfixed to the malicious, ranting call.

Vitriolic obscenities jarred Trudy's skull like a series of hammer blows. Without pause, the vicious tirade gathered intensity until the voice gave up pretensions of control, finally shrieking before the line went dead. A stunned Trudy was left sobbing in a foetal position trembling violently. Her one thought was that she must get to see Gene.

CHAPTER 88

PAVEMENTS WERE TINGED with white frost, and a chill in the air brought a healthy glow to cheeks as Trudy struggled to open garage doors frozen together by a combination of sodden wood and sub-zero temperature. Breathing heavily after her efforts, Trudy searched frantically for her keys through her well-used, leather handbag, a birthday present from her doting parents,. Finally retrieving them, she opened the car door and sat wearily down clutching the steering wheel so tightly her knuckles showed white, contrasting starkly with the black gloved wheel.

Still shaken from the horrible, disgusting phone-call, she gave an involuntary shiver, more from a feeling of being watched, rather than from exposure to the cold. A large bag of green grapes she'd bought earlier rested on the passenger seat; she picked one out of the bag and popped it in her mouth as she drove her car out onto the icy road.

She wouldn't tell Gene about the phone call, at least not yet; he had enough to worry about as it was. Perhaps she ought to tell Andy; after all, he was a policeman; he'd know how to deal with it. When the opportunity presented itself, she would ask his advice. More importantly she had a fat, bullying, mean-spirited, lovely man to see at the hospital.

CHAPTER 89

"HELLO, THIS IS Trudy Ballinger speaking. I can't take your call at the moment' but please leave a message after the tone, and I will get back to you as soon as I can."

"Bollocks," Gene expressed himself in the time honoured way. What was it with some people?—never happy unless they had a phone attached to their ear. He needed to talk to Trudy, and if not to Trudy, then it would have to be Andy Dale. The situation was getting out of hand. First, the explosion and the death of Vince; then, the murder of the porter; it could be him next. The fat slob they'd assigned to protect him spent more time eyeing up the nurses than anything else. So an indignant Nurse Patel had told him earlier, whilst angrily emptying his catheter, for a moment oblivious to the affront to his dignity, to say nothing of his acute discomfort.

"He gives me the creeps," said Rita Patel, an attractive thirty-year-old, married lady from Bangladesh, who was the temporary replacement for Joanna Harris. Joanna, still undergoing counselling after her recent gruesome discovery, was not in a fit state to empty Gene's catheter or to perform any other task for that matter.

Gene felt very vulnerable. Someone was out to kill him, and, on top of that, an outbreak of MRSA was rife in the hospital.

The words "third time lucky" buzzed around in his head as he tried, unsuccessfully, to hold back the tears while Nurse Patel made the final adjustment to his catheter. Gene's first inclination, after the porter's murder, had been to get out of the hospital and find somewhere safer and less public. His second inclination had been to get the catheter removed first.

"A real weirdo," Rita continued earnestly, taking a temperature reading from Gene's ear. One of the other nurses caught him reading a porno magazine; and far from being embarrassed, he just leered at her as if flashing his green teeth made him as appealing as Tom Cruise in *Mission Impossible*. When I came on duty last night, he was fast asleep; so don't put your life savings on him to guard you in an emergency."

If Gene had needed any further prompting to get out of hospital, this was, to quote Lord Byron, " . . . oh! Too convincing." "Tell the doctor I want this bloody catheter removed." Gene was feeling better than he had since the accident. His bombastic leanings were returning, though maybe not at full strength, enough he felt, to "kick a few arses"; and that was a quote from the editor of *World in Focus*.

"Everything working in the waterworks department?" asked Doctor Morgan cheerfully, pausing to read Gene's record sheet, before with sadistic glee he removed the catheter, forgetting to fully deflate the retaining bulb. Gene wiped the tears from his eyes blaspheming heartily as he fantasised meeting the good doctor one night in a dark alley.

CHAPTER 90

TRUDY COULD FEEL the fat police officer's eyes on her as she pushed her way through the heavy double doors. Strange, she thought, how now people came to expect doors to open automatically for them; most supermarkets had this facility. Obviously NHS made better use of their budgets. Clutching the remains of the bag of grapes tightly to her, like a cherished, irreplaceable treasure, Trudy marched down the corridor, trying desperately not to make eye contact with "Rambo" and his big gun. At least Sylvester Stallone was moderately handsome; to call this policeman ugly was an insult to ugly people. A fleeting smile tugged at the corner of her mouth at the thought.

"I ought to search you," said Rambo giving Trudy a suggestive look. "Who knows? You could be carrying a concealed weapon." The smile froze on Trudy's face as she squeezed past the leering police officer, acutely aware of his hands brushing against her thigh.

"You try to search me, and I will phone Inspector Dale and see what he has to say." said Trudy in an icy tone. "Furthermore, if you touch me again, I will report you for sexual harassment." The self-confident smirk on the officer's face morphed into a hostile glare as he reluctantly stepped aside allowing Trudy to pass.

Tension, crackling like the prelude to an electric storm, rent the atmosphere as the door of Gene's room flung violently open.

Trudy had never been so glad to see Gene, who was standing there with bathrobe loosely tied around his waist and untidy strands of hair falling almost boyishly over one eye–not exactly James Bond, but a welcome sight nonetheless. Testosterone emanated strongly as Gene and Rambo glared at each other with the unbridled hostility usually reserved for mortal enemies. Rambo finally broke the eye contact–not what Sylvester Stallone would have done in the same circumstances, but this poor man's Rambo was not of the same ilk as Sly Stallone, or even near it.

"What the f—k's going on?" queried Gene assertively, never short of a witty remark, furiously switching his gaze from Trudy to Rambo questioningly. As Trudy opened her mouth to speak she became aware that Gene was looking past her into the deep shadows of the dark corridor. The sight of a figure in white bearing down on them replaced one dramatic scenario with another far more threatening one. Brandishing a disposable bedpan, the manic figure rapidly ran towards the trio as they stood there temporarily transfixed. The horrified look on Gene's face alerted both Trudy and Rambo to the impending danger. As they turned, a banshee like scream rushed to fill the vacuum created by the tense silence. Acrid smelling liquid flew from the container as the blurred, white figure, still screaming, threw the evil contents of the bedpan over the policeman.

The agonised cry emanating from Rambo, as he tore frantically at his dissolving face, simultaneously drowned the insane sounds bellowing from the blurred, white figure. Strips of raw flesh dangling from Rambo's frantic fingers filled Trudy's vision, as a burning sensation pierced Trudy's sentience. Her scream provided a shrill descant to the agonised sounds around her. The nightmare that encompassed her became distant and hollow as it swirled ever faster until Trudy mercifully lost touch with reality, as she collapsed, ungainly, into Gene's arms.

CHAPTER 91

CONFUSION STRIPPED HIS mind of rational thought as he levered himself as near upright as he could manage in his weakened state. The cold, hard floor provided motivation to muscles protesting with every movement. He had no idea how long he'd been unconscious; it could have been a minute, a day, or even a week. He shivered as a wind, determined to chill the bones of the weak or unprepared, gusted in through a half open door. A loud explosion, like a gunshot, echoed through his confusion. His flesh crawled as he turned, heart pounding, towards the terrifying sound.

Another gust of wind, more violent than the last, slammed the swinging door hard against its unyielding jamb, causing another gunshot like noise to strike terror into his fragile senses. The door, in keeping with its now established tradition, swung open again ready for yet another demonstration of its imposing power to shock the unwary. This time the door's progress was halted suddenly. A giant, shadowy figure, temporarily framed like a monstrous silhouette against the luminous moonlight, stepped inside and the door tightly shut. This time the door remained hugging close to its jamb for protection as if paralyzed with fear of the terrible vengeance the giant shadow would impose for disobedience. It wasn't the door, however, that needed to have worried.

CHAPTER 92

BLOODSHOT EYES SNAPPED open. Eyeballs revolved in sockets, looking desperately for familiarity. As her vision gradually cleared, Trudy could see the concerned faces of Gene and Andrew Dale, hovering like glowing red orbs against a backcloth of brilliant white, cotton wool. Her arm screamed with pain, jolting her into full tortured consciousness.

"You should see the other guy," said Gene laying his hand gently on Trudy's good arm. The Phantom of the Opera doesn't even come close." Gene's much lauded tact came shining through to the disbelief of the medical observers and a grimacing Andy Dale.

"The 'other guy' happens to be the police officer who was trying to protect you," interjected Andy angrily.

"I think Professor Ballinger could manage without any bickering." Dr Sam Phillips was a good head taller than Gene, and he wouldn't brook any argument when it came to the welfare of his patients. Trudy's wan smile and vulnerable appearance brought out the caring instinct in the good doctor. Even so, Dr. Phillips' instinct at age fifty-five was still of a more selfish, libidinous nature; in short, he fancied Trudy, as he did all the attractive ladies unfortunate enough to fall within his care.

"You'll have to leave if you continue to upset my patient." Sam Phillips was now reverting to his best Dr. Gregory House mode and loving it. Not for nothing had he earned the reputation for being impatient and irascible. The impromptu demonstration of his ability to dominate ended abruptly as an elderly nurse burst into the crowded ward.

"The police officer is convulsing," she managed to utter between ragged breaths.

"Oh, bollocks!" Sam, usually precise in his use of the Queen's English, lapsed into the vulgar language understood by all as he rushed out of the room.

CHAPTER 93

IT WAS ALL wrong. This much he knew, as the realization penetrated through a panic induced haze. A vague recollection of images passed before his eyes as he ran down the corridor with people shouting everywhere—screaming bodies desperately trying to get out of the way of this manic figure rushing towards them yelling obscenities. He was running through a warren of corridors, and around each corner he found new hazards and challenges.

He screamed even louder as he ran into a trolley pushed by a frightened nurse; the trolley spilled over with a crash, the cry from the patient echoing through the corridor. The remaining acid swished about in the bedpan, still brandished frenziedly before him as he threatened to maim anyone who got in his way. A towering black security man moved resolutely to block the path of the running figure, only to collapse screaming, tearing frantically at already blistering eyes, now blind to the tumult around him. The deadly corrosive acid relentlessly destroyed bone, tissue, and nerve on contact.

Grainy indistinct images, as if taken from an old black-and-white movie, passed in slow motion before his eyes. He ran ever faster down the corridor looking for a haven where he might hide and be safe from the enemies that meant him anguish and pain—those hysterical people around him, in addition to the anguished cry of a patient in agony echoing mournfully through the hollow sounding corridor.

Frantic in his panic, fearfully glancing from side to side, he ran on blindly, the animal instinct to survive his only thought. The path ahead of him was now cleared of people, who were putting discretion before valour and rushing in the opposite direction. He turned down a gloomy corridor. Ahead, in the darkness, safety beckoned like an old friend; behind him lay certain capture by his loathsome enemies. There pandemonium had erupted, including screaming people and howling sirens.

The cacophony of sound was getting exponentially louder with each fleeting second. The crushing clamour gave an added sense of urgency to the sprinting man; still brandishing a bottle of the deadly acid. Fearful visions flashed in and out of his mind. "Momma, please stop the bad boys from chasing me," he called out. But Momma wasn't there to help him, only to punish. He recalled with terror the frightful nights spent in the dark cupboard under the creaking stairs, but then his brain came to his rescue.

A nurse's station, now deserted of personnel, flew past on the periphery of his vision as he hurtled down the dimly lit fire escape stairway. Descending deeper into the bowels of the old building, he saw a green light flickering eerily, its glow struggling gainfully to penetrate through the oppressive gloom. Designed to point the way to a safe passage for those unfortunate enough to be fleeing the ravages of fire, the sign read, "WAY OUT." Like a cornered wild creature depending on honed instinct for survival, he flung open the door with a loud bang; but then he continued his way unhesitatingly down the stairs into the blackness below.

Darkness was his friend. All those hours spent under the stairs had cemented the friendship of all three—Daniel, David, and the dark shadows.

CHAPTER 94

SIRENS HOWLED LIKE adolescent wolves trying to impose themselves on lesser pack members, despite their cracking voices. Emergency vehicles with scant regard for speed limits and even less regard for other road users shattered the early morning silence. Concerned motorists pulled into the kerbside hoping the sirens weren't howling for them and wishing that they hadn't succumbed to the tempting, but unnecessary, "one for the road." The screeching ambulances and police cars drove past the rows of well-kept Edwardian houses on Bletchworth Road as they approached the hapless victim.

"Bloody hell, someone's given this poor bloke a good hiding," said Albert Hayes, the first to arrive. He had always wanted to be a doctor. At the age of forty, he had accepted that it was now too late to realise his boyhood ambition. With the lack of a good formal education and no ambition or guidance from his well-meaning, working-class parents, Albert had wandered from job to job, never settling, or content. His life changed for the better when he married Mandy. With great support from his wife, as well as much effort from himself, he had proudly become a paramedic. Beyond that, he was also a humanitarian, who genuinely concerned himself with the well-being of others. The blood soaked bundle of rags moved shallowly suggesting that life was not yet extinct in the pathetic broken body.

A psychedelic light show, multicoloured but predominantly blue, lit up Bletchworth Hospital as an ambulance carrying the latest victim of a violent society slowly stopped outside the emergency unit. Stethoscopes dripped out of white coat pockets as emergency doctors gathered around the ambulance doors ready to continue emergency treatment where a concerned Albert Hayes had left off.

The victim saw alternating red and blue flashing lights as he painfully, through his battered face, he opened his eyes and focused on a worried looking Asian doctor leaning over him. Activity all around, blurred white walls sweeping by, shouting, and the cold feel of scissors cutting away his bloody clothing were some of the sensations he experienced before slipping into blessed oblivion.

CHAPTER 95

POLICE SIGNIFICANTLY OUTNUMBERED hospital staff at Bletchworth Hospital; or so it would appear to the casual observer, on this cold March morning. Like water on a bathroom floor, a few police went a long way, shouting orders and taking charge, much to the indignation of senior hospital personnel. The attack on a police officer, even one like "Rambo," motivated senior and junior ranks alike.

That Trudy Ballinger was also a victim provided an added inducement to DI Andy Dale. In fact, Trudy's well-being concerned Andy far more than any concern he had for that stupid, poor excuse for a police officer.

A grim smile briefly touched Andy's lips as the familiar, bulky torso of Rob Murray climbed wearily out of his car and walked slowly towards him. "You took your time," Andy greeted his subordinate impatiently, his anxiety showing through his normally cool façade.

"Sorry, Guv, but Grace has new evidence on the university murders and we were sifting through it."

"We'll talk about that later," Andy cut in abruptly. "Right now we've got a more important problem on our hands." Over the next few minutes, Andy outlined the situation emphasising the attack on Rambo," but playing down his concern for Trudy. Rob and the rest of his team would pick up the vibes soon enough without his spelling out his growing feelings for Trudy. Andy trailed off in mid-sentence, his attention distracted temporarily, as a wailing ambulance pulled up outside the emergency unit. Just another drunken road accident, thought Andy, with a shake of the head refocusing his attention on Rob.

Constable Mark Smith executed a perfect handbrake turn to bring his patrol car screeching to a violent standstill alongside the open doors of the ambulance; he narrowly missed a doctor attending the injured man. "Bloody hell, all of Bletchworth nick is here." Mark glanced across at Special Constable Graham Cole chewing furiously on a king-size Mars bar. "Nip over and find out what's happening," ordered Mark; and for f—k's sake stop chomping that chocolate; it's driving me mad."

Mark had no time for amateur special constables, as all of them who had worked with him could testify, if they dare. Nineteen-year-old Graham hurried to do his master's bidding stepping in a puddle in his haste. "Bollocks." he whispered under his breath as he ran over to the familiar figure of Constable Masters; at least Masters would fill him in without making an issue out of it. He didn't quite make it as a grim, unsmiling Andy Dale moved to block his path.

CHAPTER 96

"MOMMA, PLEASE LET me out." The familiar sound of Momma's heavy footsteps above, stomping loudly, getting ever nearer; floors creaking; doors banging—Momma must be angry with him. He shivered, anticipating the beating he would get when Momma came to let him out. Even worse, she wouldn't talk to him for days—just glower. He would even wake up in the semidarkness to see her leaning over him glaring viciously. "Please, I will be a good boy in future."

"Fuckin' get me out of here," the deeper more menacing tones of David screamed from the murky shadows before they withdrew deep into Daniel's sub consciousness allowing him to regain his tenuous link with reality. David heard more commotion—voices raised, dogs barking—until he moved further away where the creaking of cooling pipes was all that penetrated the stillness. Daniel and David huddled together behind an old, obsolete boiler still awaiting removal by contractors. David's belligerent demands for freedom went unrequited as silence gradually descended like a damp shroud reinforcing the oppressiveness of the dank cellar. A lone figure still clutching the now empty acid bottle emerged cautiously from the shadows.

David's retreat left Daniel hollow and alone, once more

trembling, not with fear but with anticipation of what was to come. But now, David must sleep.

CHAPTER 97

THE RESILIENT LIFE force clung tenaciously to the battered body. The peaks and valleys moving slowly across the heart monitor were steadily, but inexorably, becoming less mountainous, more regular. Bloodied, distorted flesh showed through swathes of white dressings. A single eye, bruised and swollen fluttered weakly then closed, the effort too much for the man to sustain.

A jolly looking nurse peeps at the prostrate man. "He's not awake yet," she calls to a colleague as she quietly closes the door. The man flinches, but is unable to communicate. His limbs are numb; the sound of his ragged heartbeat gets louder threatening to burst his eardrums. He'd scream if he could, but he's now trapped in a useless body—all he could do was hope to die.

"When will I be able to talk to him?" Mark Smith demanded in his most imperious voice. Working on strict instructions from DI Dale, who'd confronted him in the car park, gave Constable Smith an added authority; and he was making the most of it.

Senior Staff Nurse, Myra McKinney, did not impress easily, she'd heard it all before, including young police officers drunk with power that they thought the uniform gave them. Give her the more experienced officer, who knew the way to handle people, get cooperation, and not alienate the people who genuinely wanted to help. "When the doctor says so," Myra retorted, more vehemently than she intended. "I'll ask him when he does his rounds," she added, with greater civility this time. Antagonizing him any more than necessary would achieve nothing, she thought, trying to hide her dislike for the supercilious police officer.

"Ring this number when he comes round," snapped back an irritated police constable thrusting a dog-eared business card at a seething Myra. A swaggering Mark Smith walked arrogantly out of the ward as Senior Staff Nurse McKinney gave a well-used and easily recognisable finger to his departing back.

CHAPTER 98

CREAKING AND GROANING the barrier slowly raised its weary body in a slow motion salute to the university principal. Harry, out of deference for his superior, raised a grubby hand holding a grated cheese sandwich, threads of which spilled down Harry's greasy jacket.

"Bloody imbecile," muttered Ian under his breath as he accelerated violently past the gatehouse. He'd drunk himself into a stupor last night. That silly cow, Trudy Ballinger, hadn't given him an alibi; so now he was the number one suspect. He was, as they say, a prime candidate for a "fit up," to quote Regan of *The Sweeney*. It had cost him his remaining self-respect to get Goldberg's fat nephew, Vince Craig, reluctantly to tell the police that he Vince had dropped by to see Ian on a personal matter and that they were together all that night. Now the bastard was dead and that persistent fool, Dale, seemed determined to pin everything on him. Tires screamed in protest as he rounded a sharp bend leading to his private parking space. Students ambling casually toward the university portals jumped hastily on the grass verge to avoid the red Audi A4 threatening to terminate any unsuspecting pedestrians that got in the way.

If he needed confirmation, the walk from his car to the office had provided it in abundance. Staff previously affable and respectful now avoided making any eye contact with him and if taken by surprise muttered a grudging, "Good morning' before hastily scuttling about their business. Well, he'd had enough. The sooner he could get away from the bloody university and all the, self-important academics the better. The faculty were wheedling to his face but treacherous behind his back—bastards, all of them; and the Ballinger woman proved to be the worst of them all. Mind you, Helen and Deborah were no better—always demanding of him but not giving much, if anything, of themselves. It didn't matter now; they were dead anyway.

Trudy Ballinger, however, was another problem altogether—one he had to deal with sooner rather than later. Now, in the privacy of his office, his inner sanctum, he could devote himself to the problem at hand.

CHAPTER 99

"IT'S BLOODY WELL not safe here." The tone of his voice betrayed Gene's anxiety, not just for himself, but for Trudy as well. Another good reason to get Trudy away was Andy Dale; he'd been paying her far too much attention lately; the sooner they could get away the better. Perhaps he could persuade her to go away with him, away from the maniac intent on killing them. It was even more important now the maniac had turned his attention to Trudy. It had been a narrow escape; she may not be so lucky next time. Fortunately for Trudy, the big policeman had deflected most of the acid, the rest of which had spattered Trudy's arms and cheek. The events of the last few weeks—the dreams, the bombing, the attack—had left him dumfounded and scared. His blossoming friendship with Trudy was an added complication.

Vince's death hadn't helped either. He had lost confidence in the police to protect them; so, as the saying goes, "If you want a job done right, then do it-yourself"; and that was what Gene intended to do. Firstly, though, Trudy needed more time to recover. Fortunately, her injuries were relatively minor—a few more days and she should be ready to go home.

Goldberg had convinced the doctor to discharge Gene as soon as possible, arguing that it would be safer for his valued employee, but in reality more concerned with the daily cost of private rooms and medical treatment. He had enough to grieve about with the death of his nephew without adding the cost of his wayward editor's treatment to the list.

For Gene his release could not come soon enough. On the outside at least, he would have some control over the situation. Here in the hospital he was totally reliant on Andy "f—kin" Dale for protection; and judging by his current record, Gene wasn't making any long term plans for his future. Ironically, as implications of his recent dreams flashed through his mind, he wondered if there was a long term future for anyone.

Goldberg meanwhile continued to stare at the burgundy red phone several minutes after calling the person he always contacted when he wanted a special job done. And he had had many of those throughout his business life; a significant factor in the success of his business empire. His wife would be horrified if she ever found out about this dark side of his life; but she hadn't, and never would, he thought grimly, reaching for his coat as he strode purposefully to his waiting car.

CHAPTER 100

GHOSTLY APPARITIONS BURNING iridescently, tantalizingly within reach, then gradually fading from view—he could almost hear the plop as they finally disappeared, leaving an impenetrable blackness in their wake.

The warmth of pipes radiating their invisible heat did nothing to quell the icy feeling as Daniel jerked into wakefulness still curled in a foetal position, cramped behind a pile of dusty, old grey boxes. How long had he been asleep? It was all quiet now, except for the intermittent whoomph of the boiler acting in response to an insatiable thermostat's demand for heat. Creaking bones and stiff muscles gave way to adrenaline-induced energy already pulsing through his body as memories of recent events crowded his eagerly receptive mind. His body began to twitch uncontrollably as memories of the fat policeman's scream, his face dissolving, fuelled Daniel's already surging adrenaline. Rational thought gradually returned as David, emerging from the hidden depths of Daniel's mind, took control.

While Gene Harman and that fucking detective were still alive, David would have to take control and make them suffer. He was invincible. His superior intellect was more than a match for those fools; they would never catch him. These thoughts fuelled his determination as he made his way up the stairs to finish the job he'd started; only this time David's personality was in control, not Daniel's.

CHAPTER 101

"MURDERER," "HIT MAN," "executioner."—it didn't matter how you expressed it; he was just a plain killer, with a special aptitude for his chosen trade. That's why he was making a lot of money from people who could afford his services—people like Goldberg and others.

Over the years he'd led a complicated existence trying to balance his life between that of a widely respected professional on one hand and of a contract killer on the other. Well, another couple of assignments, then he'd retire and concentrate on enjoying his alter life. Perhaps he would retire to some remote island in the Caribbean where no one knew him. A warm feeling temporarily came over him, but was soon replaced by a feeling of unease, the feeling you get when you know something is about to happen, usually something bad. This unease had been getting more acute, intensifying during the last few assignments.

He'd nearly botched up his last contract; luckily for him he'd been able to make the hit and escape unnoticed—but just in the nick of time. The nearness of his escape told him it was time to get out; but first he had some loose ends to tie up on his own account. Only one living person knew about his double existence, one person with enough evidence to jail him for life or worse still, pass on information to enemies willing to pay handsomely for details of his whereabouts. As long as that one person was alive, he would never feel safe. He was already planning to remove his Achilles heel permanently as he strode from the room slamming the flimsy door behind him.

CHAPTER 102

MARK SMITH WAS angry; luckily he'd arrived, just in time, and was there when the battered man, as yet unidentified, woke from his heavily drugged sleep; but the stupid cow of a nurse hadn't rung him. Fortunately, he'd been on duty at the hospital and had decided to check for himself. Might be worth a few brownie points from Andy Dale, he thought, as he popped his head 'round the door in time to see the man straining, through swollen eyes, to see in the dimly lit room. With a quick glance toward the nurses' station, Mark quietly made his way to the now subdued man's bedside.

The sound of a chair dragging across a tiled floor alerted the blinded man to the newcomer's presence. The harsh, intimidating voice echoing in his ear identified itself as "Detective Constable Mark Smith." Images flashed through the injured man's brain like old photographs in a *What the Butler Saw* flick card machine. The images, however, were not titillating; his were those of blood, pain, and unheeded pleas for mercy. "Nurse," he croaked, his voice barely audible, as the impassive face of Constable Smith leaned closer, his breath tainted by halitosis. Frightened, the man cowered, his injured body sending messages of blinding agony to his anxious brain. If Constable Smith had any compassion, he did an excellent job of concealing it as he pressed on questioning the forlorn figure cowering pathetically among the swathe of white bedclothes.

"What's your name?" the detective continued relentlessly, moving closer to hear the weak reply. The man, tortured beyond the limit of endurance by his recent experience, could only whimper pathetically. Further interrogation came abruptly to a halt as, with a crash, the ward door swung open revealing the towering and enraged figure of Doctor Sam Phillips, followed closely by Andy Dale.

CHAPTER 103

THE TECHNICIAN NEVER knew what hit him. He was briefly aware of a shadow moving behind him, but the lump hammer wielded by Daniel was an effective weapon, dispatching the hapless man into an untidy heap on the boiler room floor, his tools scattering around him. His caved-in skull haemorrhaged, and the blood formed a rapidly growing crimson pool that lapped around Daniel's feet as he looked on ecstatically, admiring his handiwork. Snapping out of the trance, David, the practical side of a confused mind, began stripping the uniform from a dead man with no further use for it. Taking great care to avoid the stream of blood, Daniel's body followed the instructions of David's mind. Tools now replaced in their box added a final touch of authenticity to the would-be technician that was Daniel.

It was not safe remaining within the hospital complex. The thought ran through Daniel's mind although it was David controlling him. Dressed in a blue boiler suit, matching baseball cap pulled low over his face, and equipped with a hospital pass, he made his way stealthily out of the building. The hospital grounds were still crawling with police, fluorescent floodlights turning night into day. Torches gleamed like hostile eyes illuminating dark corners where floodlights, despite their best efforts, couldn't reach. Once outside, Daniel, walking with a confidence he did not feel, made his way nonchalantly across an open stretch of land leading to the perimeter car park. Swinging his toolbox, whistling, looking every inch a hospital technician, Daniel reached the comparative safety of the little-used, unlit car park. A curious police officer glancing in Daniel's direction received an acknowledging wave, to which he responded briefly before turning away to get on with the serious business of searching for the acid attacker. Throwing the borrowed overalls into a skip, conveniently placed for bottles and other recyclables, Daniel/David vanished into the night.

CHAPTER 104

"BLOODY SAFE HOUSE, is it? Bollocks." It was obvious to those accompanying him, namely Trudy, Andy, and DC Laura Thomas, that Gene was feeling more like his belligerent, lovable self. The uncomfortable journey in a blackened out van had taken nearly an hour. Under cover of darkness and with a police escort, they finally reached their destination aching and irritable.

"He's blown up Goldberg's building, killing his nephew; and we are assuming he is responsible for murdering the hospital porter," Andy said before taking a deep breath and continuing. "I've got an officer permanently disfigured, and I don't want to be responsible for any more deaths. That includes you two," he concluded, looking first at Trudy then at Gene. Laura looked on edgily.

The Boss had given the babysitting job to Rob Murray, with Laura as his second in command. Not the best assignment to improve your career prospects, she thought bitterly. It was all right for Rob; he was retiring soon. But she still had a career ahead of her, and she intended to make the most of it.

Trudy, with Laura's help, busied herself making tea while Gene and Andy, in true dominant male tradition, testosterone rising, glowered at each other from across the small, sparsely furnished living room.

"You will be safe here until we catch whoever is trying to kill you," Andy rasped, irritated by Gene's attitude. "And maybe, with your cooperation, we can get a better understanding of recent events." He made no effort to hide his hostility. "Against all my instincts, I find myself intrigued by your talk of prophetic dreams and premonitions, so let's have a discussion and see if we can make any sense out of it," Andy continued. "You obviously resent my involvement but for both your sake and Trudy's, let's try to behave like adults and work together, not in opposition."

The tension between the two protagonists visibly eased as Trudy forcibly thrust a tray of steaming coffee onto the tacky, glass topped table, slopping some steaming liquid down the sides of old china mugs that had seen better days. "We need to write down a list of all the facts as we know them," Trudy began, now in her element as a professional researcher. "If you and Gene give me the facts as you know them, I'll write them as a chronological narrative; and you can amend as necessary."

"What about Laura?" Gene tried to interject, but Trudy in full flow was not about to surrender the floor until she'd finished.

"Laura, please find some paper and something to write with," said Trudy sharply lapsing into her pedagogical role.

"Find it yourself," Laura began, but a sharp look from Andy sent her reluctantly to carry out Trudy's bidding.

"Miserable bitch—got a face liked a smacked arse." A palpable silence followed Gene's cutting comment as the trio awaited the policewoman's return. Returning with an old notebook and a couple of pencil stubs from a previous occupant, Laura ungraciously flung them on the table before flouncing dramatically out of the room. "Must be the time of the month," said Gene tactfully, drawing a disgusted look from Trudy, as she began to wonder what she saw in this ignorant man.

Andy broke the embarrassing silence. "Thanks to Laura we've got what we need, so lets get started."

CHAPTER 105

LIKE THE CUE from a Hammer horror film, the lightning created ghostly images of three faces staring incredulously at the document before them. The thunder that followed, rattling window-panes not used to such unsympathetic treatment, only added to the drama. Documents shimmering in the afterglow of the lightning strike, took on an unreal dimension, as a bemused trio poured over the chronology of events hastily compiled by Trudy. Laid out on the table before them, the events of recent weeks took on an even more baffling aspect.

Trudy was the first to speak, obviously shaken, but trying hard not to show it. "Gene's first dream fits in with the widely held theory depicting the end of the dinosaurs at the end of the Jurassic period." Breathlessly, she went on to explain theories about mass extinction that finally saw the sudden end of the dinosaurs' reign on the Earth sixty-five million years ago. Gene and Andy listened with interest, despite their natural cynicism. "It wasn't just dinosaurs that became extinct," she went on to explain; so did seventy per cent of all other species on Earth. Scientists, Trudy concluded, believe the impact of the Chicxulub asteroid, centred off Yucatán's coast in the Caribbean, was responsible for the global disaster.

"So I had one bad dream—maybe a coincidence, but what about the other dreams and the photographs?" Gene asked, addressing his two companions, but staring challengingly at Andy. "You're supposed to be the detective, so what's your explanation Sherlock?" Sarcasm was Gene's long suit, and he played it with panache.

Now in a combative mood, Andy leaned forward threateningly, "You could have produced the images yourself as a publicity stunt to sell your newspapers. I wouldn't put anything past that bastard, Goldberg," his dislike for the tycoon adding a chill to his voice.

Trudy interceded, sensing the increasing hostility. "Against my better judgment as a scientist, it makes my blood run cold to consider that maybe there are forces at work beyond our understanding. And we should seriously consider less rational explanations, instead of just dismissing them out of hand." The two antagonists turned their attention to Trudy immediately realizing that she had voiced what they both, however reluctantly, were thinking.

The faded brocade chair protested noisily under the strain, as Gene slumped heavily down on its time-soiled seat. His careworn face had aged beyond its years, as the toll of recent events left its mark. "Don't either of you fuckin laugh?" he began defensively, waiting until his companions gave him their full undivided attention. "I had plenty of time to think in hospital, and it occurred to me that my recent dreams were like disaster movies. The first dream, as we have already discussed, could be connected to the extinction of the dinosaurs, as the prof has already explained," he added sarcastically. More confident now he had their full attention, Gene continued forcefully. "I am not sure what to make of the second dream except that it looked like a major motion picture disaster, and could imagine Charlton Heston in the starring role looking out over the sea formulating a cunning plan. The volcanic eruption and the tsunami were a conversation killer for the inhabitants of the island"; the black sense of humour which lost Gene most of his friends and threatened to lose more, surfaced through the sobriety of the moment.

"What about the photographs?" Trudy interrupted. It all started with those."

"That's the biggest mystery of all." Andy abruptly cut across the two conversations. "It won't work if we don't follow our thoughts through logically; let's analyse the dreams first then try to rationalize the photographs later. Assuming that a major disaster is the common link and that the first dream is the death of the dinosaurs, has anybody got an idea what disaster the second dream represents?"

"Let's have a look at the photographs again to see if there are any clues." Gene was getting more animated now looking at Trudy. 'The game is afoot, not a word! Into your clothes and come.' Impressing his companions with a quote from his hero, Sherlock Holmes, Gene ripped opened the buff envelope spilling the dog-eared photographs haphazardly on the glass table.

For the umpteenth time Laura toured the soulless house trying windows and doors. Locks and alarms, specially installed, were next to come under Laura's scrutiny. Satisfied, she gazed out into the depths of the garden, which boasted dense shrubs casting deep, impenetrable shadows by the light of a waxing, gibbous moon.

A scurrying movement caught her eye, bringing a rare smile to her usually sullen face. An attractive young woman, she'd been told many times, by boyfriends past and present, to smile more;

but Laura was as reluctant to smile as misers are to spend money. The hedgehog, sensing Laura's gaze, looked up from its feast of bread crusts, discarded by overindulged birds and nose twitching, ran off into the perceived safety of the dark undergrowth. With a projected lifespan of six to ten years, *erinaceus* could have anticipated many more winter sleeps with long nights of eating and lovemaking. All thoughts of the future, however, came to an abrupt end as a rock propelled with terrifying force extinguished its tenuous grip on life.

The figure crouching in the shadows looked at the crushed creature with intense satisfaction, already anticipating, with relish, his next, and possibly his final, undertaking.

CHAPTER 106

POSITIONED CENTRALLY ON the small table, the laptop computer screen shone brightly, providing a focal point for four pairs of staring eyes. Intricate designs engraved on pottery, wall paintings depicting monkeys in delicate shades of blue, marble figurines pitted by the ravages of time—a myriad works of art adorned a soulless, flickering screen not worthy of displaying such a profusion of wondrous virtuosity. The people gathered around the small computer could only admire the treasures on display before them.

It had been Gene's idea to look for clues in the photographs. Frescos and pottery, hazy in the background, had provided images of greater clarity when viewed under a powerful magnifying glass wielded by himself.

Unexpected help came in the form of DC Laura Thomas. As a child, Laura had spent many summers with her aunt and uncle at their cottage in the beautiful Devon countryside bordering Dartmoor. Uncle James was an amateur archaeologist with a passion for ancient artefacts, which he collected as his limited purse allowed. Occasionally the adults' conversation would focus on her uncle's hobby. They might discuss a new bit of knowledge, or on rare occasions, perhaps a piece of cracked pottery picked up cheaply at a specialist-archaeologist auction. Although Laura did not have a great interest in archaeology, as an intelligent child she picked up a general understanding of the subject discussed. Thus, when invited to look at Gene's photographs, she was able to throw some light on the origin of the ancient images under discussion.

Trudy's fingers were a blur, skimming over the keyboard changing screens more rapidly than the eye could follow. The flickering, cavorting banners gave testament to the website creator's expertise but added little to the quality of information. Each site that Trudy visited would add snippets of relevant information to the growing inventory of knowledge; they were like pieces of a jigsaw puzzle but without the final representation as a guide. After what seemed like an eternity, however, a picture of mass devastation and loss of human life emerged dramatically before their saddened eyes.

The catalyst that led to the mysterious disappearance of the advanced Minoan civilization was reputed to be the Aegean eruption of Thera, three thousand years ago. Heavy layers of volcanic ash rained down over the Aegean, covering islands and crops. Earthquakes shook the land, and the violence of the tremors caused great stone buildings to fall into rubble. Enormous tsunamis, irresistible in their power, spread outward in every direction overwhelming all in their path. Coastal villages of Crete were flooded and destroyed. The only major Minoan structure surviving the waves and earthquakes was the palace at Knossos, far enough inland to escape the destructive tidal waves.

"So my second dream could have depicted a great disaster as well," said Gene quietly, now too shaken for bombast.

"Could be a coincidence," Andy ventured hesitatingly, although recent events had left Andy's belief in coincidence severely dented.

"I would still like someone to explain the photographs," Trudy said, feeling the need to exert herself before the whole discussion became a "man thing" and she was relegated to conversations about fluffy kittens. Her comment fell on stony ground as her male companions went on to discuss details of Gene's third dream, leaving Trudy wondering if she had somehow become invisible.

The sound of a door, taken by the wind as it crashed shatteringly against the porch wall, startled the engrossed foursome; words froze on lips and expressions on faces as a familiar figure burst into the hallway.

CHAPTER 107

RIVULETS OF WATER made an erratic trail down the rugged bumpy face of DS Rob Murray. The trail was less erratic down the gentler, smoother contours of his companion, Dr. Grace Andersen. Four pairs of eyes looked enquiringly at the two newcomers dripping in the hallway.

"Bloody hell," Andy shouted, noticing just-in time the presence of Grace, sporting a half smile, emerge from behind the stout figure of his DS.

"I've come to keep DC Thomas company for the night shift, per your instructions," Rob added sarcastically, slightly aggrieved by the welcome received from his superior. "Oh, and Grace needs to talk to you about the university murders."

Tired grey eyes snapped from the disgruntled face of his sergeant to the more pleasing countenance of his friend and colleague, Grace Andersen. "What's so important that couldn't wait until tomorrow?" Andy was suddenly aware the newcomers' intervention had severely disrupted the group's brainstorming session.

"Well, Andy, there are some interesting anomalies with the two university murder victims that I think you should know about." Grace glanced at Gene and Trudy before continuing,

"But if this isn't a good time, I will see you in your office tomorrow." The frostiness in her voice cut swathes across the assemblage, who could only look stunned, as Grace quickly turned and walked back out into the night, slamming the door behind her.

Andy made to follow but then thought better of it. There'd be plenty of time to make amends, he thought, as he marched back to join his disgruntled associates. He was wrong and would live to regret it.

Grace strode angrily out into the murky, wet night, invariably finding muddy puddles concealed by the gloom. Water sprayed out displaced by the heaviness of her tread. Good job she was wearing sensible shoes, she thought idly, her anger subsiding. Maybe she had reacted too strongly, but she could see the way that Trudy woman looked at Andy and had felt foolishly and irrationally irritated. She and Andy had been friends for more years than she cared to remember, a purely platonic relationship. Then why did she feel so resentful of the Ballinger woman's obvious feelings towards him.

Preoccupied with these thoughts, Grace was unaware of eyes watching her from the dark shadows cast by the overgrown rhododendron bush. Coincidently her last thoughts before she too became a victim were of the anomalies she had discovered with the murders she'd been so anxious to pass on to Andy.

CHAPTER 108

HE'D RETURNED TOO late—the empty bed told him that. Why hadn't that stupid bitch of a nurse told him?

It wasn't the fact that the bloke was dead that enraged him; he felt piqued the "cow" had treated him disrespectfully. After all, he was an officer of the law. That was the reason he'd joined the force in the first place, that is, to get the respect he couldn't gain any other way. It never failed to amaze him—the power of the uniform; people who would never look at him twice now had to take him seriously. One flash of the badge and people would visibly crumple. He liked that. He liked that very much; in fact, it made his miserable life worthwhile. Swearing aloud he walked furiously towards the nurses' station. Someone was going to pay for this show of disrespect.

Fortunately, for Rita Patel, but not for Mark Smith, Doctor Sam Phillips was conversing with the duty nurse when Mark, full of bombast and attitude, bustled his way to the curved, dimly lit Formica counter. These police clods hanging around hospital, asking foolish questions, when the staff had real jobs to do angered Sam Phillips, who vented his feelings on an unsuspecting Mark Smith.

"If there was any communication in your department, you

would know the patient has died, and another police officer was sitting with him at the time of his death. The body is now in the morgue awaiting the pathologist's report." With a glare, Sam Phillips turned without another word and walked angrily out of the ward leaving a shell-shocked police officer in his wake.

Completely lacking any personal charisma, the police officer stuttered and blustered when his official authority withered under the incensed doctor's tirade.

One down, one to go, the assassin thought, walking briskly to the hospital car park. It was easier than he had expected avoiding that buffoon policeman. Surprising how effective a hand over the mouth and a pinched nose was when it came to killing a frail person. One more hit, and he could retire and resume his alter life in luxury. First however he needed to go back to his university office and remove any incriminating evidence before he vanished forever with a new identity.

CHAPTER 109

HE COULD NOT wait to get this meeting over with. Bloody Andy Dale couldn't keep his eyes off Trudy. And that Laura Thomas wasn't much better, bossy little cow. Gene yawned showing a mouth full of healthy looking teeth, surprisingly white for a one-time heavy smoker. If he had a dressing gown and hot-water bottle, he would have made ready for bed to make an even greater impact. As it was, even his yawning went unnoticed. They'd been talking for hours and had made progress; in fact, they'd made much progress. They'd all agreed that his recent dreams had been depictions of great disasters, the final one being possibly an omen of the future. Nothing ever comes easy; but their discussion went on forever, or so it appeared.

They had been talking around the photographs, who and where they had come from, how the mystery person fit in. Mostly Trudy and he had bandied around theories, with inputs from the two police officers, but still no meaningful explanation had been forthcoming. He and Trudy had dominated the discussion, a fact that annoyed Andy and Laura. Fuckin' police; they were so used to being in control of proceedings that when someone else got in on the act they resented it and became obstructive.

The premonition was the most frightening. The characters in

the dream everyone agreed represented Trudy and Gene many years from now. God, but he looked terrible, not grown old gracefully at all. Trudy didn't look so bad though. But who was the child they were carrying? It looked like there had been a major catastrophe, smoking ruins and desperation all around. The bleak scene turned the dream into a nightmare of horrific proportions. If the thread of previous dreams followed through to the most recent, then this could also depict a future disaster. In the dream, if the ages of the characters were any indication, not too far in the future either—a terrifying thought they had all agreed.

It was in mid-yawn that the vision of a news headline he'd seen in hospital screamed at him. He remembered the sycophantic presenter with the supercilious grin on his face announcing the discovery of an asteroid scheduled to hit Earth twenty years from now. All tiredness forgotten and thoughts of bed passed: the now reanimated Gene and his companions set about researching the Internet for details of the supposed future catastrophe. With Trudy in control, the other three gathered 'round looking on intently as images of destruction unfolded on the screen.

Trudy's hand brushed lightly against his arm, causing Gene to give an involuntary shudder. He looked across at faces mesmerised by the alternating colours of red, green, and blue, unable to comprehend what their eyes were seeing or what their brains were telling them to believe: 2012, flash, fade, 2012, flash, fade, 2012, flash, fade.

Trudy looked towards her ally Gene, for moral support in understanding the phenomena before them. Gene still stared at the screen—a green light emanated from the TFT Cyclops giving him the appearance of an alien invader from Alpha Draconis. Suddenly with a final surge of light and a frizzle, the screen darkened until all that remained was a small circle of light flickering in the centre of a black screen. With a last defiant hiss, even that gave up its tenuous grip and vanished forever, leaving four shadowy faces gazing vacantly at a blank screen.

The pervading silence broke dramatically as a high-pitched wail rent the air. Four people simultaneously jerked out of their mesmeric state, becoming aware for the first time of others around them.

"Fucking cats!" The spell was broken as a familiar voice shouted venomously from the kitchen. Expletives exploded from Rob's lips as he gazed through the darkened window that looked out onto the impenetrable black void that was a shadow cast by an overgrown rhododendron bush. Funny how the undergrowth was shaking; there didn't seem to be any wind. It must be the bloody cat, thought Rob, turning away from the window to concentrate on more important matters, like making a cup of tea.

CHAPTER 110

MOZART'S *HORN CONCERTO*, testing polyphonic ring tones to limits unheard-of a year ago, rang out in all its majesty from Andy's mobile phone. A look of concern replaced the irritation he had been feeling as a smug sounding Mark Smith told his superior of the battered man's death. Self-importance exuded with every word as he went on to reveal the deceased's identity. Grudgingly, as Andy pressed the constable for more detail, Mark revealed the hospital pathologist had contacted Grace Anderson suspecting the death may not be from natural causes. Dr. Anderson is doing a full post-mortem in the morning, Mark concluded, unable to disguise the self-satisfaction in his voice.

Strange, buzzing noises droned from Andy's phone. "Bloody mobile," he muttered, his ear still pressed to the dead, plastic earpiece. It must be electrical interference, he supposed, now turning his attention back to his companions, who were still discussing in hushed tones recent phenomena. Giving bad news was part of his job, and goodness knows he had done his fair share and watching the crumpled looks on faces as loved ones received bad news that would change their lives forever. It was never easy, but this time it would be even more difficult. The bad news he was about to pass on would affect someone he was extremely fond of.

Trudy gave an involuntary shudder. The grave look now on Andy's face as he walked hesitatingly back towards the now silent trio, brought an unnatural chill to the room. Trudy knew it was bad news; she also knew the bad news would affect her. Like a dream sequence from an old movie, Andy appeared to glide in slow motion towards her. While the others looked on bemused, Andy took the shaking Trudy by the arm and led her silently from the room.

CHAPTER III

HAVING REMOVED ALL evidence from his office the assassin aka Ian Mason made his way stealthily back to his waiting car. A sense of guilt lay heavily on his shoulders—another sign it was time to get out. His final target was someone he knew and had built up a relationship with. He would do the job, but it would be his last; and he hoped his conscience would not lay too painfully on him in the future. The grey outline of his car, stationary in the far corner of the university car park, showed dimly against a background of murky, grey mist.

"Bloody remotes are useless," he grumbled pointing the control in the general direction of his car but receiving no response to his frantic pressing. Funny how inconvenienced one felt when having to put the key in the lock and open the car door manually. Another thought suddenly occurred to him—of all the cars he'd had with remotes, this was the first time one had failed him. He temporarily froze in his tracks as feelings of deep apprehension rolled over him in waves. His intuition had saved him many times in the past. The reassuringly solid Beretta Model 93R, nestling in his pocket, felt good as it pressed against his thigh.

Now alert, his senses heightened, and stooping low, he ran for the cover of a tall beech hedge bordering the car park. Pressing back to the hedge, he sidled slowly, glancing frantically around, toward his darkened car. The small torch on his key ring gave only a small glimmer as he tried to penetrate the darkness of his car interior. Crouching low, he moved silently peering in through darkened windows as he circumnavigated the desolate car. He thought he heard a car door bang; but looking around, he saw that his was the only vehicle left. Although satisfied there was no one in the car waiting to surprise him, he still he felt uneasy. Unhurriedly he pushed his key into the lock turning slowly and deliberately until with a final clunk the door opened.

"A faulty key after all," he muttered with relief. Talking to himself was a disturbing habit he'd picked up recently, another indication of his pressing need to retire. Sliding behind the wheel, he flicked on the interior light, still needing confirmation that he was alone. Looking around, his eyes focused on a light yellow binder leaning up against the back-seat. Red spidery writing adorned the light-grained cover, its message simple but chilling. "Help." The assassin's head started spinning as the words appeared to take on a life of their own dancing soundlessly over a light, textured dance floor. They cavorted first one way and then another, as the eyes of the onlooker grew steadily heavier gazing at the increasingly frantic hypnotic performance.

Overwhelmed by the mesmeric effect, a head heavy with sleep slumped against the comforting headrest into a deep trance-induced sleep.

CHAPTER 112

THE STRANGE NOISE grew louder as he woke from a deep sleep. He didn't know how long he had been incognizant; but judging by the stiffness in his limbs and the brightness of a watery sun, shining through his car windows and temporarily blinding him, it must have been several hours. A strange, dark silhouette blacked out an April sun as the disturbing sound came ever nearer. It was a moment frozen in time as a strange beating, like the wing-beats of giant moths amplified a thousand times, threatened to shatter his sensitive eardrums. He breathed an audible sigh of relief as a news helicopter, reporting on a major traffic accident, passed overhead.

The sun once again flooded his car with an exquisite light. It was then he noticed the package still leaning against his back seat. Memories came flooding back as virgin white notepaper defaced by red spidery writing fluttered like a demented albino leaf at his feet. A shaft of diffused light cast a flickering shadow, animating the menacing, reclining package, mockingly daring him to rip open its cover and view the contents within. In films and books, professionals in his line of business are portrayed as ruthless, calculating, and fearless. This is not true. His first instinct was to throw the package out of the car and drive off as fast as he could. The package, mottled with light and shadow, fugaciously faded in and out of his vision. Summoning his remaining courage, he reached behind for it.

He couldn't put it off any longer. As soon as the rain let up, Harry knew the time had come. He had been hoping Sid would do it for him. Sid had not obliged, so Harry set off reluctantly to do his rounds, with security key in one hand and a partly eaten Mars bar in the other. His shift ending in half an hour, Harry walked briskly, or as briskly as Harry ever walked, tentatively checking doors and locks hoping fervently not to find anything amiss. The recent murders linked to the university had left everyone jumping at shadows. Harry wasn't the bravest security man in the land before the librarian's murder; he shook with anxiety now, after it.

Like Dr Who'sTardis, it shimmered in the distance, its blue and red lights making abstract patterns on the wall. Harry walked towards the ever-changing cacophony of lights—a familiar haven in the darkness. His sweaty hand clutching a fifty pence piece and his mind excitedly anticipating yet another Mars bar, he walked unhesitatingly towards the comforting glow of the university vending machine. Another chocolate bar regurgitated with a clunk from the automated candy store, only to be snatched voraciously by an impatiently waiting Harry. Leaning against the traditionally painted, cream-coloured wall, contentedly chewing the remainder of his king-size Mars bar, he could barely see the distant car park in the murky darkness.

The solitary car had been there all-night, probably a car left by a staff member, off for a clandestine liaison with a colleague. Lucky buggers thought Harry bitterly, these secret affairs always happened to someone else. He'd never heard of it happening to security men, just the university nobs. A sudden movement dancing on the periphery of his vision drew his attention once again to the solitary car. Giant concentric circles distorted the space surrounding the deserted vehicle. Whirling ever faster like a mini tornado the circles became a blur until vanishing as suddenly as they had appeared. Harry did not hear the clatter of keys as they slipped through his torpefied fingers. He stood silently transfixed, his brain not believing what his eyes beheld. Harry blinked. The average duration of a human blink is about fifty to seventy-five milliseconds; but by the time Harry opened his eyes, the vision had gone, leaving a stunned security man wondering if he had imagined the whole incident.

CHAPTER 113

IT WAS LIKE a bad dream—worse than that; it was a nightmare. Trudy sat down heavily. The kettle now simmering on a low gas whistled tunelessly, mockingly happy in the background. Trudy's métier had always been her ability to think and work logically. Even so, she still subscribed to the widely held view that bad news such as she had just received always happened to someone else. When, in fact, the worst does happen, your first port of call is denial. However you phrased it, Trudy was now at that stage. "But it can't be. I saw him only a few days ago," she sobbed, not wishing to believe what she knew in her heart to be true.

Andy leaned across and placed a big, comforting hand on Trudy's arm, a surprisingly gentle gesture for a man dispassionate by both training and natural inclination. "I am afraid there's no doubt, although we still need someone to identify the body." Andy's visage dissolved in a mist of her tears. Without warning, the irregular outlines of his face filled her vision as he moved uncomfortably close. Reacting instinctively, Trudy turned her head away, leaving Andy first puzzled then hurt at her obvious rejection of his premature advance. The tension that had built up between them eased when the door suddenly burst open and an angry looking Gene filled the doorway.

"What the fuck is going on? Is this a private party, or is anyone invited?" It was a poor effort for a master in the art of withering sarcasm; but it still had the desired effect, as a relieved Trudy stood up and walked unsteadily towards him.

"He's dead," blurted out Trudy between sobs as with faltering steps she walked into Gene's arms.

"Who's dead Trudy?" asked Gene quietly, sensing the deep sorrow within her.

"It's Mike, my friend Mike Powell; he died today in Bletchworth Hospital." Her sorrow turned to anger. "Some bastard mugged him and left him for dead in an alley." She slumped deeper into Gene's accommodating arms, her energy visibly drained by the sheer effort of her outburst.

From across the room Andy looked on helplessly, immediately regretting his clumsy and inappropriate overture. His increasing dislike of Gene almost immediately replaced his self-admonishment as he gazed across at the subject of Trudy's affection. As if in sympathy, the steaming kettle abandoned its taunting wail in favour of a gentle bubbling—the source of its energy removed. The moment lost its impact, as with a flourish, Laura, now feeling her feet within the group, walked imperiously into the room, curiosity triumphing over waning patience.

"What's up, Doc?" Laura's attempt to lighten the atmosphere with a poor impression of Bugs Bunny not only fell on stony ground, but, even more sorely, invoked a look from Andy designed to kill at twenty paces. Tumbleweed blowing down the hallway was all that was missing during the ensuing silence as Laura's erstwhile confidence began to melt like the permafrost in Greenland.

Trudy swallowed the rage that was building up inside her. With chilling calmness she glared across at Andy, her eyes like cold, green stones, moist with her salty tears. "Well, what the hell are you going to do about it, Mr. Policeman?" she snarled through clenched teeth, denial turning to hostility, looking for someone to blame.

Without thinking, Andy trotted out the well-used phrase, which tells you nothing but sounds pompously official, used by police everywhere: "We are actively pursuing our enquiries." Sounding like Joe Friday from *Dragnet*, he immediately realised his mistake, as Trudy's face contorted first with hurt and then with anger.

"You arrogant bastard, this might be just another day at the office for you; but this is my life we're talking about here." Gene, who in the past had made conversation-killing remarks an art form, now stood there silent but glowering at the two antagonists.

Suddenly aware of the tension, crackling like the build up of an electric storm and pervading the room, Trudy summoned the will to move away from Gene. "Well, let's get on with the research," she mumbled to no one in particular as she walked a little unsteadily towards the glowing Cyclops.

CHAPTER 114

HE HAD NOT intended to kill this woman, but opportunities like this didn't present themselves everyday; and as he'd never been one to look a gift-horse in the mouth, he had killed her. What's more, he enjoyed it; oh, he'd enjoyed it all right. They say that practice makes perfect, and there is no doubt he'd been getting better. He had killed many people over the years, but recently he'd made a concentrated effort to increase his tally.

David's influence, of course, had helped him; in fact, he wasn't sure whether he or David had killed the woman. Even more disturbing, he wasn't even sure who he was. As their personalities were melding, so the boundaries of reality and fantasy became increasingly obscure. The only clear thought in his head was that the two people he hated most were in this house. He did not intend to let them get out alive. To be fair, he and David would die as well; but the more of those flawed examples of the human race they could take with them the better.

He didn't want to die; but if he could go out in a blaze of glory, his Momma would be pleased. She would finally realise he was a son to be proud of not despised and abused as he had been when a little boy. Come to think about it, the bitch he had just killed looked a bit like his mother did before his father left. She had then been nothing like the hateful hag she became in later years. The orgasmic enjoyment he got from killing the woman had surprised even him, as his mother's face morphed with the struggling, dying woman. Pity he and David would have to die with the loathsome enemies inside. Just when they were about to achieve the zenith of their nirvana, life as they knew it on this mortal plane would end just as quickly as it had begun; at least he would have the satisfaction of taking them with him. A sensual feeling flooded his loins, the same feeling he'd experienced after watching his first victim die all those years ago. Subsequent kills had progressively less impact on him; and the need to recreate the ecstasy of that first kill, just like a drug addict, became increasingly acute. The next few hours would be the defining time of his life—the time when the essence of his very existence would culminate in glory beyond the reach of mortal men.

CHAPTER 115

HIS FACE REGISTERED the boredom he felt as his glazed eyes stared fixedly at the flickering laptop. He didn't know how people could spend so much time at the computer. His nephews were the worst, spending all their spare time playing those mindless games instead of getting out playing football or cricket with their mates. They had a weight problem now; God knows what they would be like in a few years time. His job now revolved more around paperwork and records than catching criminals. What with that as well as the political correctness bollocks, the job was getting impossible; and he was glad to be getting out of it. Roll on next year when he could spend more time in his beloved garden and, occasionally, in his beloved pub.

Pity Grace went off in such a huff, he thought, his mind desperately looking for sanctuary from the mood of tedium generated by the group of people crowding around the animated screen. She hadn't told him, despite his cajoling, what she had discovered, preferring to tell Andy first. And it wasn't just because of his rank; everybody at the station knew she fancied him. They'd been friends for years, and whether the relationship was purely platonic was the subject of much speculation between coppers and admin alike. Lucky bugger—his missus wasn't a bad looker either. Still, Andy was all right when you got to know him; and Rob knew that when he retired, he would miss their daily banter and would have to confine himself to conversations with his plants. The thought saddened him. He'd miss the job more than he realised—most people did. He remembered his father's sombre warning: "Retirement always appeals more when you are working; the reality is vastly different."

As a teenager Rob had watched his father's sense of worth progressively dwindle until his self-esteem and confidence reestablished themselves only through the comfort given by prodigious quantities of alcohol. Specialists at the Liver Disease unit, his father's final resting place, attributed excessive alcohol consumption over many years as a major cause for the liver failure that finally killed him. The background drone of sleep inducing voices suddenly rose, jolting him from a semisoporific state.

Gene's voice boomed above the supporting background of chatter: "That's it! That's exactly as I saw it in my dream."

CHAPTER 116

THE STORM WAS sudden. A crack of lightning heralded the opening of floodgates releasing a deluge of torrential rain on an unprepared and clearly unimpressed world. Across the country, storms raged, fuelling the global warming debate in which everyone had an opinion. People talked about it, paying it lip service, but no one was willing to give up anything that would inconvenience them in the slightest—a selfish world full of selfish people.

A wall of water from a sagging gutter obscured Rob's view as he peered morosely into the murky night outside. It was the kind of night that thriller writers had described 'ad nauseam' as a prelude to whatever grisly crime they had thought up for their eagerly awaiting public. Fuckin' weather, thought the detective to whom retirement couldn't come soon enough. Another course of Prozac beckoned, he thought, the dreariness of the weather reflecting his mounting depression. A temporary break in the water wall allowed him a clearer view of the quagmire that was once a garden. Funny how the light plays tricks—the way that bush moved seemed out of synchronization with the rest of the gusting undergrowth. From a stormy sky lit up by a myriad of lightning strikes, a silhouette appeared briefly from behind the rain obscured bush, only to vanish as quickly as it had appeared.

If Rob had younger eyes, he may have noticed the brief outline. As it was, with a sigh he turned away from the darkness of the night and walked back to join his companions basking in the laptop's inviting glow.

From his concealment outside, he'd seen a vague image outlined in the dim light struggling to penetrate the storm-exaggerated gloom. The impression at the window was that of an old man. The hidden man was no respecter of age—in fact, far from it. This old fucker would die along with the rest. The thought brought a sinister smile to his face as he set about his deadly work in earnest.

CHAPTER 117

WITH A DEEP breath, he tentatively opened the package and spilled the contents untidily on the passenger seat beside him. Disappointment creased deep lines into his face, already etched by time and stress. He didn't know what he expected, but something more exciting than a collection of old photographs—a few colour, but mainly black-and-white. The clarity and sharpness of the images impressed him though, as he rifled through the photographs like a mutoscope from arcades of old.

Sifting through a second time, he was drawn to a coloured eight by ten, depicting an elderly man and woman against a backdrop of smoking rubble. This is dramatic, he thought, obviously a scene from some disaster movie the Hollywood machinery served up with increasing frequency to a gullible public. Strangely though, the woman in the photograph appeared vaguely familiar, like an older version of someone he knew. She appeared older definitely, but the likeness was there nonetheless. Perhaps it was her mother or even grandmother—he had never been good at judging the age of women. Yes, that would be it. Satisfied with the explanation, he shuffled disinterestedly through the remaining photographs.

Unnoticed at first glance, a drawstring pouch, still nestling within the nearly empty package, came to his attention. Someone's rubbish, he thought, emptying the contents tentatively into the palm of his clawed, gloved hand. His first notion was quickly dispelled as he gazed quizzically at the small items nestling comfortably against the black backdrop of his leather glove. One of the objects he recognised immediately as being a much smaller version of the Phaistos Disk.

The clay object was a replica of the much larger version of the legendary artefact, the subject of much discussion and conjecture during his early training as an archaeologist. Exquisite hieroglyphics decorated the mottled surface of the coin like disk. Although crowded on an area not much larger than a modern day fifty pence piece, the etchings were clear and distinct even to his eyes. He remembered from university lectures that the Phaistos Disk dated back to the burning of the Minoan Palaces on Crete about 1600BC. He impressed himself remembering such facts; it must have been at least twenty years since that particular subject had occupied even the remotest corner of his mind, but the knowledge came flooding back to him.

A volcanic eruption on the island of Thera had been instrumental in destroying the advanced Minoan civilisation. A feeling of unease swept over him, as he flicked back to an image depicting panic stricken men, wearing loincloths and boots of ornamental leather, trying to escape from an unseen danger. The terror on their faces he'd seen before on the faces of people who knew they were about to die. His heart told him this was as real as it gets, no acting here.

A chilling thought niggled at the back of his mind, but logic and reason soon regained their dominance, dismissing the idea as quickly as it had begun. With a shake of the head he turned his attention to the remaining items. Partially obscured by the

Minoan relic the small black item, about one centimetre long, looked inconsequential. The man's eyes gleamed, recognition winning its battle with curiosity, as the form of a small insect like creature emerged, as if woken from a deep sleep. Picking up the small object, the man placed it gently on a sheet of white paper. Moving it closer, squinting at first while the complex lens system of his eyes fixed its focus on the small, black object contrasting against the white background of the paper.

Eyes focused, the man now recognized the black object as a trilobite fossil. Surprisingly this fossil was a complete dead trilobite, not the more usual moulted exoskeleton. Coincidently, he had attended a lecture given by Trudy on this very subject about six months ago— ironic, he thought sardonically, given the current circumstances. The unease he had felt previously surfaced again as he shuffled through the purse looking for a photograph that could provide the link to his latest discovery. A picture of fleeing beasts, like a shot from *Walking with Dinosaurs*, caught his eye. The drama of the image was heightened by the fiery object dominating the doom laden sky.

Strange, but when the adrenalin begins to flow, the brain makes logical leaps many moves ahead, like a chess grand master playing for the world title. The link fell inexorably into place. If this trilobite fossil linked back to a dinosaur age and the disk artefact linked to the extinction of the Minoan civilisation, what then was the link with the small, pulsating green object still nestling in his gloved hand? Futuristic images of the devastated buildings and the familiar face of Trudy Ballinger leaped through to the forefront of his mind as he picked out several coloured, more detailed photographs from an ever decreasing pile.

Science of the past was his speciality; science of the future left him cold. If, indeed, these were futuristic images, then the link between this and the green, pulsating capsule completely eluded him.

He suddenly became furious with himself for losing focus. He needed all his concentration and objectivity to complete his final job before retirement. Still, instinct, which had served him in the past, now told him danger loomed. Myriad questions invaded his mind. Why would anyone send this package to him, what did it mean, and most important of all who had sent it? If someone had wanted to capture his curiosity, he or she had succeeded commendably well. There was no letter of explanation and no name; someone was having a laugh at his expense, although his instinct told him there was more to it than that. The filing system of his mind worked overtime trying in vain to identify anyone of his acquaintance with the skill and expertise needed to produce the photographs and make these exquisite objects.

The perpetrator of this hoax might yet live to regret such folly.

CHAPTER 118

LITTLE DID THE man in the car realise it, but at the same time that he made his logical leap, five other voices, six miles away, rose with excitement at making a similar discovery. A scarred fist violently punched the air; simultaneously a throaty "Yes" shook the room startling the astonished occupants gathered around the dispassionate computer. Four heads turned as one, towards the triumphant Gene Harman, before they too joined in, adding their voices to celebrate the sudden breakthrough.

A sad half smile flitted across Trudy's face, grudgingly replacing the cheerless frown she had worn since hearing of her friend's death. Trudy's recognition of the small disk dangling from the terrified man's naked chest, startling on the black and white photograph, had started a train of thought leading to a chilling realization. The potential significance of the message contained in it rapidly altered the first feeling of elation they had felt at piecing together the puzzle.

Andy, the first to speak, looked obviously shaken. "There's some mistake; it's just a coincidence," he said, seeking to reassure himself before continuing. "You can always create links, no matter how tenuous, if you try hard enough." Three faces turned towards him, none of them convinced by his weak argument. As a police officer, Andy had to deal in facts. Nothing else would stand up in court as evidence. But human intuition now drove Andy, as he realised the weakness of his own arguments in the face of compelling evidence to the contrary.

Sensing Andy's indecision, Trudy fell easily into the role of lecturer and summarised the evidence of their recent research, pausing occasionally to emphasise specific relevant points. Easily deflecting attempts by the others to interrupt, Trudy finished her diatribe, sat down, and folded her arms across her chest, daring anyone to disagree with her conclusions. There were no takers.

"So I had a vision of the future, as well as dreams of the past; and the one common denominator is that each event ended with a mass extinction." Spurred on by Trudy's nod of agreement, Gene continued—"the dinosaurs by a cataclysmic asteroid, the Minoan civilisation by a catastrophic volcanic eruption, and then the future, which doesn't look too rosy does it?" Rapt in their own anguished thoughts, the impact of Gene's sardonic wit went unnoticed.

"What we have overlooked in all this is that some unidentified force could be trying to warn us of impending danger," Laura interjected, her voice shrill with emotion, reflecting her growing anxiety. "What can we do about it?" Laura's commanding officer felt the full force of her hostile glare, as she demanded a response to a question that neither Andy nor anyone else in the room could answer. The one person who did have the answers that Laura sought was unaware of the question and didn't care about the answer. That person was six miles away and getting closer.

"I don't have an explanation any more than you, but I do know we won't get anywhere by panicking." Andy's riposte did little to soothe the group's emotions, which were now running high.

The sound of Trudy's chair scraping on the bare wooden

floorboards broke the brief, uncomfortable silence. "The only clue we have to this so-called premonition is the old couple carrying a baby surrounded by devastation." Trudy once again had the floor. "If the couple is, as we suspect, Gene and I, then we are looking at least twenty years in the future, probably fifty years in Gene's case, she added with rancour, "so there is still plenty of time."

"That's assuming your conclusions are correct," Laura butted in, still stinging from Andy's curt riposte to her earlier question.

Determined not to lose her composure, Trudy persevered. "Without any hard facts, we have to theorise and then prove or disprove the hypothesis with any evidence we get hold of."

"Don't patronise me; I'm not one of your students," Laura fired back, infuriated, the tension clearly mounting between the two women.

Gene, not a stranger to conflict himself, sensed the growing feeling of hostility within the room and intervened. "I don't know about the rest of you, but Trudy and I are getting out of here." Gene, after the initial euphoria of discovery, felt chilled, as the full impact of the situation struck him. "I need time and space to think, without coppers busy-bodying around as if they are the only ones with any answers or opinions." Since the explosion and his resulting stay in hospital, he had been subdued—by his standards; but now, he felt the need to take control of the situation and specifically, to save his own skin. "So we are off, unless we are under arrest, of course," he added looking to Trudy for support. A smile signalled her concurrence as she reached for the pink cotton jacket left hanging carelessly over the back of her chair.

"You're free to go; but remember, we can't protect you if you leave," said Andy, resignedly realising he had no power to hold them, even for their own safety.

"If he was still alive, the porter at the hospital could vouch for the effectiveness of your protection," Gene said bitterly.

For once Andy didn't react, realising the recent murders and now the impact of their discovery had left nerves frayed and feelings edgy. "You will have to wait until I can arrange for transport back to town: I'm not compromising the anonymity of this safe house by getting a taxi to pick you up," Andy asserted with a finality that brooked no argument.

Unexpectedly delayed, the man with the answers they all craved, resumed the journey to his date with destiny.

CHAPTER 119

HIS LOINS HAD a life of their own. Uncontrollable energy surged magnificently through his body. He was on fire. The thought of killing so many people flooded his body with adrenalin so powerful that his muscles made ready to burst.

In his early life, he, as Daniel, had killed many times before, each occasion involving only a single victim. Now, with his friend David, he could achieve his dream. They'd had great hopes for the bomb in Goldberg's building. But unfortunately there was only one death, and that fat slob, Vince, didn't count. The look on their faces as they faced death would be worth a lifetime of waiting in the shadows. After spending what seemed like hours, but in fact was only forty-five minutes, the plan that would ensure David and Daniel's immortality, alongside such legends as Michael Robert Ryan and Charles Manson, was ready.

When on his killing spree in Hungerford, one of the weapons Michael Ryan had used was an AK-47 assault rifle. Poetically Daniel and David would use a similar weapon. It had taken most of his life savings to get the weapon. However, it will have been money well spent when they became famous, his and David's names mentioned in the same breath as their heroes and role models. Daniel jerked out of his reverie, David insisting that he maintain his focus to enable them achieve their destiny.

Much time happily spent practicing the assembly of the weapon on the floor of his flat did not allow for the awful conditions prevalent on this cold, wet, windy night. Frozen fingers struggled determinedly to assemble the many pieces by feel, eyes useless in the murky darkness and adrenaline fuelled muscles twitching with a mind of their own. Finally, after much fumbling and cursing, the magazine locked in place with a reassuring clunk. The gun, now assembled, was ready for what lay ahead.

CHAPTER 120

"WHAT'S THE MATTER, Rob, you miserable sod?" Andy's tone registered his annoyance, as he addressed his gloomy looking sergeant. "You weren't much help in there; after all, you are Laura's boss, at least for the next few weeks," Andy added, still smarting from Laura's hostile questioning. Amid the excitement and furore created by recent discoveries, Rob had remained impassive and withdrawn until Andy had posed the question.

"Well," began Rob, feeling distinctly uncomfortable under the glare of his superior's darkly grim face. "I think you were too hard on Grace; she was only trying to help after all. We are all on the same side you know." Rob, his growing confidence correlating positively with his rising anger, had nothing to lose, with retirement looming soon anyway. He continued emotionally: "Everyone at work knows that Grace thinks the world of you; but for some unknown reason you denigrate her at every given opportunity. She is a doctor after all, for Christ's sake, and a bloody good one at that—too good for you, if you want my opinion.—And furthermore . . . ." Rob's voice trailed off mid-sentence. Breathing heavily he walked away before he lost control and compromised their relationship forever.

For once Andy's sharp wit and renowned cutting ripostes let

him down. Dumbfounded, he couldn't believe that Rob had spoken to him in such a disrespectful manner. Despite his growing anger, though, Andy still respected his sergeant's opinion. Rob's words had struck a chord with him; maybe he had been bad tempered and offhand; but he reasoned it was due to the pressure he'd been under recently. Feeling partly absolved by his rationale, Andy decided that he would ring Grace later to apologise. After all, they had been friends for many years, perhaps another reason he had reacted in such an offhand manner. Looking at his watch, he calculated she had flounced out about an hour ago and should be home by now. He'd give it another ten minutes; allow her time to cool down; then ring her, turn on the charm, and hopefully, everything would be all right. Then, too, maybe Rob would look happier and less reproachful; and they could get on with their job.

What Andy didn't realise, but would find out soon, was that the last words Grace had heard before her death were cold and dismissive—words delivered by her friend and former lover, Andy Dale.

CHAPTER 121

SIRENS WAILED IN the distance, getting nearer, drivers dropping their phones guiltily, tentatively looking to see if the flashing, blue lights of rampant police cars had focused their self-important attention on them. Thoughts raced through minds, such as, Was that last drink one too many? Feet instinctively released pressure from accelerators, trying desperately to keep under the speed limit so as not to attract unwelcome police attention.

The man behind the wheel of the speeding car had no thought for anyone around him. A casual onlooker might well believe the expressionless face, hovering like a ghostly presence, stark against the car's dark interior, was that of a dead man. In another time frame the same onlookers might well be right in their judgment. For the moment, however, the man was alive and had a mission to perform that would change many lives forever.

The shimmering iridescence of wasted energy, unashamedly lighting up the sky, now retreated, becoming smaller, as the man glanced anxiously towards his rear view mirror. The diminishing glow of the city was replaced rapidly by the white orbs of starkly glaring headlights approaching much too fast for safety. The lights momentarily released their mesmeric hold on contracted pupils, now dilating frantically in their effort to harness all available light necessary for navigating the constricting and savage darkness ahead. Behind him, the violent contact between bumpers more designed for cosmetic reasons than protection jerked him forward, restraining seat belt groaning and complaining under the unaccustomed stress created by the heavy man. Brakes jammed on instinctively invoked another thud of metal-on-metal contact, as unprepared, the hostile vehicle rammed into the back of the car driven by a man now cold with fury.

Jimmy Weiss was a small-time criminal and self-styled hard man. Feared by those who had the misfortune to cross him, he thrived on the notoriety his reputation gave him. The ragged scar trekking down from his left ear lobe to the point of his jaw was regarded as a badge of honour by his few loyal friends. Two of these friends, too hard to use seat belts, careered violently forward, propelled by the force generated by colliding cars. Their tyres screeching, two cars locked their bumpers like rutting stags, as they shuddered to a halt amid the ghostly backcloth of stunted trees and rampant hedgerows. Momentarily the world stood still, before the doors of Jimmy's car, groaning under the strain, slowly opened. Jimmy Weiss paused while his eyes adjusted to the gloom, the pounding need for revenge blocking out any reasonable thought.

Frank Simmonds emerged next, blood pouring from a nose badly misshapen by its recent contact with an unyielding dashboard. Finally, the short, wiry body of Aaron Young stumbled into the roadway, an open razor at the ready, his need for violence burning brightly through an alcohol fuelled haze.

The rear view-mirror framed the three pathetic figures as they stood shakily, full of righteous indignation and hate. The man watched emotionless as the vengeful trio, cursing roundly, approached and crowded his vision with hate filled faces. Like a gunfighter of old, Jimmy's hand flashed to his side reaching for an ancient but trusty claw hammer—a tool that had served him well in the past, as many broken fingers and toes could testify. As if choreographed, Jimmy reached the driver's door as his cohorts cut off any means of escape on the passenger side.

Serving his apprenticeship on one of the roughest estates in Bletchworth, Jimmy was no stranger to the seedier side of life. He had rubbed shoulders with many hard men, and he'd learned to give them respect. No one, however, had ever filled him with the dread he now felt looking into the eyes now locking his gaze with terrible intensity. His cocky self-assurance melted like microwaved ice, coinciding with the warm stream now flowing down his leg, as both bladder and prostate surrendered to the natural laws of gravity. The hammer slipped through his nerveless fingers, its slow motion descent ending abruptly on the mud splattered road with a muted splash. The round hole that appeared like a third eye, only added to Jimmy's look of surprise as he followed his hammer, which slid into the slimy, wet mud.

Frank Simmons, not renowned for his high intellect, made a decision that might have saved his life. It didn't, however. He ran; in fact, he ran faster than he'd ever run before in his life—faster probably than even Linford Christie, but not faster than the bullet fired from the killer's gun. A powerful blow from behind sent him sprawling, his face ploughing a furrow in the sodden earth. The El Paso gunfighter had Feleena to comfort him before he died. Frank Simmons had no one.

For once in his life, Aaron Young was glad he was short. At school friends had grown tall and continued to do so all through their teens. Most of his friends and enemies towered above him. Some short people may develop an inferiority complex; others try to make up for their lack of size by being overly aggressive. Aaron went one step further and developed a sadistic streak that even his much taller contemporaries were wary of. Known in the neighbourhood as "Weasel," he had a reputation as a vicious street fighter. Consequently he made few friends; those he did have feared him rather than liked him.

The Evolution 45 is highly effective at suppressing the sound emitted while firing a large handgun. So effective was the silencer that Weasel barely heard the first shot, which took out Jimmy: but he witnessed the devastating effects of the second, as Frank Simmonds collapsed face down in the mud. Unlike his fearless namesake, Weasel's first reaction was to panic and run. His second reaction was to drop to the ground and roll under the car. On this occasion second was best, that is, until the car wheels drove over him, ruining his love-life, and any other life he may have had, forever.

CHAPTER 122

"YOU HAVE REACHED the phone of Dr. Grace Anderson. Sorry I'm not available at the moment; but please leave your message and phone number after the tone, and I will get back to you as soon as possible."

Listening to the message for the third time, Andy was now beginning to worry. Automatically glancing at his watch, hardly recognising his distorted reflection leering back at him, his mind began to work overtime. Mobile switched off, no one at home—most unlike Grace to be incommunicado. Knowing it was him, she probably was not answering the phone, just to prove a point. Well, give her another ten minutes; then, he'd get a patrol car to look in on her. That will teach her when old Sid Cole knocks on the door demanding entry. He smiled sadly, now strongly regretting the hasty words he'd made to his friend earlier.

With a crash, a glass once perched precariously on the Formica topped table now lay in pieces at his feet. "Oh, bollocks," Andy fumed, as shards of glass scattered over the kitchen floor. A little water goes a long way when spilled over a floor; the same physical law applied to glass, thought Andy cynically, surveying the glinting debris around him. He'd get Laura to sweep it up—about time she did something useful; it would get that bloody chip off her shoulder. Andy smiled, gender discrimination still alive and well in Bletchworth.

All heads turned as one towards the open kitchen door. The sound of breaking glass rapidly followed by an emotional expletive prompted a buzz of conversation by the group still sitting around the computer. Cramming the last of the papers into his briefcase, Gene paused and said, “Hadn’t you better see what’s happened to your boss?” Gene looked pointedly at Laura then moved his gaze to Rob.

Fuck him, he thought. Still smarting from his earlier altercation, Rob was not in the mood to pander to his superior; Laura’s silence signalled that those were her sentiments as well.

CHAPTER 123

GENE STARED IN blank amazement at the sight of Andy surrounded by broken glass, holding his mobile phone, gazing through a soulless kitchen window into the dark night. "Bloody hell. What's happened here?" Gene's loud, unsympathetic voice broke Andy's reverie.

Preoccupied with his own dilemma, the senior police officer resisted the temptation to fence verbally with a belligerent Gene Harman. Reigning in his instinct to react aggressively to a question, which even the questioner didn't expect to be answered, Andy said quietly, "Grace isn't home yet; I'm worried."

Andy's uncharacteristic response to Gene's question, invoked a predictable reaction from Gene. "Well, it's your own fault; you shouldn't have been so bloody unpleasant to her." Not known for his sympathetic ear, Gene lived up to expectations.

"You sound like my sergeant," Andy retorted hotly, pointing a threatening finger at the sneering figure before him. The two protagonists glared at each other, neither willing to back down. Even the sound of the kitchen door opening detracted from the hostility built up between the two men.

"Come on, Gene; let's go for a walk to clear our heads, before we end up fighting," Trudy demanded, trying to ease the tension.

Momentarily, the eyes of the two men remained locked, neither willing to back down from the confrontation. Finally, the watery blue eyes of Gene turned reluctantly towards Trudy, "Okay, sooner we get out of here the better." The cold wind gusted through the kitchen as Gene and Trudy walked out of the door into the cold night.

CHAPTER 124

HE WAS SURE that he had heard the door open. Loud voices from within contaminated the now still, night air. The glow emanating from shadeless, incandescent light bulbs penetrated deep into the darkness beyond. A corridor of light sent flying insects into a frenzy, trying desperately to find the source of an intrusion, which had forced its way, uninvited, into their world. The pink eyes of a large grey rat peeked timidly out from the wet undergrowth, alerted to potential danger by the sudden light. Unaware of the confusion they had created among the garden's residents, two figures emerged into the cold, dark night swathed in heavy coats, huddled together for protection against the elements.

One of the garden's less desirable inhabitants surveyed the scene unfolding before him, the deadly AK-47 weighing heavily at his side. This was not going according to plan. He recognised the looming figure of Gene Harman, about to escape into the night, with the smaller figure of Trudy Ballinger clutching his arm. How touching, he thought, a malevolent smile briefly touching his lips before vanishing as quickly as it had appeared. Perhaps he, David, should kill them both now; but, then, that would go against his plan to take out all the people in the house at the same time. They obviously would be coming back; there was no place for them to walk to from this remote spot. Well, he could wait until they came back; it would give him more time to anticipate and savour the final act to come.

Gene and Trudy, oblivious to the murderous human predator skulking deep in the bushes, walked, collars up, tentatively down the dark, eerily shadowed garden path. Trudy, suddenly becoming aware of her vulnerability in threatening, unfamiliar surroundings, grabbed Gene's arm, the feel of a once hard, but still reassuringly firm, muscle giving her a degree of comfort, albeit temporarily. Little realising that the countdown towards an event, which would shape their destiny, had already started, Trudy and Gene vanished into the darkness beyond. And the countdown clock ticked remorselessly on.

CHAPTER 125

THE INTRUSIVE SOUND of a cell phone's plaintive cry finally penetrated Gene's consciousness, as he and Trudy passed through the rickety gate heroically protecting the old house from an unfeeling outside world.

"Gene, can't you switch that mobile off for once." The ring at long last penetrated the fleece lined upturned collar and resounded around an eardrum, sparking off an irritated reaction from Trudy. "You're one of those irritating people for whom there was no life before mobile phones," Trudy said, her pet hate rising bitter to the surface.

Surprised, even though he was accustomed to accepting blame for many misdemeanours, Gene objected strongly on the rare occasion he was not to blame. "Bloody hell, Trudy, it's not mine; I haven't even got it with me."

"Well, it's not mine either," Trudy whispered, the realization dawning on them both at the same time. Just as quickly as it had begun, the ringing stopped; the silence was almost unbearable as Gene and Trudy stood silently, in that instant not daring to move.

A cracking sound pierced the night air breaking the comforting silence that had engulfed, however fleetingly, the two companions as they stood transfixed in the faint night glow.

Without warning, the phone began its pleading cry for attention once again. Two figures held their breath as Grace's phone, insistent in the gloom, continued remorselessly. The hand of a third figure, listening to the shrill chirping, clutched ever more tightly the gun weighing heavily at his side.

A fourth figure, for whom the phone, or anything else for that matter, held no interest at all, lay dead on the ground less than six feet away from the motionless pair. Partially hidden in the slimy mud, a blooded Dr. Grace Anderson lay unceremoniously behind the night blackened rhododendron bush. Her favourite shrub in life became now, her shroud in death.

CHAPTER 126

TWIN ORBS, CASTING shafts of light that cut dramatically through the darkness, dimmed briefly before fading altogether. They left only a memorised image, burnt temporarily on the retina of the lone man. With a final shudder, the engine, still hot from its forced labours, also died. Steam rising from the overheated bonnet provided a clue to the car's untimely death.

A pattering rain still drummed rhythmically on the car roof as the driver's door creaked slowly but inexorably open. A black, handmade leather shoe, once shiny, but now wet from earlier activity, stepped out into the soggy undergrowth. Cold brackish water, seeping over footwear inappropriate for the terrain, went unnoticed by the ruthlessly focused man easing out of the car. A distant, faint glow singled out the object of the disquieted man's attention. Parking this far away and approaching on foot would give him the opportunity to approach his targets unobserved.

As a professional he had learned many years ago the value of surprise and not to give the potential victim any opportunity to react in defence. He'd learned earlier on in his career how people cornered and faced with death found hidden depths when battling for their own life or the lives of loved ones.

Reaching into his pocket, he found the small torch he always carried with him. Surprising how technology had moved on, he thought, his small laser torch cutting through the gloom effortlessly. Its beam came to rest upon a well-located stile, which defined the beginning of his trek towards the distant light. A wave of dizziness almost overwhelmed him. Steadying himself by leaning his arm heavily against the cold, wet roof of his car, he saw flashing images, which blinded him to the outside world and sapped his mental energies.

Sliding slowly down wet metal into a sitting position, he was oblivious to the momentary distortion surrounding him like a shroud. As he slept, conflicting thoughts dominated his unconsciousness. Subliminal messages competed for their host's approval. His mind became a battlefield with two opposing armies fighting for control. At last control was established. Unhurriedly, the man raised himself from the muddy earth and began to walk with a steady gait towards the distant light

CHAPTER 127

HER CRY WAS one of terror. The events of the past weeks had undermined Trudy's previously cool, logical disposition, leaving in its place vulnerability and anguish. Frantic rustling of bushes followed by the sudden appearance of a dark, threatening silhouette invoked from her an involuntary scream. The silhouette metamorphosed into a human figure as Trudy's eyes adjusted to the evening twilight. A gloved hand reached out to grab Trudy.

The looming form of Gene Harman moved instinctively between Trudy and her menacing assailant. The butt of a heavy rifle temporarily ended Gene's heroic intents crashing down with a sickening thud on a shoulder still recovering from earlier mistreatment. Coincidently, although the irony was lost on Gene, the person responsible for the previous carnage and destruction was the one who stood menacingly over him, now intent on completing the job. Blinding pain blurred his vision. Kneeling before the evil being, who screamed foul abuses to a world he was losing contact with, Gene, calling up his remaining strength, flung himself forward and grasped the waist of the raving madman.

Acting on instinct, Gene clung frantically to his attacker, oblivious to the sound of the bullet that buzzed dangerously close to his ear. Both Daniel and David as a single entity, however, became aware of it, as a bullet simultaneously tore a savage passage through unyielding flesh. The writhing mass of human flesh threatening to break free from Gene's adrenalin fuelled grip, suddenly became still, before crumpling into an untidy heap taking a disoriented Gene Harman with it. Daniel Weston, now a crumpled heap on the soggy turf lay, the victim of an unknown assassin, anonymous in the faint diffuse light beyond the trees

The sounds of slamming doors and raised voices gradually penetrated the miasma overwhelming Gene Harman, who was frantically hugging the inert mass of rags heaped on the muddy turf. "Get in here quick," Andy's commanding voice shouted from the doorway, not keen to venture out into the line of fire. A helping hand reached out for Gene's arm invoking an involuntary gasp, as pain from the damaged shoulder registered in his protesting brain. Another hand, this time stronger and more forcible, grabbed Gene's other shoulder; between them, Rob and Trudy hauled Gene unsteadily to his feet and dragged him through the kitchen door to a waiting Andy Dale.

Flashing blue lights heralded the arrival of the police backup. Ten minutes after a call put out by the frantic police inspector, three cars and a van carrying heavily armed police polluted the night environment. The sound of shouting men and heavy bodies crashing through unresisting undergrowth sent panicked wildlife scurrying for the safety of the woodland beyond. The barking of men shouting orders competed with the sound of distressed creatures of the night fleeing for their lives. After thirty minutes a thorough search of the grounds and surrounding area revealed the mutilated body of Dr. Grace Andersen, partially hidden beneath the rhododendron bush, where she had spent her final moments on earth. The lunatic that had come so close to killing Gene had vanished as had the firer of the bullet that had stopped him.

A shocked editor and an even more shocked university professor sat in the lounge barely able to comprehend the horror surrounding the night's events. They say your whole life passes before you when you face with death. Gene had lived every moment of his ordeal, but thoughts of past life hadn't entered his thinking. His only thought had been for his survival and that of Trudy. Psychologically, Trudy's brush with death and recent happenings would affect her for many years to come, manifesting in nightmarish dreams and cold sweats. But that was in the future. Not surprisingly, both Gene and Trudy had refused the offer of hospital treatment, relying instead on a cursory check by a surly paramedic, unhappy at their refusal to accept his advice. After all, he was the professional.

Still trembling from her ordeal, Trudy glanced slowly around the room; her eyes alighted on Gene, the man who had saved her life. Moist tears formed in the corners of her eyes as, with a sudden rush of emotion, she realised how much she loved this big ignorant man. She reached across and took his hand, feeling only a momentary resistance before he responded, briefly squeezing her hand tightly, causing her to wince for the split-second before his grip relaxed. The magical moment vanished almost as soon as it had begun when a desperate moan emanated from a corner of the room where the disconsolate Andy Dale sat alone.

Andy's anguish at the discovery of his friend Grace's body left little room for anything but self-reproach and pity, which would later metamorphose into a lust for vengeance. He'd make someone suffer, if it was the last thing he did. Meanwhile, however, he could only sit staring vacantly into space berating himself as he thought of what might have been. Sensing someone's stare on him, he looked across at Trudy's face and saw only pity in her sad eyes. She displayed none of the fondness she had felt just a few days ago, a few days that now seemed a lifetime away. Resolutely unfolding from his slumped posture, Andy replaced his anguish with steely determination as he slowly rose to his feet and, without a word, walked out into the night.

CHAPTER 128

THE DEBILITATING NUMBNESS was beginning to wear off, replaced cruelly by searing pain cutting through his side like a hot knife. Daniel, for it was now Daniel and not David in control, let out a stifled cry, which threatened to give away his hiding place deep in the eerie, forbidding wood. Sitting behind a pile of logs conveniently stacked by a local woodcutter, Daniel, his strength failing, leaned back heavily against the wet, uncomfortable timber. The once white, but now crimson, shirt felt icy cold against his trembling body; the congealed blood created a macabre starch effect to the cotton fabric clinging to his skin. Until now he'd felt invincible. Now, cold and wet and racked with an intense throbbing in his side, his feeling of invincibility melted away with each passing minute.

Deserted by David, Daniel sat and waited for his father to come and make everything all right again. He knew his mother wouldn't come because she despised him. She'd nearly died during his birth, and she'd hated him since then. She'd driven his father away—he was there one minute and gone the next. Daniel would never forgive her for that. Now, David had abandoned him, too; he felt alone in the world. Pain and the threat of approaching death produced in him clarity of mind he had not known before. Images of him and David in happier times—playing in the fields that surrounded his house—flashed through his mind with an intensity that took precedence over the pain of his shattered body.

Memories were coming back fast and furious as he remembered one summer's day. David was teasing him, laughing. "Please don't laugh at me" he had pleaded; but David wouldn't stop. A cold rage enveloped him as he grasped his friend's throat with the superhuman strength that only supercharged adrenalin can give. Locked together, they had slid down the muddy bank into the lake. His hands clawed at David's scraggy throat as he tried desperately to stop his friend's terrified screaming. He felt the surge of omnipotent power as David stared up uncomprehending into the face of his friend, who was forcing him under the clear water of the lake. He shuddered at the orgasmic pleasure he'd felt seeing David struggling for life, his eyes bulging and his body frantically thrashing to no avail. Daniel had blocked the deed from his consciousness, only recalling glimpses of the happiness he'd felt at the time

No one blamed him for David's death. In fact, at first he'd had praise for sounding the alarm and, then, sympathy for the death of his close friend. In the days and weeks that followed, friends and neighbours were kind to him; even those hateful bullies, who usually made his life hell, left him alone, though temporarily. Most adults were supportive in their own way, except, of course, his mother, who looked at him as if she knew the truth of what had happened that day. In fact, about this time he became aware of his mother's increasing vindictiveness towards him.

Over the years he'd tried many times to recapture that first thrill he'd experienced watching David's frantic reaction to his impending death, but it had always eluded him. Strangely though, now with his own impending death, he felt something akin to that first blissful contentment. Through dimming eyes, he thought he saw a faint, glowing wave in the distance; but it had gone as quickly as it had appeared. The pain was less intense now, a slight numbness moving through his legs and gradually inching its way up his body. Daniel waited with his memories.

While Daniel waited, his body weakened by shock and loss of blood, another shadowy figure, more sinister and deadly, prowled the woods looking to finish the job his bullet had started just an hour before. Like a jungle predator stalking his prey, silently he moved deeper into the unwelcoming woods. He stopped and listened, his body still, as if frozen in a time warp; paradoxically, it was.

The sound of trees creaking, as they battled against the driving wind, assailed his eardrums and formed a barrier to other less natural sounds. The longer he listened the more he became aware of the rhythmic pattern that the sound of nature was providing for his benefit. But it was not the natural world, or its workings, that interested him. His interest was borne of a practicality that had kept him alive when many others in his profession had died. Reasoning that any sound not in keeping with this recurring musical beat of nature would provide clues to the whereabouts of his quarry, he continued his lonely waiting and listening vigil.

CHAPTER 129

ANDY DALE JUST had to get out of the house and away from those people trying to make the right noises but failing dismally. It riled him to see Trudy and Gene looking like two young lovers, as well as Rob's accusatory look laying the blame for Grace's death squarely on Andy's shoulders. No shades of grey with Rob—it was either black or white. Dealing with the burning wretchedness of his friend's death was devastating enough; but condemnation by his peers as well was more than he, Andy Dale, the great, tough detective, could stand. Times like this sorted out who your friends really are. Andy was beginning to realise he had few if any real friends. The thought made him even more depressed. Laura, after her earlier outburst, had gone back to the station; he'd deal with her later when he had more time.

Billowing like the giant sail of a ghostly galleon, the forensic tent fought bravely against the elements to protect the area where Grace's body had lain. Slowly and deliberately Andy walked towards the temporarily erected monument to his friend's death. A tear that had started its journey from the corner of his eye was soon joined by many others, which cascaded in rivulets as they merged with the trails of rain.

"Forgive me, Grace," he choked, before his words, carried away by an unsympathetic wind, metamorphosed into uncontrollable sobs.

CHAPTER 130

A GHOSTLY APPARITION in humanoid form stands motionless, braced against the biting wind. Onlookers would have strongly supposed they had ventured on a figure turned to stone. Seconds ticked by slowly, combining into minutes before suddenly, like a raptor sensing its prey, the head turned towards sounds that were out of synchronisation with the natural rhythm of the dark, windy night. The distracters effect instantly reverses Medusa's curse, as the once stone like figure now moves forward with all the grace and ease of a jungle cat. Stealthily, as one with the night, the Hunter remorselessly hones in on his unwary prey with the accuracy and deadly intent of an Exocet missile, disturbing neither branch nor undergrowth as he moves ever nearer his quarry. Clouds scudding across the stormy sky briefly allow a sliver of moonlight to light up neatly stacked logs. Clouds quickly resume their position, blocking out the moonlight but now the Hunter's prey in his sights.

Images fade in and out of his delirium induced fantasies. Family holidays by the sea, fishing in rock pools with nets, digging in the sand with buckets and spades—he could almost feel the warm sea breeze blowing through his hair already lightened by the sun. He could see mother and father walking hand-in-hand along the seashore, watching him splash in and out of the foaming water. He could hear childish laughter sounding above the gentle murmur of the tide, which flowed gently over the welcoming shore, tickling his toes as it swamped his sand encrusted sandals. Suddenly all goes silent around him as myriads of arms reach out grabbing, clawing, pulling him down beneath the waves. He struggles and struggles but to no avail, his gasping breaths drawing water, not air, into his bursting lungs. The murky, black depths draw him, frantically struggling, deeper and deeper into their deadly embrace.

Suddenly, when he feels he can stand no more, the scene changes around him. Back in the clearing, he does not feel the hard logs pressing against his back, nor does he feel the discomfort of a biting wind. What is real, and what is fantasy? Paralysis mercifully denies all feeling to his broken body. He is back in the dark wood, but this time the spectre before him appears only too real. Hello, Daniel, whispers a voice he knows well. I've come to take you home. The words surround him, pressing into his subconscious mind, chilling beyond mere physical cold. Feeling unyielding metal pressing hard against his forehead, the doomed man smiles. The face is Daniel's death mask. A split second later a bullet enters his forehead, taking with it most of his brain on its way through to the wet impenetrable logs behind.

Two inert bodies lay still in the log circled clearing. Continuous rain and cold wind persuasively added to the growing atmosphere of desolation. One of the corpselike figures had lost all interest in earthly matters, seeping blood and grey splatter and providing clues to Daniel's early demise. A second grey shape rose slowly from the quagmire, silently, like a spectre emerging from its grave after centuries of confinement in a worm infested, rotting coffin. Without even glancing at the pile of bloody rags that was Daniel, the figure gazed slowly around, his eyes settling once more on the distant, yellow glow. The figure's eerie silhouette stood out in bas-relief against the thundery sky. It was lit by a sudden lightning flash followed almost immediately by the deep rumble of thunder rushing to fill the vacuum left by the monumental electric discharge. As if waiting for a sign, the silhouette detached itself from the stormy backcloth and set off once more in search of its original target.

CHAPTER 131

ROB FLINCHED AS the door, caught by the wind, slammed shut after Andy's hasty exit. What was Andy thinking, not insisting that Gene and Trudy return to the station? Bloody hell, there could be more than one maniac around waiting to finish off the job they'd started earlier. Andy's theory that the killers would be miles away by now was just conjecture and taking too much of a risk with other people's lives. If he'd been more considerate towards Grace, she may still be alive. Guilt weighed heavily on Rob's shoulders; if only he'd insisted that Andy listen to what Grace had to say, instead of standing there like a dumbstruck fool. It wasn't until it was too late, after she'd left, that he'd found his tongue and remonstrated with Andy.

The story of his life—as his mother used to say, he'd be too late for his own funeral. The thought blackened his mood even further–a mood not improved by the prospect of babysitting the lovebirds all night. Rob watched the big man lying uncomfortably on the small sofa with his girlfriend sitting opposite, a fond smile on her face. Bloody pathetic, he thought, acting like a pair of lovesick kids. Rob's irritation, borne more out of jealousy than any prudish principle, did little to improve his current psychological demeanour. It had been more years than he cared to remember since he and his wife, Martha, had done any cuddling; maybe when he retired, they should have more fun. A tired smile briefly touched his face at the thought. Ah well, he could but dream. A loud snoring, emanating from the recumbent Gene Harman, jolted Rob back to grim reality.

Many people before Trudy Ballinger had tried to get comfortable in the large lumpy armchair; many, like Trudy, had failed. After a period of fitful restlessness, she finally sat, one leg tucked under her and her head resting against the greasy wing of the chair. Trudy glanced enviously across at the reclining, untidy figure before her. Seemingly settled into restful sleep, Gene's snoring, interspersed with the occasional garbled shout, guaranteed there would be no sleep for Trudy in the near future.

Sleep would be at a premium for more than Trudy—this night and many more nights to come.

CHAPTER 132

THE BODY LAY in a cold, depressing room, deep beneath the bowels of the hospital building. A thin, white sheet provided but a flimsy cover, giving the deceased some final dignity. A hunched figure, dressed in the green garb of a mortuary attendant shuffled wearily over to the ghostly shroud, gloomy in the inadequate light of an energy saving bulb. Like the re-enactment of a scene from *The Body Snatchers*, the stooped figure honed in on his target, mumbling to himself, alone in the empty mausoleum except for the spiders and the occasional rat.

Gentle whispers of air, displaced by sudden movement, ruffled the white shroud, momentarily giving life to the inert body reclining beneath its voluminous spread. Green garb and black Wellingtons stopped in their tracks; mumbling stopped mid-mumble. Statue like, the old attendant froze, his staring eyes fixed like lasers on the gently moving cotton sheet. Speechless for a split second, his voice now broke its silence. An expletive starting deep in the throat ended in a high-pitched "Bollocks', bouncing off the mausoleum walls like echoes resounding from the turntable of a demented disc jockey.

Imperceptibly at first, then as if viewed through a time-lapse camera, the ghostly shroud started to slide off the corpse, recumbent on the cold trolley. Reaching forward as quickly as his advanced years would allow, the old man grabbed at the falling sheet; his rheumy eyes dreaded to see what lay beneath its protecting cover. Frantic effort to no avail, the white cover continued its inevitable journey ending in an untidy heap on the cold, stone floor. The grey form of a man lay exposed, now devoid of its protective cover, eyes alive, wide open in dead rotting flesh. Looming big, filling the old man's vision, the face, one he recognised, transfixed the onlooker, the scene frozen in time.

The image changed once more. This time the perspective transformed from that of the old man to an aerial view encompassing the whole scene. The camera panned out until the old figure and the shroudless body were just insignificant specks in a barren wasteland. From the wasteland panning continued, rushing by with ever increasing velocity and forming a vortex through space and time through which the free mind could travel endlessly. Images, worlds, speeding by, in alternating light and darkness, an endless cycle, flashing by ever faster until all merged into one twilight zone. Still the journey continued through semi light, rushing sounds getting louder until all other senses ceased to exist, obliterated by the thunderous roar. Reaching a point beyond endurance of mortals, suddenly a magnificent pure light blotted out all else, including the noise. The silence was deafening in its intensity, the light blinding in its radiance.

CHAPTER 133

THE LIGHTNING BOLT flooded the room with its radiance; the intensity awoke Gene with a start. His whole body shook uncontrollably, the dream still real in his befuddled mind. A vicelike grip clamped his shoulder sending tremors of pain down his body, still sore from previous exertions.

"Wake up." Another violent shake—"Are you all right?" Rob didn't care whether Gene Harman was all right or not; he just wanted him to stop that bloody, unnerving moan. Gene's lolling head jerked rigidly upright; his white, rolled up eyeballs transformed with a blink, as the watery, pale blue irises, still uncomprehending, tried desperately to focus on the scene around him. Like Phobos and Deimos hovering around Mars, the faces of Rob and Trudy floated in and out of a trembling Gene Harman's blurred vision. In the netherworld, hovering between fantasy and reality, Gene tried desperately to gather his scrambled thoughts.

A sudden gust of cold air broke the spell, as Andy burst into the room, his face pinched with cold and rain coursing down his face and neck. "Come on, get ready; it's time we got out of here," he gasped his voice staccato through ragged breaths. Gene, sleep still lingering in his befuddled brain, blinked vacantly at the bedraggled figure before him. A lingering ambience of pure white dominated Gene's vision, reluctant to give up its purity for the drabness of reality about to envelop him.

The drama of Andy's entrance startled both Rob and Trudy. Rob was the first to react. "Bloody 'ell, Guv, what's happened?" said Rob glaring at his boss.

Known for his logical common sense approach and not given to panic or flights of imagination, Andy was reluctant to divulge his feelings to the two people confronting him, who were demanding an answer. Trudy recently had become one of his greatest critics, and he wasn't about to satisfy her by letting her see him bow down to their demands. Uncharacteristically stuck for words, he glared back, holding his sergeant's gaze momentarily before turning back to a challenging Trudy Ballinger.

"Is the killer still out there?" Trudy inquired shrilly, panic adding asperity to her voice. Andy turned briefly away from the grim, questioning looks on the three faces confronting him.

"There is a feeling of menace lurking close, and I think it will be safer if we leave," said Andy, asserting himself, in the long established manner of police officers everywhere.

"What's made you change your mind?" Gene was now fully awake and in a combative mood; he temporarily banished images of his recent dream to the torpid recesses of his mind.

"There was a gunshot over in the woods," replied Andy, reluctant to admit that the sound he'd heard could be a car backfiring or even a poacher trying his luck, unaware of the proximity of a police presence. As far as conversation killers go, on a scale of nought to ten it rated at least nine with the assembled group, as they stared incredulously at the harassed police officer. "Rob, you stay here and radio in for backup while I take Trudy and Gene back to the headquarters; they'll be safe there," he ordered. Andy was trying to convince himself as much as anyone.

The drama of the last few days had been dramatically different from anything he'd encountered before in his twenty years as a police officer; he only hoped he'd emerge unscathed, both physically or mentally. His job, to which he'd devoted his entire working life, became less attractive with each passing hour. The last time he'd felt this way was when, as a young detective constable, he'd investigated the mass murder of a young family in London. Witnesses swore the killer had faded into thin air before their eyes. He'd doubted their credibility then, but now anything seemed possible.

Gene made to object, but seeing the determined look on the police officer's face he realised his objections would be overruled. Moreover, he wasn't going to leave her alone with bloody Andy Dale and his cronies. His head swam, and the ancient sofa soughed as he levered his heavy body into a sitting position. It was hard to believe that two days ago he'd been resting comfortably in a warm hospital bed, his every whim, well almost every whim, catered to by pretty, attentive nurses. That had been until the attack; now look at him, aching all over on a greasy sofa with springs threatening to bore their way through to his vital organs. If they ever survived this ordeal, he would take Trudy on a bloody good holiday. She would soon soothe his troubled brow—and a lot more besides. Luxuriating on these thoughts, he slowly unrolled himself to his full height, towering over an anxious looking Trudy Ballinger.

"Come on, you two; let's get out of here while we still can. Rob will bring your possessions later," prodded Andy, trying desperately to instil a sense of urgency into the stupefied couple. Deliberately, offering token, face saving resistance, Gene slumped back down on the sofa and slowly laced up his mud encrusted trainers, refusing stubbornly to make eye contact with the visibly agitated policeman. Leaving the two adversaries to follow in her wake, Trudy paused to snatch up her coat and purse before walking in an arrhythmic gait towards the waiting car. Lashing rain swept over the car as it pulled away slowly down the muddy road into the murky dawn light.

Jumping at shadows, Rob competed bravely with the dissonance outside and struggled with the poor quality reception on his mobile as he urgently requested backup teams to the remote house. Shivering, he suddenly felt very alone. But he wasn't.

The man had no name. What's more, the man did not know his name, nor, for that matter, where he came from. What he did know, instinctively, was that the lives of two souls inside the distant house linked inextricably to his own destiny and the destiny of many others. An inner compulsion drove him on, ever nearer, to face a danger he could not even begin to comprehend. The figure walked rapidly, focused unerringly on the lone house looming bigger in his vision with each resolute step.

CHAPTER 134

ALTHOUGH THE WEATHER was cold, the atmosphere generated by the three people in the speeding car was several degrees cooler. And it was getting frostier by the second. Trudy was the first to break the silence, Andy being the target of her vituperative attention. "Pardon me if I doubt your sagacity, but I remember your assertion that the domiciliate where we were attacked and nearly killed was regarded by you as a safe house." When angry, Trudy's higher lexicon kicked in, vastly annoying her addressees, who were struggling to understand. "Thank God you didn't shack us up in an unsafe house," she concluded. The vehemence of her tone added a hard dimension to Trudy, which neither Gene nor Andy had witnessed before.

The previous luckless victim of Trudy's immoderate anger found himself jilted and homeless three weeks before the planned wedding having spent the previous year living with Trudy and two dogs. The dogs stayed but her partner Jack went.

Both Andy and Gene began wishing they were somewhere else other than cooped up in a cramped Ford Focus speeding into the portentous night with an irate Trudy Ballinger spoiling for a fight with anyone daring enough to speak out of turn. The two men's silence communicated their decision to put discretion before valour. Gene's body language reflected his boredom, his eyes wandering in all directions but never catching Trudy's gaze. Andy, teeth clenched, concentrated furiously on the road ahead as if mesmerised by the dancing headlights he would never catch. Shadowy outlines, rendered like demented aliens against the mordant sky, flashed by as the car with its three silent occupants sped through the twilight lit roads.

The ghostly delineation of a large man loomed in the headlights before vanishing as quickly as it had appeared, leaving onlookers doubting whether overactive imaginations were playing tricks.

Unnoticed by the trio speeding through the night, a car waited patiently in the blustery twilight like some prehistoric dinosaur ready to pounce on unsuspecting prey. From the cover of dark forest undergrowth, the man watched as the car zoomed past, its headlights momentarily lighting up the road ahead and its escaping occupants unaware of the sinister figure watching them fade into the distance. For the first time, the man temporarily lost his focus, pausing several minutes before walking back into the dense undergrowth. It wasn't the devil stalking through this fateful night, but a near disciple, intent on evil of great magnitude.

CHAPTER 135

HE COULDN'T WAIT to get home to see Martha; even her constant chatter about the day's events would be welcome. The backup would soon arrive; then he would get home, have a nice warm bath, and take Martha out for a meal at that new pub the lads at the station raved about. He could imagine her surprise. The last time they'd been out on their own was nearly twelve months ago, on her fifty-seventh birthday. With luck, it could be his birthday tonight; he'd better call her—give her time to get over the shock and dress up ready.

Martha Murray picked up the softly chirping phone on the second ring. She always carried the handset with her now. Her fifty-eight-year-old legs did not allow her the luxury of rushing anywhere, let alone to answer the phone. "Hello, Martha Murray speaking." Hearing her husband on the end of the line, she smiled inwardly. *What does the old fool want?* she thought fondly. Martha knew Rob would be grimacing, hearing her best telephone answering voice; he always said that her own accent was good enough, and it wasn't necessary to put on a posh voice to impress callers. As usual, though, she made up her own mind.

"Hello, Luv; I'm about to wend my weary way home." The tired sounding man, distorted on the end of the crackly line, was her Rob. Even after all these years, it was good to hear his voice. Stressed and tired, he needed a good long rest, and she couldn't wait for his retirement. Earlier in their married life she would worry endlessly until he arrived safely home. Now, with only a few more months to go before he finished work for good, she was a little more philosophical.

"We're going out tonight, so get your glad rags on." Rob's voice conveyed rather more enthusiasm than he felt. Given the choice, he'd rather go home, have his tea, and nod off watching the TV until bedtime; but he knew Martha would love to go out, so he would make the sacrifice.

The warm glow that accompanied Rob's heroic, unselfish train of thought was disturbed by the sound of the kitchen door handle, creaking. In front of the incredulous policeman's eyes, it started to turn slowly and inexorably in a clockwise direction, pausing momentarily before renewing its journey until the door, unfettered by the catch, would spring open.

Temporarily mesmerised, Rob's years of training to deal with minacious situations kicked in, as he placed his mobile, now clammy with his sweat, down gently on the grimy kitchen work surface. A gentle click signified the end of the door handles journey. Rob braced himself as the door began to inch open, creating a gentle movement of cold air, its coolness vexatious on Rob's sweat soaked face. "Rob, are you still there?" A disembodied voice called frantically from between dirty dishes, piled high on the greasy work surface, where Rob's discarded mobile unceremoniously lay. Fleetingly distracted by his wife's frenetic intonations, the detective reached for the chattering phone just as the kitchen door burst open.

CHAPTER 136

STANDING MOTIONLESS, THE menacing silhouette filled the open doorway. Papers flapping on the kitchen table tried to escape the restraints of an empty tea mug carelessly placed by a thoughtless user. A sudden bolt of lightning provided a contre-jour effect, backlight throwing the framed silhouette into a sharper relief, adding to the mood of menace pervading the room.

"Oh, my God, Rob, are you still there?" The squawk emanating from the forgotten phone broke the menacing silence. Hidden from view, sheltered among grimy dishes, a disembodied voice hysterically demanding an answer fleetingly attracted Rob's attention. Glancing at the stacked dishes shrouding the flickering phone, Rob's attention briefly left the intruder. A clap of thunder jolted his attention back to the imminent threat facing him. Like a badly exposed black-and-white negative, lightning lit up the now empty, open doorway.

His eyes, semi blinded in reaction to the lightning strike, flitted frantically around trying to locate the spectral figure who only a second before had filled the open doorway. Dark hiding places and dimly lit shadows could harbour God knows what. Imagined or real, but terrifying nonetheless, the situation caused Rob to tense up, as he prepared for the deadly assault to come.

Silence overwhelmed the room, the phone stopped its nettlesome chatter, the night outside became deathly silent like the eye of a hurricane pausing before unleashing its devastating fury. It was a moment frozen in time; a moment etched in Rob's mind forever. He realized that he was alone in the room, as if the spectre had only existed in his imagination; the figure had vanished.

The open door, groaning with the wind, was the only testament to the antecedent drama. Sounds of nature's fury returned, thunder and lightning once again dominating the night. The high-pitched screaming sound of a voice trapped in the electronic circuitry of a mobile phone returned, demanding the listener's attention.

"Bloody hell, you bastard, I'll get you." Another voice—this time Rob's own—filled the air.

On the verge of panic, the aged detective ran out into the darkness screaming at the unwelcoming night shrouding his invisible enemy. A flashing blue light, its effulgence filling the night sky, shimmered at the end of the driveway. DC Mark Smith, more intent on stepping 'round the mud, climbed cautiously out of the police car.

"Hello, Rob; are you all right?" Having successfully manoeuvred on to firmer ground, the young detective gave his governor full attention. "Backup is on its way," he added quickly, trying desperately to hide the shock at seeing the wild look on his superior's face. For his part, Rob still stared into the unforgiving night.

CHAPTER 137

IT LOOMED COLOSSAL, although obnubilated by the enshrouding mist. Great eyes appeared in the evening twilight, their twin coronas of overlapping, yellow luminance blinding the three occupants sitting transfixed on the erratically speeding car. Like a giant ship's horn, communicating its arrival in port, the boom filled the car with ear-splitting sound. An involuntary, high-pitched scream of panic broke from the smallest of the passengers, instantly joined by a lower, but no less frenetic, vociferation from a startled Gene Harman.

Reaction time normally gets slower as you get older. In times of dire need, however, the human body and its reflexes still manage to surprise. This was such a time.

With a manoeuvre that would have put Michael Schumacher to shame, Andy yanked the leather-covered steering wheel hard to the left allowing the car to mount the muddy grass verge. Oblivious to the loss of a nearside wing mirror, shattered against the trunk of an unyielding tree, the steering wheel, as if with a life of its own, reoriented to the right amid the sound of screeching tyres.

The twin red lights faded rapidly into the distance as three badly shaken people crouched in shock, facing the ghostly outline of the rapidly retreating lorry, their car now stationary. Burning rubber, combined with the sour smell of fear-induced sweat, polluted the car's interior making breathing difficult for the hapless occupants, who were desperately attempting to escape into the mist infused night air.

Coughing, the big man was the first to stagger out, clutching his side; he emitted a stifled cry as in his haste he stumbled ungainly, rolling over in the wet, muddy scrub. The leaves rustled, noisily buffeted by the gusting wind, as Andy heaved open his door. Consciously flexing his stiffening muscles, he was relieved that his body functioned in the approved manner. Black in the vanishing twilight, a spreading patch of blood dappled starkly against the white shirt of the injured Gene Harman, his low moan distinct above the wrath of the stormy night. Skittering and sliding in the mud soaked undergrowth, Trudy was the first to reach the injured man, his moaning fainter as consciousness slipped away. An erratic, faint pulse still throbbed under Trudy's probing finger, now resting reassuringly on Gene's carotid artery.

"We've got to get help," Trudy gasped, not turning as Andy approached, clutching his useless mobile phone.

"There's no signal," shouted Andy with more than a degree of antipathy. "Must be a dead spot," he added, barely able to control his frustration.

"You're the policeman who's supposed to deal with emergencies, so do something!" The hard edge to her voice testified that she wasn't about to brook any argument from Andy. As Trudy refocused her attention back to the injured man beside her, lying unceremoniously in the mud, she felt that his cheek was cold.

"Perhaps if I get beyond these trees, the signal will improve;

and I can phone for help."

Trudy didn't hear Andy's suggestion as she cradled Gene's head in her arms. Neither did she hear Andy walking briskly down the gloomy road, a glimmer of moonlight filtering through the trees and forming a ribbon of light to guide him through the thick canopy.

Less than a mile away, another vehicle started on its journey—a journey that would have a long lasting effect on the three persons stranded in the wood.

CHAPTER 138

With every step he took, his ragged breathing bore an overwhelming testament to his lack of fitness. Cursing loudly, he stumbled on into the night. Run one hundred strides, walk one hundred strides, he thought, recalling that as a youth he and his friends would travel great distances round the neighbourhood using this technique. Now, many years later, Andy made an early, unilateral decision to abandon the tried and tested method of his youth and to walk steadily the rest of the way. Still, a mile down the road, shoes not meant for long-range walking started to pinch feet also not used to walking—not since he was a beat copper, many years, and much fitness, ago. Still no bloody signal, he noticed; the bars on the mobile twitched momentarily giving false hope before complacently settling back indicating no network coverage.

He saw a glimmer in the distance—was it his imagination or could that be a car heading his way? As quickly as it had appeared, the distant light vanished, leaving only the dim, eerie light rendered by filtered moonbeams in the twilight. Andy laboured on, the sinister canopy closing in more with every step—or so it appeared to an imagination wildly influenced by the spookiness of the night. There they were again—bigger this time—two pinpoints on the horizon twinkling like binary stars in space. Gone again—it must be the light playing tricks, his mind began to doubt what his eyes were striving to tell him.

Head down, Andy drew his coat tightly around him in a vain effort to keep out the drizzling rain. The pace of his stride was governed by the breath in his body. A break in the dark outline of the tree canopy appeared ahead of him, signalling hope that maybe his mobile would have strong enough coverage to make the vital call. His stride quickened with a goal in sight; like an Olympic sprinter going for the tape, Andy hurried towards the break in the trees.

The intense brilliance of the rampant lights fixated the police officer like a caught rabbit. This time, however, it wasn't a rabbit caught in these speeding headlights; this time it was DCI Andy Dale.

CHAPTER 139

RESISTING THE ALMOST overwhelming urge to scream, Trudy flailed frantically about her head. Black outlines of night creatures, only visible when flying across the faint backlit sky, displayed their incredible aerobatic skills, narrowly missing her uncovered head. She fantasised creatures tangled in hair and clawing at faces, a phobia heightened in the atmospheric semi light of near dawn. High-pitched sounds all around stretched her imagination beyond the bounds of reality. As if on cue, a low moan broke the hypnotic spell, which had threatened to envelop and dominate the mind of the frightened woman.

Despair mixed with panic weighed deep within him; he watched helplessly as the speeding outline of the lorry swept past him. Red lights like the eyes of a demon, mocked him, finally vanishing hidden behind the hilly contours of the country road. Instinctively, he knew the speeding lorry was heading back to where Trudy and Gene waited for the help that would never come. His legs running heavily and his heart beating faster than could be good for a middle-aged detective, Andy ran, his mind focused on getting back to Trudy before it was too late. Powerless, unable to summon help, he felt rather than heard the polyphonic orchestrations of the *William Tell Overture*, permeating above the sonorous voice of the wild, stormy wind. Realization dawned. His bloody mobile was ringing, competing gallantly with the night. Frantically fumbling, not daring to believe, relief flooded Andy as a single press of the connect button confirmed his high expectations.

"Hello, Andy, where have you been? I've been trying to get you for ages." Never before, and possibly never again, would Andy be so pleased to hear the cultured voice of DC Stephen Green.

Out of the gloom, without warning, startling Trudy by its size and nearness, a grim silhouette manifested itself. The enormous lorry had returned, black and impenetrable, sinister in the near dawn light. The motionless, forbidding shape began to show signs of life as the cab door slowly opened, breaking up the grim outline and revealing a dark, humanlike figure. A throaty laugh broke the silence, as a large figure climbed out, indistinct against the shadowy backcloth of the brooding vehicle.

CHAPTER 140

EARLY MORNING LIGHT was beginning to cast its cool shadows across the rutted ground where an hour previously the near fatal accident had occurred. The car was still leaning drunkenly against the dispassionate tree. Trudy and Gene, however, had vanished. Rutted impressions in the wet mud and a blood soaked handkerchief bearing the initials TB screamed out their woeful message to the bewildered observers.

"Trudy"—his voice battled bravely against the wind, which seemed to vent its ire against the human intruder. "Gene"—another call, this time laced with panic, rebounded dully from the impenetrable surrounding screen of trees, standing like silent guardians to the unknown. Two dark figures, their collars turned up against the elements, stood desolate, desperately waiting for an answer that would allay their worst felt fears. The reply never came. Only the mocking wind and creaking trees voiced any reaction to Andy's frantic calls.

"They couldn't have gone far on their own," Andy's voice quavered as he spoke to his silent companion. "They had no valid reason to move from this spot," he added, thinking aloud, neither expecting nor getting a response from his DC. The pervading silence increased the tension surrounding the two men.

"Someone must have been here before us—perhaps taken them to hospital," Stephen Green finally contributed, his voice trailing off at the improbability of his remark. His superior's look of disbelief reducing Stephen to his previous, silent, abject state. Deeply rutted and still pronounced, despite the best endeavours of rain to wipe out all trace, tyre marks bigger than those of the average car, told their story—a story Andy didn't want to hear.

"Get in; we're going for help," Andy called forcefully to his subordinate. He needed to gather himself, calling on every ounce of his experience and training to deal with emergencies like this. Partly running, partly sliding, mud spraying with every maladroit step, Andy rushed frantically back to the waiting car; his uncoordinated DC slid along in his wake. Pounding impatiently on the steering wheel, Andy waited while a dishevelled Stephen Green clambered into the passenger seat beside him. Passenger door not yet shut, the car slewed off with the squeal of tyres trying to get traction on the wet slick surface and spraying mud like brown rain in all directions.

As he cursed to himself, the man's face contorted with rage. So close, then that bloody lorry turns up, he muttered to himself. Preserving a discreet distance behind, he followed the lorry's red lights hazily shimmering in the distance.

CHAPTER 141

EVERY BUMP SENT a shudder down her spine. God knows what it was doing to the injured man beside her. He'd stopped groaning now, the effort too much for the once physically strong, seeming invincible, Gene Harman. The radio playing quietly in the background, Winston drove faster than his employer would approve of through the narrow country lanes. Bletchworth Hospital—the sign loomed ahead, and then just as rapidly faded into the distance.

"Soon be there, love," Winston said reassuringly to his fraught passenger. "Another five miles or so; let's hope there's not much traffic," he added in a cheerful voice, in no way appropriate for the direness of their predicament. Still the radio played on. Trudy recognised the gangster rap music, and the violence frightened her.

"Please, could you turn the music off?" If Winston heard her request, he chose to ignore it; instead, he put his foot down hard on the accelerator causing the lorry to jerk forward even faster. His face lit up like a grotesque mask as the low, early morning sunlight flickered briefly through the cab. And still the music played on.

Focused fixedly on the road ahead, Trudy could feel his eyes penetrating her skull. His hand brushed her thigh, fleetingly at first, almost accidental, as Winston pushed home another gear. Trudy's instinctive reaction was cut short as something heavy leaned against her; she turned in time to see Gene slipping sideways in his seat, the belt no longer restraining his heavy bulk.

It appeared suddenly. Sharp bends usually do, but this one was the daddy of them all. As the wheels squealed and the centrifugal force irresistibly had its way the speeding lorry lost its grip on the greasy road., Trudy felt herself sandwiched between Winston and Gene; then, in an instant, positions reversed as the same force flung them around the cab like rag dolls. The sickening sound of tearing metal filled her eardrums assuaging the sound of shattering glass as the lorry bounced off the verge, miraculously regaining its purchase on the tarmac surface before finally clanking to an unceremonious halt in the middle of the bleak country road.

Winston's luck was out. On the scale of nought to ten Winston's luck was unquestionably nought. His mother had said he would always "land on his feet." Mostly, for the previous twenty-four years she had been right; she was wrong this time however. This time his head took the full brunt of a vengeful branch, pile driving its way through the unresisting windscreen, determined to extract retribution for the damage caused to its parent tree. And the caved in look didn't suit Winston at all; even his mother would have to agree.

CHAPTER 142

A PIERCING SCREAM filled the steaming cab. Endlessly resounding, bouncing around the small compartment, seeking out every nook and cranny to infiltrate with its distasteful vociferation. Blood running down his smashed skull in a repulsive winding stream, Winston slid slowly sideways depositing an ugly, red smudge, adding a kaleidoscope of colour to the spider-web crack in the remaining glass window.

Her bloodied hands pressed tightly to blooded ears as Trudy tried to shut out the animal like screeching still filling the confines of the small, metal prison with its terrible feral sound. Distorted, suspended in space, a cavernous mouth levitated, defying gravity in its attempt to bring it to earth. Vaguely familiar, reality suddenly dawned, as Trudy recognised the crazed face staring back at her from the splintered mirror as her own. Abruptly the screaming stopped, immediately replaced by an arrhythmic sobbing as the gaping mouth closed, leaving a more recognisable, though webbed, image of herself.

Forgotten, barely alive, a low moan emitted from the crumpled figure still restrained by the greasy, twisted seat belt. Searing pain coursed through her body as a neck damaged by whiplash turned slowly towards the injured Gene. A spectrum of blue and red alternated across the leaning body of Gene giving an other-worldly effect to a face already devoid of human colour. Trudy's sobs of despair changed to cries of relief as the police car skidded to a halt spraying mud in all directions. Vociferously critical in the past of police preoccupation with catching easy, middle-aged speeding targets instead of solving real crime, Trudy was on this occasion overwhelmed with relief upon seeing a police uniform emerge from the flashing car.

Undistinguished in post-dawn light, the car slowed down pulling over to allow the speeding police car to pass. The driver's face, partially hidden in the shadowy interior, glowered with rage—a rage that would only be satiated by the death of Trudy Ballinger.

CHAPTER 143

THE RED LEATHER chair protested noisily as a heavy bulk shifted across its surface, worn by years of constant use. Placing the ivory handset back on its matching cradle, the bulky man leaned back amid further protests by the long-suffering office armchair. Rage welled up within him. Soon the Davies and Son suit rose slowly, as the upholstery expelled sighs of relief, released from a prolonged state of compression. A worsted wool-covered arm paused briefly before, with a flourish, sweeping the contents of the Victorian oak desk violently to the floor, sending a hand-rolled Cuban cigar, still smoking, spinning erratically on the polished block floor. It was not the news he wanted, or expected, to hear. Still seething, he unlocked the hidden desk drawer, a tribute to Victorian craftsmen, with his shaking hand and paused a moment before transferring a cold, heavy object into the finely tailored pocket. A sea of heads bowed over desktops with the well-practiced pretence of working busily, as, walking erratically, the man in the fine tailored suit walked out of the building towards his waiting car. He didn't hear the hum of voices chattering excitedly, heads raised, all pretence at work forgotten.

CHAPTER 144

THE RED LIGHT shimmered hazily through the steamy car window, metronomic wipers striving heroically to keep windscreens clear of the cascading rain expelled from a murky sky. The police driver muttered impatiently, waiting for traffic lights, seemingly trapped on red, to change their colour to liberating green. Instinctively he fixed his eyes on the two silhouetted heads levitating ahead of him. The driver in front, now locked in the officer's gaze, was doing what all drivers do when followed by a police car, that is, obey all the rules—no edging forward waiting for the green light when normally they would be halfway across, anticipating the change. One of the perks of the job was watching people squirm; he cheered up at the thought.

Looking at his watch, he realised that his shift should have finished half an hour ago, so the sooner he could drop these two off at the hospital the better. A couple of hours overtime would be useful to help pay off his "flexible friend," if his sergeant sanctioned it. He couldn't be sure these days of budget cuts and financial restraint. Still, pulling a couple of easy mark motorists for speeding, after he'd dropped off his passengers at the hospital, should cover his overtime claim and appease his sergeant.

He felt like a taxi service driving the professor and her boyfriend to hospital. Sadly the job had changed recently and not for the better. At one time the job was about catching crooks; now it was admin and paperwork. Politicians ran the force, not the experienced officers, who really knew about fighting crime. All his thoughts of a better world without politicians vanished, as a demonic face appeared at his window.

CHAPTER 145

HE'D FOLLOWED AT a discreet distance hoping for an opportunity; now, it had arrived. An icy coolness spread over him like an Arctic wind. He would savour this long-awaited moment for many years to come in his retirement. Luckily the outside lane was empty as he drove up silently alongside the stationary police car, its driver impatiently drumming cold, stubby fingers on the simulated leather steering wheel. Unnoticed by the preoccupied man still beating a staccato rhythm, he peered anxiously through the misty windows trying to locate his target. With recognition, a cruel smile touched his face; finally he could complete this last job, collect his money, then go away forever. Red and amber—the lights changed as he levelled his Walther PPK 7.65 mm at the startled face distorted in the misty glass.

For the first time in ages, Trudy felt safe. She and Gene were travelling to hospital, relatively secure, in a police car. Andy was following with Stephen Green in an unmarked car behind. Belt and braces sprang to mind, but just as quickly the image was dismissed as a half smile crossed her face. Another time Trudy would have laughed at all the fuss; but after what they'd been through recently, she felt only gratitude. Gene had risked his life saving her from that madman. To quote one of her students, "She owed him big-time." *And she would pay him back "big-time"*, she thought and smiled.

Surprisingly, Gene was looking better; considering all that had happened recently, he looked positively healthy. He was a strong man, unlike some of her past boyfriends, wimps from academia, whose idea of a good-time was a night discussing their current project.

Sadness suddenly dominated her feelings as her thoughts turned to Mike; he was different from the others as well. She and Mike had been good friends until recently, before his personality had changed. But latterly he'd been a different person, one she hardly recognised. Did his change coincide with her meeting Gene? Was he jealous? Too late to ask him now, she mused sadly.

Her deliberations vanished instantly as a strong hand grabbed her shoulder, roughly pulling her down away from the window. Protest froze on her lips, as the sound like a deranged hornet was followed by the dull thud of a 7.65mm bullet as it burrowed its way through the hard backed upholstery before flattening itself against an unyielding, metal, car door.

DC Stephen Green knew from experience when his boss was angry. This was one of those times. Stephen also knew when it was advisable to say nothing and keep your head down. This was also one of those times. Following the "jam butty," he and Andy had exchanged no more than a dozen words the whole time. He stole a sideways glance at the unsmiling man sitting stiffly at his side. Stephen took comfort knowing, as a fast track university graduate he would be in the boss's seat in a few years. His reverie was shattered when Andy sprang to life as if suddenly infused with pure adrenalin.

"Look out," Andy wrenched the door open as his words,

beaten back by the elements, went unheard by all except Stephen. Startled by Andy's cry, the shadow moved quickly, like a silent illusion, towards his car, its engine still revving, expelling clouds of smoke to an already over polluted atmosphere.

"Let's get the bastard!" His boss slammed the door shut as he rasped out instructions. Reacting instinctively, Stephen pulled out, wheels spinning, to catch the assassin's car, which was already just a blur in the distance.

CHAPTER 146

Still smouldering, the rubble that once was the Goldberg Building, home to the prestigious Goldberg Publications, looked like a scene from devastated Beirut. Graffiti already adorned the barriers and hoarding erected by emergency services anxious to keep out the public. Forensic investigation still underway would begin again in the morning, but meanwhile the smouldering rubble remained the domain of the night creatures. Between the remains of a decimated Goldberg Building and the Star Insurance headquarters, the alley in post dawn looked drab and forbidding. Blocking the dark alleyway's exit, a car with its lights extinguished stood silently like some minatory predator.

The hooded figure did not move as twin beams of halogen light heralded the arrival of another car. This one, much smaller, drove part-way up the alley before juddering to a halt amid the debris and bins. Twin beams were doused abruptly, leaving an inky blackness till eyes used to light adjusted to the sudden darkness.

At each end of the dark alley, two car doors thirty metres apart opened slowly revealing the opponents—their fates inexorably linked, their date with destiny nigh. Light from a passing bus temporarily lit up the scene casting eerie shadows and making monsters out of bins piled high with yesterday's waste, before passing on its journey into the early morn. The muted sounds of early morning traffic provided an unwelcome accompaniment to the drama. Another passing vehicle, this time a lorry, temporarily lit up the dark recesses of the alley sending a rat scurrying for the relative safety of obscurity.

Terrible in its intensity, an appalling wail resonated out of the gloom as a tomcat, disturbed from its early morning endeavour, gave vent to his feelings before scampering over the hoardings and vanishing into the night. The illumination this time briefly revealed outlines of two shadowy figures, indistinct, even in the temporary light, less than twenty metres apart. Another flash and they were ten metres apart. Another and it was five metres.

"Well?" a muffled voice, confined within a black hood, emanated from the impenetrable void.

"I've got it if you have completed your end of the bargain," came the curt reply as another flash of light lit up the two figures. Inches separated them as the hooded figure reached slowly into the pocket of his bulky anorak. The round crimson rain, spattering randomly on the bulky envelope, closely matched the blood spurting from the black hood, as it and the rest of the body fell backward into the darkened void from which it had come.

CHAPTER 147

ANDY AND STEPHEN Green were the first to arrive. In the nearly deserted streets of early morning, it had been relatively easy to follow the car. They knew they should wait for backup; but reacting instinctively, they had pursued the would-be assassin to this desolate alley.

The sun peeping tentatively over the horizon cast the first rays of morning light on the dramatic scene. Two figures eerily indistinct in the grim shadows suddenly transformed into high contrast silhouettes as the sun broke free of the shielding horizon and cast its low morning light blindingly down the alley. Transformed by daylight, the antagonist's battleground was no less dramatic set among the bins and graffiti.

Still shrieking, the tyres left their skid marks on the tarmac road as the car carrying Andy and Stephen skidded briefly before stopping with a judder at the end of the darkened alley. The familiar sound of burning rubber tainted the early morning air, as Andy, the first to react, leaped from the steaming car. The scene before him stood still momentarily, and with it came the sudden realization of the dangerous reality posed by the two silhouettes. A sudden glint of light on metal focused Andy's attention on the metal gun barrel now pointing unwaveringly in his direction.

Time stood still as Andy, intently focused on the danger ahead, didn't hear the sound of more cars arriving on the scene; neither did he hear the sound of the bullet as the Walther spewed out its deadly load. What he did feel, however, was the searing pain as the leaded missile burrowed its way spitefully into his ribs, smashing bone and tissue before lodging dangerously in his chest cavity.

Held upright against the alley wall, Andy looked on helplessly as the figure moved slowly towards him gun aiming steadily at his head. Were there two figures coming towards him? He could see two guns. No there was only one; his vision wavered, moving in out of focus as he slid further down the greasy wall. His legs trembled weakly trying to support the weight his body pressed on them.

Surprisingly, he wasn't afraid when the cold barrel pressed hard against his forehead. What did surprise him, however, was the look of panic on his assailant's face, as he struggled to resist and then turned the gun barrel back towards himself. A voice distorted by fear cried out in terror as the finger white with pressure squeezed the trigger of the Walther pistol. The light from a bedroom window suddenly illuminated the alley revealing the remains of a face that Andy knew well.

Was this going to be the last face he saw in this life? Why had this man tried to kill him; and, now, why had he turned the pistol on himself? These were the last thoughts of Andy Dale before he lost consciousness, sliding slowly to the alley floor.

CHAPTER 148

THE DESERTED LAY-BY with its overflowing rubbish bins was an unlikely sanctuary when Constable Matthews pulled in shaking, knuckles white, still tightly clenching the steering wheel. His eyes stung viciously as perspiration ran down his face, finally absorbed by the snug fitting collar of his shirt. PC John Matthews's speciality was catching unwary motorists speeding on the motorway, or speeding anywhere for that matter. Young or old, fat or thin—he'd caught them all in his time. However, a shooting was different altogether; it required bravery and dedication to duty—a quality that John Matthews didn't realise he had—until now.

Gene was the first to recover from the shock, releasing his grip on a petrified Trudy gasping for breath, face pressed into the dusty, smelly car seat. She struggled to pull herself upright, unaware of her narrow escape from the assassin's bullet. "What the bloody hell do you think you're doing?" she blurted out, still in shock, her voice trailing off as she saw the stunned look on Gene's face. Following his gaze from the shattered window to the smouldering ragged hole adorning the car seat, suddenly the realization hit her. Burying her head in her hands, she sobbed uncontrollably as Gene drew her gently to him. "It's Ian. Oh, my

God, Ian tried to kill me," she cried out incredulously, her salty tears mingling with the blood clotting on Gene's shoulder. Gene didn't feel the sting at first, among the other aches and pains picked up over the last few days; but later he would realise how close he had come to death.

He hesitated, but for only a moment, when the radio crackled into life grinding out its request for all cars within the area to proceed to the Goldberg Building. John Matthews, acting on instinct, oblivious to his passengers, who still sat shocked in the back seat, pulled out of the lay-by, wheels screaming and the wailing siren warning other road users to get in the way at their peril.

A crowd was already gathering when PC Matthews, along with his traumatized passengers, arrived at the scene. Pulling up alongside the alley, he could see that "fast tracker" Stephen Green was hovering around trying to look important, but leaving the dangerous work to his boss, Andy Dale. Bloody typical to get a top job just because he went to a posh university, while the rest of us were working for a living. These thoughts flittered through John Matthews mind while he propelled himself out of the flashing car. "You two stay where you are," he called back, his voice drowned by the myriad sirens as he pushed his way through the gathering throng.

Trudy and Gene, shaken by the night's events, either didn't hear or chose not to heed the warning, as they followed John Matthews through the crowd.

CHAPTER 149

CARNAGE WAS ALL around, blood splatters running down walls to form miniature lakes on dirty, cobbled ground. A blooded figure twitches uncontrollably on the concrete floor—the final throes of a dying man played out dramatically in a dark, depressing alley, against a backcloth of garbage bins and graffiti. Gawkers gathering at the scene, like vultures around carrion, were transfixed by the convulsions of the wretched, blooded creature writhing before them—royal entertainment to pleasure the human animal's lust for blood.

Unnoticed by onlookers, enthralled by the paroxysms of the convulsing figure, another gravely wounded man, collapses silently and slowly to the ground, with surprising dignity, in this desolate alley of death.

Emitting a low, distressed mewl, a grey shadow breaks from the gathered crowd and rushes to embrace the second figure, now lying in silent repose on the fetid alley floor. Grief-stricken and oblivious to her surroundings, the woman kneels to cradle the head of the dying man. The air is rent with her piercing scream as with a final choking cough, the man dies, eyes wide as if embracing the full horror of his last seconds on earth. The loud, agonised caterwaul of the distraught woman attracts the attention of the silent crowd. Heads turn as one, focusing their gaze on the previously unnoticed drama now unfolding before them. Blood washes down in red rivulets weaving in and out of the garbage littering the alley's cobbled street.

The welcoming sound of sirens filled the air as police cars raced to the scene full of importance and pomposity. Spectators, normally not welcoming police intervention, made an exception as they turned expectantly towards the approaching saviours in blue. The engine was still running as Rob Murray, not dressed in blue, but wearing an old gabardine mack and a trilby, pulled down low over his face, clambered from the steaming car aghast at the scene in front of him. Laura Thomas eased herself from the driving seat and joined her governor trying to comfort the woman, sobbing uncontrollably, still cradling the head of the dying man. A look of horror and disbelief crossed Laura's face as she recognized the inert body now in silent repose lying among the debris littering the alley floor. For Trudy, the events of the last two days proved too much as she sobbed, shaking uncontrollably, and tried to comfort the prostrate figure.

CHAPTER 150

FOR SEVERAL DAYS, all the major news networks and newspapers carried stories and features detailing the violent death of prominent business leader Jason Goldberg. The nation mourned the death of such a fine man. News of his good works, spread over the last thirty years, became a source of inspiration to the nation and the business world alike. Lobbyists hassled MP's with talk of posthumous awards to mark the philanthropist's passing. Even the Prime Minister, after consulting his PR man and seeing that political capital was in the offing looked suitably sombre as he paid tribute to, "the man he called a friend."

Surprisingly the death of Jason Goldberg created more concern in government than the deaths of a myriad of soldiers currently fighting in a futile war. Just as journalists and their editors tired of the war story and moved on to pastures new, so did the early headlines of Jason Goldberg's untimely death move to the inside pages, ending finally as a minor feature in weekend reviews. Journalists soon forgot about Jason Goldberg and all his good works—all journalists except one; an old friend of Deborah Moon.

Darren Brown was of average height, slightly overweight, without any distinguishing features. Darren, everybody agreed was a bloody good journalist. Even those who didn't like his abrupt manner, still rated him highly as a professional. Working as a journalist for many years, Darren knew the value of a good story, especially when you had scooped the opposition for it. And that's what he had done.

Darren had been a family friend of the Moons, mother and daughter, for many years, not romantically involved with Deborah, just plain good friends. So several weeks after Deborah's tragic death, Enid Moon invited Darren around to help sort through her dead daughter's possessions. It was an onerous task, and at eighty-two Enid was too fragile emotionally to attempt it on her own. So Darren, thoughtful despite his abrupt manner, had devoted this weekend to helping Enid sort through Deborah's possessions, with the strict instruction from Enid that he should choose something for himself as a keepsake. Why do librarians collect so many books and folders, thought Darren, sifting through another pile of dusty, old hardbacks?

He'd spent the afternoon helping Enid and he felt sorry for the old woman's sadness at seeing her daughter's possessions sifted through like this. He'd conscientiously glanced in all of the dusty folders filled with equally dusty papers; he did not want to overlook anything that might be of value to the old lady. With a sigh of relief he reached for the last pile of folders, eagerly anticipating a few drinks down the pub later to lay all the dust he'd breathed in during the afternoon's labours.

The thick, red, box folder on top wasn't dusty like most of the others. Must be a current folder, supposed Darren, as he undid the clasp and raised the lid. Typical of Deborah—neat as always, he smiled, looking at the thick sheaf of papers and news cuttings tidily held together in sections with paper clips. Well, well, you sly old girl, he thought, seeing the photograph of Jason Goldberg looking grimly up at him from the depths of the folder. So you fancied him all the time. Let's have a look and see what other souvenirs you've collected of the old bastard. Discoloured by age, its glaze cracked, the next image showed an upright man in a uniform—more precisely, the uniform of a Nazi soldier. The soldier, laughing and smoking a cigar, stood on the edge of a trench containing myriads of pathetic skeletons untidily heaped together. Darren Brown wasn't laughing now, as he recognised the uniformed soldier—much younger but with an unmistakable arrogant look; trembling with excitement, Darren reached for his mobile phone.

The newspapers had a new headline the next day, and this one wasn't as complimentary to Jason Goldberg as the previous ones had been. Now the headline blazoned: "Newspaper Tycoon Jason Goldberg, aka Mass Murderer Friedrick Hauptman, Nazi Camp Commandant." Needless to say, the Prime Minister kept a low profile, as did his PR man.

CHAPTER 151

THE BLACK, SHADOWY outlines of mourners could be seen huddled around the graveside listening to the sombre tones of an old priest as he made his final discourse: "May his soul and the souls of all the faithful departed through the mercy of God rest in peace." He had been presiding over burials for the last fifteen years, but it was still harrowing for the reverend John Snowden. John had come to the priesthood late in life and had experienced the rigors of survival in the real world.

After extended service in the armed forces, John's life experiences had shaped his cynical nature, particularly seeing young lives "snuffed out" in their prime, their orders given by those in high office who had never experienced the true hardship such carnage invoked. Life—so temporary and fragile, thought the old vicar; graveyards—such depressing places. How many spirits lingered there waiting for the next visit of loved ones? Weekly visits become monthly; monthly turn into once a year on anniversaries; finally, even these stop—their next visit being when they themselves have the starring role. He looked around at people with sorrowful faces and heads bowed, their collars turned up against the rain. Those with forethought enough to bring umbrellas stood silently like weathervane figures waiting for the sun to come out. It was at times like this that he questioned his calling. Burials typified the grimness and harsh reality of life. Young or old, good or bad, death held no favourites. All were welcome.

Lost in her own internalisation, Trudy slowly became aware of the droning voice beseeching the departed to rest in peace. *What about the living?* she thought. *Shouldn't they have the right to peace?* After the torment of the last week, Trudy thought she would never find peace again. Previous constants in her life had crumbled, challenged and found wanting. Now the terrible uncertainty of the future haunted her.

Glancing at her companion, Trudy could see the same troubled look on his face that looked back at her each time she caught sight of her own reflection. Where had it all gone wrong? Past events flashed through her mind, each merging into the next, until boundaries became obscure and memories ill defined. What was certain, she had lost good friends in violent circumstances; and her world would never be the same again.

To think it had all started with silly photographs and her indignation at the thought that someone had leaked her discovery. It all seemed so irrelevant now. With death all around her and the prospect of a bleak future for the world, with politicians not looking beyond the next electoral round, what chance did humankind have? She knew where they must go for any hope of survival, but whom should she tell? Who would believe her anyway?

As in the X-Files, governments only let you know what they deem good for you or, more precisely, good for them. Fat cats at the top protect their own interests first; they have little or no conception of, or even more worrying, do not care about, the plight of the ordinary person. The state would not hesitate to discredit, or even remove, anyone posing a threat to its affluence and stability.

As if reading her mind, a big, comforting arm engulfed her. "It's all right, Trude; we'll get through this together," said Gene Harman, his voice reassuringly strong. Lost in his own thoughts, Gene's mind, made weary by the vicar's irksome monotone, strayed inevitably to the future. If the recent warnings were true; and he believed they were, life on earth would change for everything and everyone. Would society break down and new orders spring up, or would the same dominant dictators seize power to further their own interests? For that matter, would anything change? The rich would still "get richer," and the poor still "get poorer." Maybe the cataclysm would be an opportunity to change a society that flourished on greed. Was avarice the basis of humankind's success, or was the essence of man something higher?

A lone figure in a wheelchair flanked by two hospital attendants watched the proceedings without any display of feelings. Andy Dale would be confined to this wheelchair for the rest of his life. He had no emotion left to give.

CHAPTER 151

Rob Murray trudged wearily up the wet path leading to Trudy's front door. He'd rung earlier so he knew she was expecting his call. The door opened before the aging detective even rang the bell and Trudy's careworn face smiled as she ushered him into the back room where Gene lounged on the big armchair.

"How's retirement treating you?" said Gene as Trudy placed three steaming mugs of coffee on the table.

"Retirements not all it's cracked up to be" Rob replied cautiously sipping the steaming liquid. "The wife say's I spend too much time moping around the house but Grace's murder hit me and the wife hard." It could easily have been me centre stage at the funeral last month." "Anyhow I saw the Superintendent yesterday and he told me they've pieced together the mystery of the last few months." Two pair of eyes were firmly focused on Rob as he continued.

"The difficulty was we were dealing with two murderers, Ian Mason and Daniel Weston." The old detective paused momentarily, lost in his own thoughts, then he gathered himself together and continued.

"Ian Mason had a secret life as a paid assassin and was responsible for the murder of Helen Baxter, Deborah Moon as well as Mike Powell." "Dr Mike Powell was treating Mason for depression. During one of the sessions Powell had become suspicious of Mason's activities and became a risk to the assassin-he was killed in the hospital." Helen had learnt his secret and threatened to expose him, so she has to be disposed of. His other victim Deborah was a hit paid for by Jason Goldberg. Deborah had evidence to incriminate Goldberg as a Nazi commandant so he had paid Mason to find out if she had told anyone else and then kill her.

Rob's face looked drained of emotion as he reached for the now tepid mug of coffee.

"What about Daniel Weston?" Gene demanded rudely, glaring at the old detective.

Ignoring Gene's hostile stare Rob continued. "Daniel Weston was psychotic with a dual personality. "It appears that he murdered his best friend David when they were both very young but in his mind David still lived."

"So he was responsible for blowing up the Goldberg building and putting me in hospital?" questioned Gene butting in.

"Yes and the murder of Grace at the safe house," Rob looked across at Trudy trying to avoid Gene's challenging stare. "And many more we haven't identified yet I wouldn't wonder" added Rob struggling to his feet, signalling the end of the discussion.

Rob paused pulling up his collar. "Those photographs are still a puzzle and those dreams of yours, we still haven't an explanation for them either." And maybe never will, he added walking back down the path to his waiting car.

CHAPTER 152

THE BIG MAN was ready for the worst. He'd known for many years that this time would come. Now it was almost upon them; others would start to believe and take him seriously. Years of ridicule and scorn had left its mark on him and his family.

The azure blue sky shimmered, the heat rising from the earth like a gossamer curtain. He turned his gaze towards the heavens, peaceful at the moment, but concealing, albeit temporarily, a deadly secret.

In the twenty-first century, successive corrupt governments had succumbed to commercial interests and refused to take rising tides and unstable weather patterns seriously. Those that did take it seriously committed the even bigger sin of hiding the facts just to keep their paymasters happy. "Natural climate change" was the standard, glib reply from patronising heads of state all over the world, all sharing the same commercial pressures and personal greed.

Family dynasties ploughed untold wealth into ensuring that the "right people" were in positions of power. Dishonest governments and politicians had blighted the world since the dawn of time, but never more so than at the beginning of the twenty-first century. Techniques of mass persuasion, designed for those in power, were refined after many years of research and used to convince gullible nations of the righteousness of their crusades. These leaders gave no heed to the deaths and suffering of innocent people.

All the lies and deceptions, hidden truths, and avarice would not count for anything, as another unstoppable destructive force drew ever nearer. Now, temporarily hidden by the giant planet Jupiter, ominously primed to make the final lap of its cataclysmic journey, there lurked FX21, its final destination a medium-sized, blue, fertile planet, ninety-three million miles from the sun. It is called planet Earth.

A much younger and even bigger figure carrying a small child joined the man, who was still gazing intently skywards. He too looked up inquisitively, following the older man's intent gaze on the heavens. "Do you think we'll survive?" the younger man muttered, turning his head away as if not wanting to hear the reply from his older companion.

The weary, careworn face of the patriarchal figure slowly turned toward his son. "We've got to," he said emphatically. They turned slowly and trudged wearily back down the hill. No other words passed between them as they journeyed home. Now, all they could do was wait—and hope.

Lightning Source UK Ltd.
Milton Keynes UK
21 October 2010

161675UK00001B/6/P